This volume contains ten Usborne titles which are also available separately: Things On Wheels; Things That Float; Things That Fly; Our Earth; Things Outdoors; Rockets And Spaceflight; Sun, Moon And Planets; Where Food Comes From; How Things Are Made; How Things Are Built.

THE USBORNE FIRST BOOK OF KNOWLEDGE

THINGS ON WHEELS
THINGS THAT FLOAT
THINGS THAT FLY
OUR EARTH
THINGS OUTDOORS

ROCKETS AND SPACEFLIGHT
SUN, MOON AND PLANETS
WHERE FOOD COMES FROM
HOW THINGS ARE MADE
HOW THINGS ARE BUILT

Kate Little, Annabel Thomas, Jane Chisholm, Eliot Humberstone, Lynn Myring,
Sheila Snowden, Janet Cook, Shirley Bond S.R.D., Felicity Brooks, Helen Edom

Designed by
Steve Page, Roger Priddy, Iain Ashman, Kim Blundell,
Chris Scollen, Robert Walster

Illustrated by
Peter Bull, Guy Smith, Martin Newton, Louise Nevett, Joseph McEwan,
Basil Arm, Malcolm English, Bob Hershey, Gordon Wylie, Kuo Kang Chen,
Philip Schramm, Teri Gower, Chris Lyon

CONTENTS

THINGS ON WHEELS

What are gears?
What makes the wheels turn?
How does an engine work?
What is four wheel drive?
Which trains are the fastest?

Going places on wheels

This part of the book is all about different types of things on wheels. It shows what the first bicycles, motorbikes, cars and trains looked like and explains how they work. You can also find out about different types of racing vehicles.

You can find out how this train works on page 20.

These are the working parts of a car. You can find out how they work on pages 6 to 9.

On page 16 you can see the differences between an old-fashioned high-wheeled bicycle and a modern bicycle.

This is a Formula 1 racing car. Find out about other motor sports on page 12.

The very first motorbike was made of wood. On page 17 you can see how much they have changed.

The wheel story

Before wheels were invented, tree trunks were used as rollers to help push heavy loads along the ground.

The first wheels were made of solid wood about 6,000 years ago. Later, they were fixed to carts pulled by horses and oxen.

Then wheels were made with wooden spokes, which made them lighter. An iron rim round the edge made them last longer.

What makes them go ?

Person power

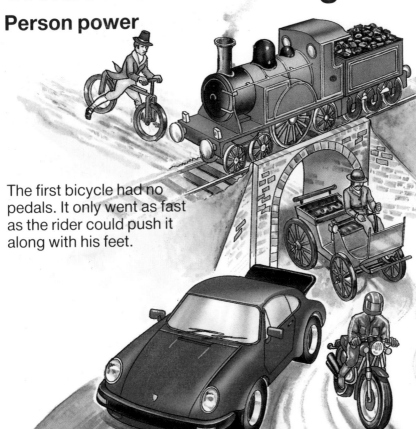

The first bicycle had no pedals. It only went as fast as the rider could push it along with his feet.

Steam engines

Steam trains burned coal or wood. The fire heated a tank of water. Steam from this pushed a rod which made the wheels turn round.

Gas power

The engine in a car and a motorbike is called the internal combustion engine. It burns gas inside it to make the wheels turn.

The first four-wheeled car was a horse-drawn carriage with an engine fitted to it. It was built in 1886 by a German called Gottlieb Daimler.

Later, wheels were made with metal spokes. They were much stronger and lighter, so were good for bicycle wheels.

Train wheels are made of very strong steel. They have a ridge on the inside to stop them running off the track.

All car and bicycle wheels have air filled (pneumatic) tires. These make riding over bumps in the road more comfortable.

3

Parts of the car

In a car factory, all the pieces needed to make a car are arranged in order. As each car moves along a line, all the parts are fitted to it. This is called an assembly line. At the end the car is finished and needs to be tested for any faults.

These strong steel bars lower the car body down on to the chassis.

The chassis

The engine, clutch and gearbox, driveshaft, rear axle, rear differential and suspension are all supported in a steel frame called the chassis. (This has been left out of the picture to make it clearer).

The engine is cased in and fitted to the front of the car.

The driveshaft joins the engine and gearbox to the rear axle.

Engine

Gearshift

Gearbox

Bumper

Radiator

The clutch and the gearbox allow the car to be driven at different speeds and to go backwards.

Clutch

Lights

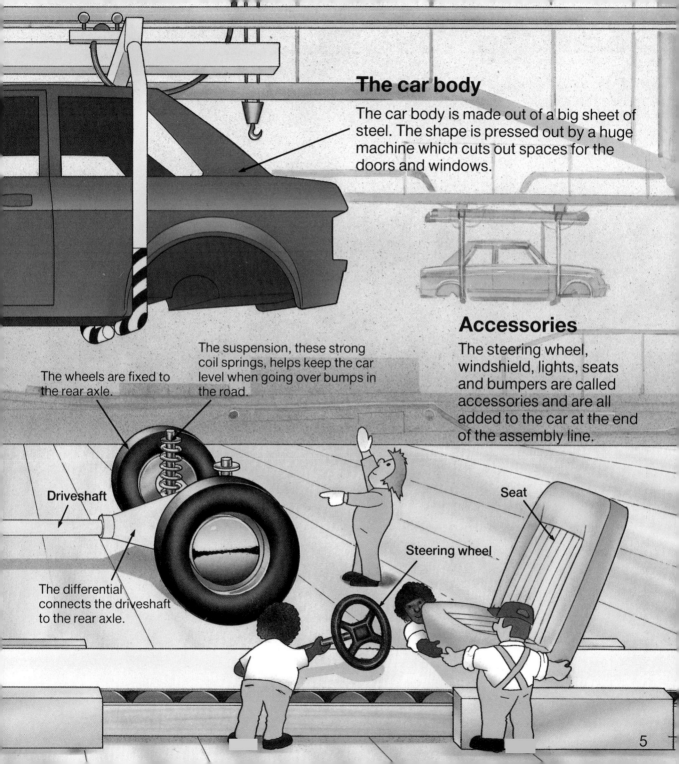

The car body

The car body is made out of a big sheet of steel. The shape is pressed out by a huge machine which cuts out spaces for the doors and windows.

Accessories

The steering wheel, windshield, lights, seats and bumpers are called accessories and are all added to the car at the end of the assembly line.

The suspension, these strong coil springs, helps keep the car level when going over bumps in the road.

The wheels are fixed to the rear axle.

Driveshaft

The differential connects the driveshaft to the rear axle.

Seat

Steering wheel

5

How an engine works

A car engine has many different moving parts that need to be kept oiled to keep it working well. Car engines run on a mixture of gas and air which burns explosively inside the engine.

When the engine is switched on, the pistons move up and down inside the cylinders. This up and down movement turns the crankshaft around. The crankshaft turns the driveshaft, which makes the wheels go around.

Spark plug

Cylinder

Piston

Carburetor

Radiator

Crankshaft

Connecting rod

The carburetor

Gas is mixed with air in the carburetor before it goes into the cylinder.

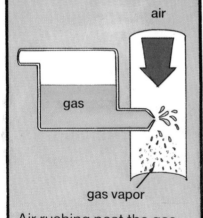

air

gas

gas vapor

Air rushing past the gas breaks it up into tiny droplets so small you cannot see them. This is called gas vapor.

1. Gas vapor is sucked into the top of the cylinder when the piston moves down.

2. The piston moves up and squeezes the gas vapor into a small space in the top of the cylinder.

3. An electric spark from the spark plug sets light to the gas vapor. It explodes, pushing the piston down.

4. Exhaust fumes are pushed out along the exhaust pipe by the piston moving up.

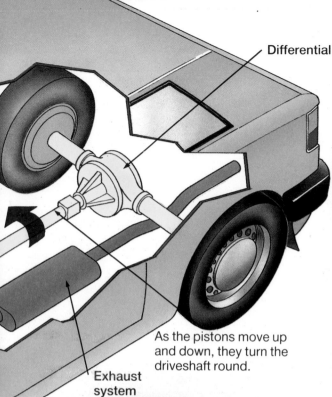

Differential

As the pistons move up and down, they turn the driveshaft round.

Exhaust system

This engine has four cylinders. More powerful engines have as many as six or 12 cylinders.

Piston power

The force that fires a cannonball from a cannon is similar to the force which pushes the pistons in the cylinders. When the gunpowder is lit, it explodes and hot gases force the ball out.

Driving the rear wheels *

At the end of the driveshaft is a cogged wheel or gear which connects to a larger gear on the rear axle.

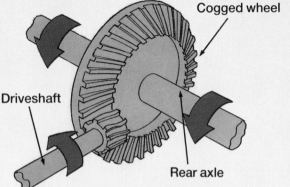

Cogged wheel

Driveshaft

Rear axle

The teeth of one gear fit into the other to make it turn. This makes the power from the engine drive the rear axle and rear wheels.

Hot engines

The radiator is a narrow metal box which contains water. Water is pumped around the engine to keep it cool.

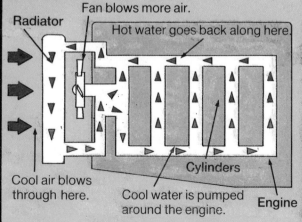

Fan blows more air.

Radiator

Hot water goes back along here.

Cool air blows through here.

Cool water is pumped around the engine.

Cylinders

Engine

*This picture is simplified. There are actually many more gear wheels in this part (the "differential"), to allow the rear wheels to go at different speeds around corners.

On the road

On these pages you can find out how the clutch and gears make the car go at different speeds and how the brakes work.

What are gears?

Gears are cogged wheels which fit together and turn at different speeds depending on the number of teeth they have.

This gear has 10 teeth.

This gear has 20 teeth.

The small one turns twice as fast as the big one.

Gearshift

Gearbox

Brake pedal

Most cars have four forward gears and one reverse. Trucks can have as many as 16 gears.

How the gearbox works

The top row of gears inside the gearbox are turned by the engine. They turn the bottom row, which make the wheels go around.

Most cars have drum brakes on rear wheels.

Using the gears

When starting off, the driver puts the engine into first gear. It needs a lot of power to get the car moving.

Second and third gear help the car to gain speed.

Fourth gear is used for driving along at a fast, steady speed.

Reverse gear changes the direction of the wheels so the car goes backwards.

How the clutch works

To change gear the driver has to press the clutch pedal down. This separates the two discs and stops the engine from turning the wheels.

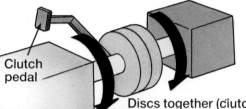

Clutch pedal

Discs together (clutch engaged)

Discs apart (clutch disengaged)

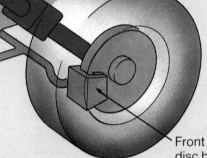

Front brakes are usually disc brakes.

How the brakes work

When the driver presses the brake pedal, pads are forced to rub against all four wheels. When they rub together, a force called friction stops them moving. Friction between the brakes and the wheels makes a car slow down.

Drum brakes

The brake drum is fixed inside the wheel. So when the brake shoes press out against the drum, the wheels slow down and stop.

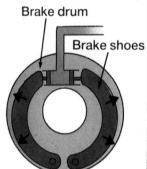

Brake drum

Brake shoes

Steering a car

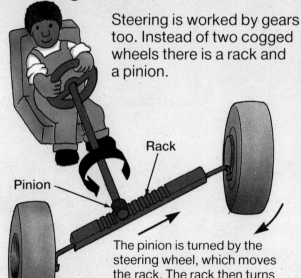

Steering is worked by gears too. Instead of two cogged wheels there is a rack and a pinion.

Rack

Pinion

The pinion is turned by the steering wheel, which moves the rack. The rack then turns the wheels.

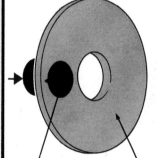

Disc brakes

A steel disc is fixed inside the wheel. When the brake pads press in on the disc, friction stops the wheel moving.

Brake pads

Steel disc

Grand Prix racing

Winning the Grand Prix Championship is the greatest achievement of all motor racing. Drivers and cars battle for ten months of the year on race tracks all over the world. They cover 5,470km (3,400 miles) during the 16 Grand Prix races. The drivers score points if they are among the first six to finish each race. There are two world championships, one for the cars and one for the drivers.

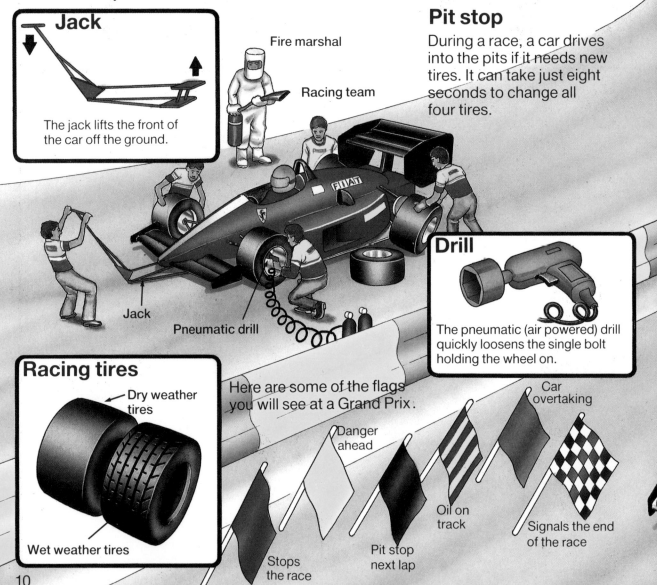

Jack

The jack lifts the front of the car off the ground.

Fire marshal

Racing team

Jack

Pneumatic drill

Pit stop

During a race, a car drives into the pits if it needs new tires. It can take just eight seconds to change all four tires.

Drill

The pneumatic (air powered) drill quickly loosens the single bolt holding the wheel on.

Racing tires

Dry weather tires

Wet weather tires

Here are some of the flags you will see at a Grand Prix.

Danger ahead

Car overtaking

Oil on track

Stops the race

Pit stop next lap

Signals the end of the race

Driving seat

The driver's seat is molded exactly to his shape.

The engine is so powerful it uses 4.5 liters (1 gallon) of gas every 8km (5 miles). The cheapest Formula 1 engine costs as much as six family cars.

Air pushes down on the airfoils at the front and back to keep the car on the ground.

Air pushes down here

The driver has a radio fitted inside his helmet so he can talk to his team during the race.

Airfoil

The car is only 76cm (30 inches) high. It cuts through the air easily because it is so long and low.

Brake duct

Safety

The driver wears a fireproof hood under his helmet to protect his face.

Different styles of racing helmets.

Gas is carried in rubberized tanks all around the driver.

The rear tires are nearly 48cm (19 inches) wide. They are smooth and sticky to touch, and grip the track well. The driver can race around corners at up to 152km/h (95mph).

The brakes can slow the car from 290 to 65km/h (180 to 40mph) in under three seconds. As they get very hot during a race, these ducts let air blow on to the brakes to cool them down.

Motor sports

There are many types of motor sports. Here are just three of them. The cars are all different and have been specially prepared in some way for their particular sport.

Airfoil

Drag racing

Drag racing is a test of speed between two dragster cars. They race on a straight track over 400m (1/4 of a mile).

A drag race

Slicks

The driver makes the rear tires spin around. This makes them hot and sticky so the car gets a good grip on the track when starting.

In just two seconds the car accelerates from 0 to 160km/h (0 to 100mph).

At the finish it is travelling at 320km/h (200mph).

Parachutes help slow the car down.

Start

Finish

Stock car racing

In stock car racing, old cars are raced on oval shaped dirt tracks.

Different classes of races are held for different types of cars.

All windows and back seats are taken out for safety.

Powerful brakes, suspension and engine are fitted.

Safety

Roll bar

Safety harness

Safety harness and roll bar protect the driver if the car turns over.

Slingshot dragster

The rear tires, called slicks, have no tread and are made of very soft rubber. The front wheels are very light and thin, like bicycle wheels.

The high airfoil at the back and the one between the front wheels stop the car lifting off the ground.

Airfoil

Funny cars

This dragster is called a Funny Car. It has a top speed of 418km/h (260mph). To make the car go fast it burns rocket fuel in its engine.

This old Ford Anglia has been fitted with a special engine and fat rear tires to race in a mixed class.

Rallying

Rallies are held on snowy mountain roads, across rough country and through deserts all over the world.

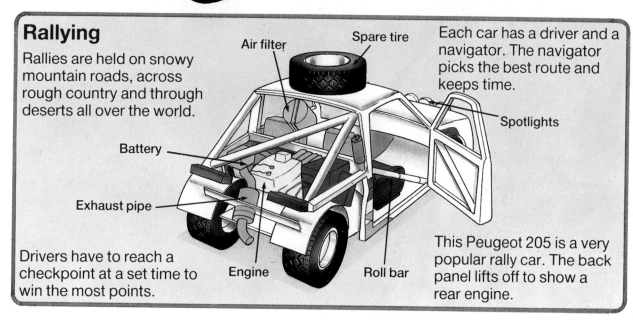

Air filter

Spare tire

Each car has a driver and a navigator. The navigator picks the best route and keeps time.

Spotlights

Battery

Exhaust pipe

Drivers have to reach a checkpoint at a set time to win the most points.

Engine

Roll bar

This Peugeot 205 is a very popular rally car. The back panel lifts off to show a rear engine.

13

Off the road

Some cars are specially designed to travel over very rugged ground where there are no roads. An ordinary car is designed to run on good roads and would soon break down in conditions like these. The exhaust pipe would be knocked off, the tires would burst and it could not go through rivers.

'County' Station Wagon

The Land Rover was designed for driving in rough country. This one looks very much like the first Land Rover ever built in 1948. The design has not changed much because it is so good.

The car body is high off the ground. It is bolted together in sections, so it will not bend or twist.

Spare tire

Rear axle

Folding side step

Tough aluminum body

Front differential

Front axle

Rear differential

Extra springy suspension cushions the driver and passengers from bumps.

Big, chunky tires help the car grip uneven ground. They are made with very thick rubber so they will not split.

What is four wheel drive?

An ordinary car has one differential which drives either the front or the rear wheels. A four wheel drive car has a differential at the front and the back so the engine turns all four wheels. This means that four wheel drive vehicles travel well over mud, snow or sand.

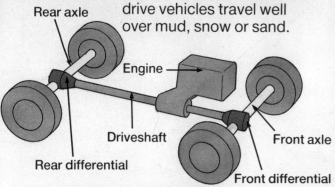

Rear axle

Engine

Driveshaft

Rear differential

Front axle

Front differential

Tires

Heavy duty tires with deep tread for going over rocks and sand.

What can four wheel drive do?

These are some of the things that four wheel drive (4WD) cars can do.

This Land Rover can be driven through rivers up to 50cm (20in) deep.

This pick-up truck can climb very steep slopes because of the extra power in its wheels.

This jeep can be driven on steeply banked tracks without it tipping over.

Other 4WD vehicles

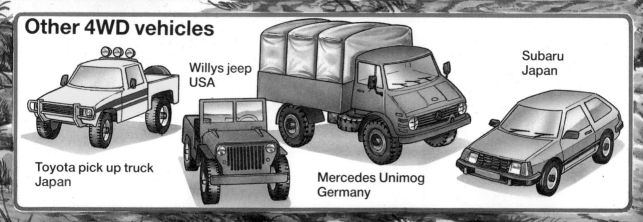

Willys jeep USA

Subaru Japan

Toyota pick up truck Japan

Mercedes Unimog Germany

15

Bicycles

The first bicycle, called a hobbyhorse, was built about 150 years ago. It had a front wheel that could be turned but no pedals. Later, pedals were fixed to the front wheel to make the bicycle go faster.

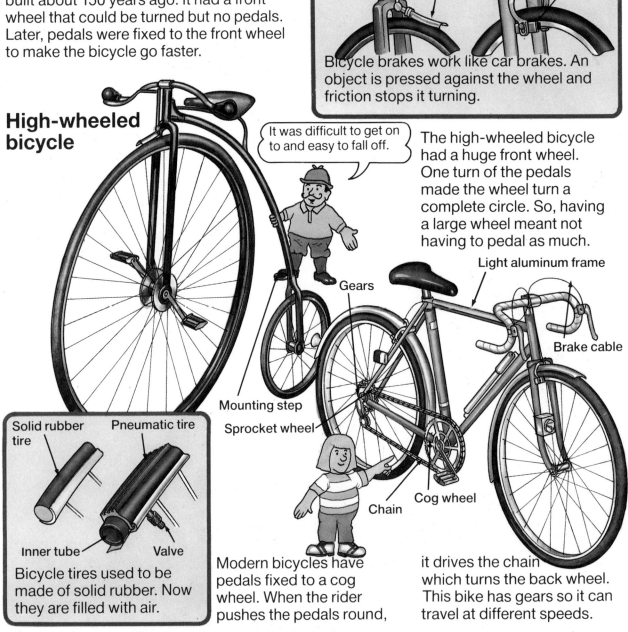

Spoon brake

Brake block

Bicycle brakes work like car brakes. An object is pressed against the wheel and friction stops it turning.

High-wheeled bicycle

It was difficult to get on to and easy to fall off.

The high-wheeled bicycle had a huge front wheel. One turn of the pedals made the wheel turn a complete circle. So, having a large wheel meant not having to pedal as much.

Light aluminum frame

Gears

Brake cable

Mounting step

Sprocket wheel

Cog wheel

Chain

Solid rubber tire

Pneumatic tire

Inner tube   Valve

Bicycle tires used to be made of solid rubber. Now they are filled with air.

Modern bicycles have pedals fixed to a cog wheel. When the rider pushes the pedals round, it drives the chain which turns the back wheel. This bike has gears so it can travel at different speeds.

Motorbikes

The first motorbike was built about 120 years ago. It was a bicycle fitted with a steam engine. Now there are many different types of motorbike for different racing sports.

Road racing

A Grand Prix racing bike is the fastest bike built today. The engine is covered in so the bike can cut through the air.

YAMAHA

Arrows show the movement of air over the bike.

The rider crouches forward so the wind rushes over him.

Sidecar racing

Low, streamlined shape

During a race, the passenger leans right out of the sidecar to balance it as it speeds round corners.

Trials bikes

Strong suspension

Trials riding is a cross-country competition which tests the skill of the rider. The bike has strong tires to help it grip over rocks and through mud.

Dragbikes

Wide rear tires (slicks).

Dragbikes have very powerful engines. The rider lies right across the bike so it travels faster through the wind.

Types of trains

The first railway tracks were built about 400 years ago, when animals were used to pull heavy loads along rails. At that time, the rails were made of wood.

The very first engines were driven by steam. Today trains are pulled by diesel engines and electric motors. On these pages you can see all three types.

Steam trains

American type 4-4-0

The American type 4-4-0 was one of the first steam trains to cross America.

The smokestack catches sparks from the fire.

Boiler

Bell

The tender carries wood for the fire.

How steam turns the wheels

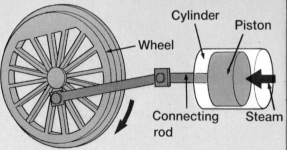

Wheel

Cylinder

Piston

Connecting rod

Steam

Burning coal or wood heats water in a large tank, called a boiler. Steam from the boiling water pushes pistons in a cylinder. The pistons are connected to the wheels.

Driving wheels power the train.

Leading wheels guide the train around bends.

Cowcatcher to push stray animals off the track.

Electric trains

Electric trains are the fastest in the world. They pick up electricity from overhead cables or from a third track on the ground.

Hikari express

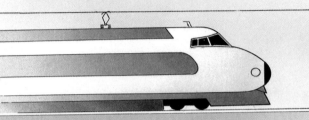

This Japanese train, nicknamed 'The Bullet' can travel at 209km/h (130mph).

Diesel trains

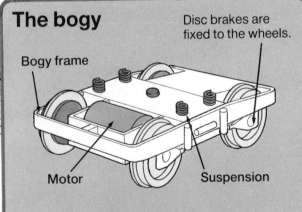

British Rail Inter-City 125

This train has a diesel engine. It is the same as a car engine but burns diesel oil instead of gas. The diesel engine produces electricity in a generator. Electricity goes along cables to motors which turn the wheels and work the heaters and lights.

Underground railways

The guide wheels keep the train on the tracks.

Steel beam

On the Metro, the Paris underground, the trains run on pneumatic tires. The trains are faster and quieter with rubber wheels.

The bogy

Disc brakes are fixed to the wheels.

Bogy frame

Motor

Suspension

The train carriages rest on top of bogies like this one. It lets the train bend as it goes around corners.

19

Trains today

Today's high speed trains are built for fast inter-city travel. This French TGV (Train à Grande Vitesse which means 'high speed train') has an average speed of 260km/h (161mph), which makes it the fastest passenger train in the world. A special track was built for it, without sharp bends and steep hills.

There are no signals on the TGV track for the driver to look for. Instead, electronic signals are sent to the driver's cab. They tell the driver what speed to travel.

The driver has a radio-telephone in the cab and there are emergency telephones beside the track every 1km (0.6 miles).

There is a locomotive carriage at each end of the train. This is what powers the train.

Driver's cab

Concrete sleepers

SNCF

Tracks

Steel rail

The distance between the two parallel tracks of a railway line is called the gauge. Throughout the world there is a standard gauge which is 1.43m (4ft 8½ inches).

Electric motors here turn the wheels.

SNCF

The track is raised on one side so that the train can speed around corners.

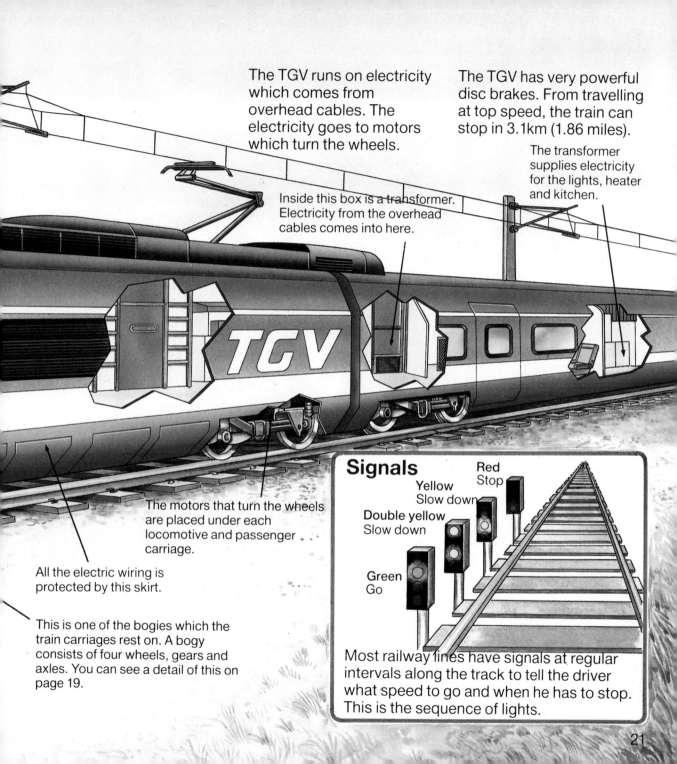

The TGV runs on electricity which comes from overhead cables. The electricity goes to motors which turn the wheels.

The TGV has very powerful disc brakes. From travelling at top speed, the train can stop in 3.1km (1.86 miles).

The transformer supplies electricity for the lights, heater and kitchen.

Inside this box is a transformer. Electricity from the overhead cables comes into here.

The motors that turn the wheels are placed under each locomotive and passenger carriage.

All the electric wiring is protected by this skirt.

This is one of the bogies which the train carriages rest on. A bogy consists of four wheels, gears and axles. You can see a detail of this on page 19.

Signals

Red
Stop

Yellow
Slow down

Double yellow
Slow down

Green
Go

Most railway lines have signals at regular intervals along the track to tell the driver what speed to go and when he has to stop. This is the sequence of lights.

Fastest on wheels

The first cars and motorbikes travelled very slowly. A hundred years ago, cars in Britain were only allowed to go at 6.4km/h (4mph). A man had to walk in front of the car to make sure the driver kept within the speed limit.

Fastest on the road

**Aston Martin
V8 Vantage**

The Aston Martin V8 Vantage is one of the world's fastest and most powerful cars. It can accelerate from 0 to 161km/h (0 to 100mph) in just 11.9 seconds.

It has a top speed of 270km/h (168mph).

Car factories, like British Leyland, produce one car every six minutes. An Aston Martin takes 16 weeks to produce because each car is hand-built.

Fastest on rails

These trains are the fastest steam, diesel and electric trains in the world. They have all set speed records in the past and have been responsible for cutting down journey times between main cities. Here you can see how far each could travel in one hour.

Flying Scotsman (UK)

LNER Mallard (UK)

96km (60 miles)

161km (100 miles)

The Flying Scotsman was the first steam locomotive to provide a non-stop service from London to Edinburgh.

In 1938, Mallard set a new record for steam engines, travelling at 203km/h (126mph). No other steam train has travelled faster.

22

Kawasaki GPZ1000RX

One of the fastest motorbikes on the road today is the Kawasaki GPZ1000. It can travel at over 260km/h (161mph).

The rider is protected from the wind by sleek panels. Holes in each side panel let cool air blow on to the engine to stop it from overheating.

World Land Speed Record

This is a test of speed run over a straight mile (1.6km). The vehicles competing must make one run in each direction within an hour.

Car class

Thrust 2, broke the speed record in 1983. The car travelled at an average speed of 1,019.4km/h (633.45mph).

Motorbike class

This very unusual motorbike, Lightning Bolt, broke the speed record in 1978, travelling at an average speed of 512.7km/h (318.59mph).

Inter-City 125 (UK)	Hikari express (Japan)	TGV (France)
200km (125miles)	210km (130miles)	260km (161 miles)

The Inter-City 125 is the fastest diesel train in the world. It can reach a top speed of 231km/h (143mph).

Japanese National Railways built a new track for this train which speeds along at over 210km/h (130mph).

This is the fastest train in the world. During tests it reached an amazing top speed of 390km/h (236mph).

THINGS
THAT FLOAT

What is a hydrofoil?
How does a hovercraft work?
What powers a cruise liner?
How fast is a speedboat?
How does a paddle boat work?

All about ships and boats

This part of the book tells you about lots of different ships and boats. You can find out how they float, what makes them go and what they do. It also tells you about some unusual ships and boats around the world, as well as those that have broken records for speed or size.

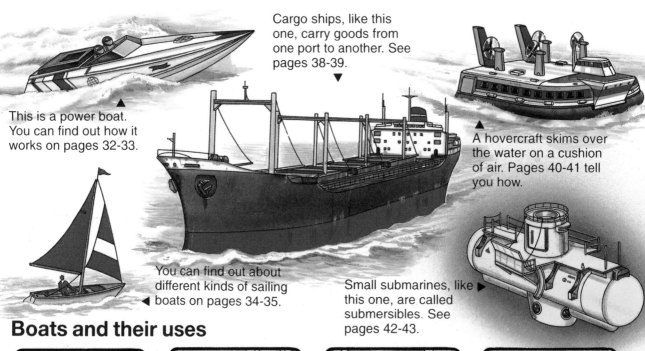

Cargo ships, like this one, carry goods from one port to another. See pages 38-39.

This is a power boat. You can find out how it works on pages 32-33.

A hovercraft skims over the water on a cushion of air. Pages 40-41 tell you how.

You can find out about different kinds of sailing boats on pages 34-35.

Small submarines, like this one, are called submersibles. See pages 42-43.

Boats and their uses

Some large ships, called liners, are built for holiday cruises. They are like floating hotels.

Huge naval ships have a runway on the deck where planes can take off and land.

Some ferries have ramps so cars, trucks and buses can drive on and off them.

Lifeboats are specially built and equipped to save people from drowning at sea.

Floating and sinking

A big steel or wooden boat is very heavy. When it floats it pushes some of the water aside. The water round the boat pushes back. This push (force) of the water holds up the boat if the boat is not too heavy for its size.

A heavy boat needs to have high sides so lots of water can push against it.

Wood is light for its size and floats easily. ▼

Although metal is heavy, a steel ship can float. ▶

Hull

Because it is hollow, the metal shell or hull of a boat weighs less than a solid amount of metal of the same size. Both push aside the same amount of water, but the force of the water can support the weight of the hull because it is hollow.

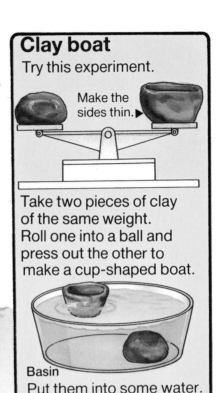
Boat power

The earliest way of moving a boat along was by a person's muscles, using paddles or oars.

For thousands of years, sails were used to catch the wind and push the boat forward.

Now most large ships have diesel engines, but some use steam turbine engines.

Many modern submarines use nuclear power to turn steam turbines.

27

Steamboats

The first engines were invented at the end of the 18th century and were powered by steam. Here you can see an early steamboat engine. The steam is used to turn paddle-wheels either side of the boat. As they turn, they push against the water. This makes the boat move forward.

What is steam?

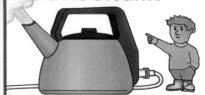

Steam is very hot and can burn you.

Steam is a gas which is made when water boils. You can see the powerful way it spouts from a boiling kettle. It is this power which works a steam-engine.

Steamships

Savannah

In 1819, the first sailing ship with an engine crossed the Atlantic. An American ship, *Savannah*, only used its engines for 8 hours of the 21 day journey.

Sirius

The first steamship to make a crossing without using its sails was the British ship, *Sirius*, built in 1837. It took 18 days.

1. Coal is burnt to heat water in the boiler.

2. The steam is piped from the boiler into a cylinder.

3. As steam enters the first cylinder, the piston is pushed up, turning the crankshaft.

The turning paddles dip into the water, moving the boat along.

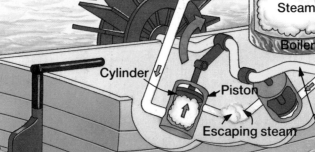

Paddle-wheel

Steam

Boiler

Cylinder

Piston

Escaping steam

Crankshaft

4. A small hole lets the steam escape so the piston can fall back down again.

5. The first piston goes down while steam enters the second cylinder, pushing its piston up.

6. The up and down movement of the pistons turns the crankshaft which turns the paddle-wheels.

Screw propulsion

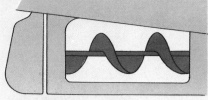

Early type of screw propeller.

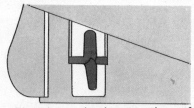

Later type of screw propeller.

In the 1840s screw propellers were invented and fitted to the back of boats. Although they were smaller than paddle-wheels they made the boat go faster. Like paddle-wheels, they were powered by steam engines and were turned by the spinning motion of the crankshaft.

During the trial run of a boat, the end of a long screw propeller broke off. It worked better so propellers were made shorter.

How propellers work

The *Great Britain* was the first iron ship to use a screw propeller rather than paddle-wheels.

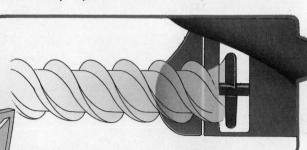

Propellers work by going through the water like a corkscrew goes through a cork. As the blades of the propeller turn, the water is forced backwards. This thrusts the boat forwards.

Steam turbines

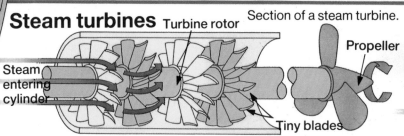

Turbine rotor

Section of a steam turbine.

Propeller

Steam entering cylinder

Tiny blades

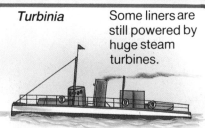

Turbinia

Some liners are still powered by huge steam turbines.

In 1894 Sir Charles Parsons invented the steam turbine. It turned faster and so produced greater speeds.

The hundreds of tiny blades turn with the turbine rotor as steam rushes past. This turns the propeller.

Turbinia was the first turbine powered boat. It was launched in 1897 and had three turbines and three propellers.

Liners

Liners are very big ships. In the past people had to travel by sea if they wanted to go to another country. Nowadays airplanes take much of the passenger traffic and liners are used mostly for holiday cruises.

The biggest passenger liner in use is the *Queen Elizabeth II,* or *QE2.* It is like a small city, with shops, restaurants, movies and even a hospital.

These are kennels where passengers can keep their pets.

This is the ship's theater.

The *QE2*

There are four swimming pools.

Tennis court

In the ship's shopping center, passengers can buy things, such as clothes, food and flowers.

The *QE2* has two propellers, each with six blades.

This is the ship's laundry.

The ship's health club is here.

This is the ship's control room – a huge computer works out its speed and direction.

This is the turbine room, where all the ship's diesel powered turbine engines are.

Measuring speed

At sea, speed is measured in knots. The name comes from the time when a sailor would throw the end of a knotted line into sea. As the ship moved forward, the line unravelled and the knots, which were equally spaced, were counted over a period of time.

The average travelling speed of the *QE2* is 28½ knots.

Nowadays a knot is a speed of one nautical mile per hour. A nautical (sea) mile is different from a land mile. It

is 1852 meters, so a knot is 1.85 kilometers an hour (1.15 miles an hour).

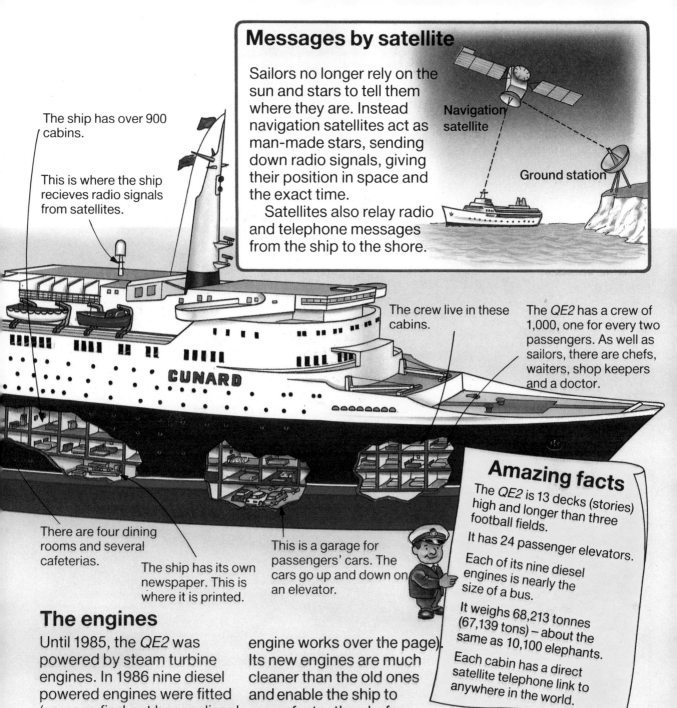

Messages by satellite

Sailors no longer rely on the sun and stars to tell them where they are. Instead navigation satellites act as man-made stars, sending down radio signals, giving their position in space and the exact time.

Satellites also relay radio and telephone messages from the ship to the shore.

Navigation satellite

Ground station

The ship has over 900 cabins.

This is where the ship recieves radio signals from satellites.

The crew live in these cabins.

The QE2 has a crew of 1,000, one for every two passengers. As well as sailors, there are chefs, waiters, shop keepers and a doctor.

CUNARD

There are four dining rooms and several cafeterias.

The ship has its own newspaper. This is where it is printed.

This is a garage for passengers' cars. The cars go up and down on an elevator.

Amazing facts

The QE2 is 13 decks (stories) high and longer than three football fields.

It has 24 passenger elevators.

Each of its nine diesel engines is nearly the size of a bus.

It weighs 68,213 tonnes (67,139 tons) – about the same as 10,100 elephants.

Each cabin has a direct satellite telephone link to anywhere in the world.

The engines

Until 1985, the QE2 was powered by steam turbine engines. In 1986 nine diesel powered engines were fitted (you can find out how a diesel engine works over the page). Its new engines are much cleaner than the old ones and enable the ship to move faster than before.

Boats and their engines

Most small boats have a gasoline engine fixed at the back. They are called outboard motors because the engine can be lifted off the boat. Larger boats have powerful diesel engines, housed inside the hull. They are called inboard motors.

This boat is called a power boat. It has two diesel engines and two propellers.

Panel showing boat's speed and how much fuel there is.

Steering wheel

Deck

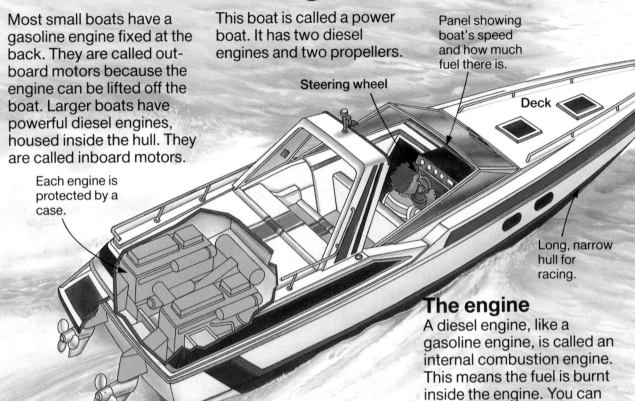

Each engine is protected by a case.

Long, narrow hull for racing.

The engine

A diesel engine, like a gasoline engine, is called an internal combustion engine. This means the fuel is burnt inside the engine. You can see how on the next page.

Pilot boats

Pilot boats take sea pilots to large ships. The pilot then guides the ship through dangerous and unfamiliar water.

Motor cruisers

Motor cruisers are often big boats, with living quarters on board. They are used for cruising holidays.

Tenders

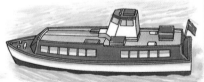

A tender, such as this one, is kept aboard large ocean liners for carrying passengers from the ship to the shore.

The diesel engine

The diesel engine was invented by a German, Dr Rudolph Diesel, in 1897. It uses a special type of fuel called diesel oil.

A boat engine can have between two and twelve cylinders. The more cylinders an engine has, the greater its power.

This engine has four cylinders. Each cylinder shows one of four things that happen to turn the propeller.

2. The valve closes and the piston moves up, squashing the air. This makes the air very hot.

3. The injector squirts fuel into the hot air. The mixture explodes, pushing the piston down.

1. Air enters the cylinder through the inlet valve and the piston moves down.

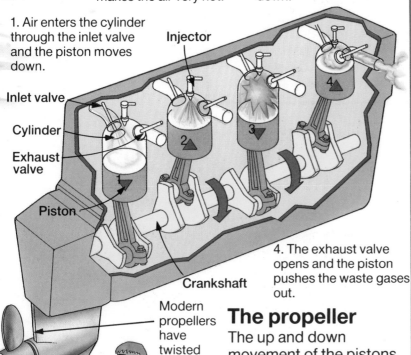

Injector

Inlet valve

Cylinder

Exhaust valve

Piston

Crankshaft

Modern propellers have twisted blades.

4. The exhaust valve opens and the piston pushes the waste gases out.

The propeller

The up and down movement of the pistons turns the crankshaft which turns the propeller. Its blades push the water backwards and the boat is driven forwards.

Power boat racing

Power boats are designed specially for racing. The fastest have jet engines, the kind of engine an airplane uses.

A famous racing event is the Bahamas Powerboat Grand-Prix.

Record breaker

It took 3 days, 8 hours and 31 minutes to cross a distance of over 5,000 km (3,000 miles).

In 1986, a British power boat, *Virgin Atlantic Challenger*, crossed the Atlantic in record time. It won the Blue Riband, previously awarded to liners for the fastest Atlantic crossing.

Sailing boats

For thousands of years boats with sails have relied on the power of the wind to push them along. The sails "catch" the wind and the force of the wind pushing against the sails moves the boat forward.

An arrangement of sails is called a rig. You can find out about the development of rigs on the opposite page.

The first sails

wind

wind

About 5,000 years ago, the Egyptians used square sails. When the wind blew from behind the boat was pushed forward.

For thousands of years the Arabs used triangular (lateen) sails. They used ropes to curve the sails round to catch the wind.

The mainsail is joined to the boom and mast.

The jib is an extra sail which catches the wind. It helps to steer the boat and turn it round.

Nowadays most sails are made of a light, waterproof material.

Mainsail

Jib

Mast

Boom

Tiller

Rudder

Centerboard

Hull

Modern sails are triangular with a curved outside edge. This style is called Bermudan.

Small boats like this sailing dinghy only use a mainsail and a smaller sail, called the jib.

Steering the boat

The boat is steered by the tiller, which acts like a steering wheel. The tiller is joined to the rudder which changes the direction of the boat.

When the tiller is moved to the right, it moves the rudder and the boat turns left. When it is moved to the left, the boat goes right.

The centerboard keeps the boat going straight. It helps to stop the boat drifting sideways, when the wind pushes on the sails.

The catamaran

The trimaran

A catamaran has two hulls and a trimaran has a central hull with two smaller hulls either side. Both have less boat in the water than an ordinary boat and so they float high in the water. They skim over the water and can go very fast.

Tacking

Sail

Direction of wind

If a sailor wants to go in the direction the wind is blowing from, he steers in a zig-zag. This is called tacking. On each part of the zig-zag the wind is blowing on the side of the sails and pushes the boat forwards.

The America's Cup

The America's Cup is a yachting event which takes place every four years in the country of the last winner. In 1986-87 the races were held in Australia and were won by the American yacht *Stars and Stripes.*

America's Cup trophy

Story of rigs

Chinese ship

In the 9th century, Chinese ships were built with several masts and sails made of bamboo matting. This design lasted for hundreds of years.

Three-masted ship

In the 15th century, three–masted ships were built in Europe. These ships were used for sea battles, exploring and trade.

Clipper

In the 1820s cargo ships called Clippers were made. They had many large sails, a long slim hull and could go very fast.

35

Muscle power

Long ago people used their hands like paddles to propel their boats along. Then they made wooden paddles which were bigger than their hands and worked better.

Later long oars were used, like the ones in the picture. These worked even more efficiently.

Rowing boats like this one are made from very light but strong material, such as fiberglass.

The cox shouts instructions to the crew and steers the boat.

Racing crews often practice several hours a day to make sure they work well together to make the boat go faster.

The cox

Rowlock

Pushing water aside

The way you move a paddle or oar through water is similar to the way you move your arms when you swim. As the paddle or oar pushes the water backwards, the boat moves forwards.

Each oar rests on a rowlock, so the oar works like a lever.

Ships with oars

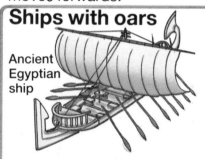

Ancient Egyptian ship

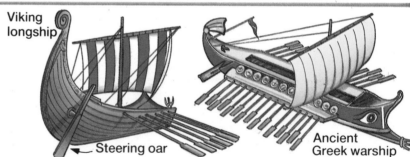

Viking longship

Steering oar

Ancient Greek warship

As long as 5,000 years ago, the Egyptians rowed their ships along with oars when there was no wind or it was blowing the wrong way.

About 800 years ago, the people of Scandinavia, called Vikings, built long, narrow ships, called longships. They had up to 25 oars on each side.

The oars of an Ancient Greek warship were usually arranged on different levels so that the oarsmen did not get in each other's way.

Going faster

People soon discovered that the length of the oars was important. A single pull on a long oar pushes the boat further forward than a single pull on a short oar.

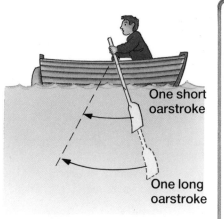

One short oarstroke

One long oarstroke

The boat's streamlined shape enables it to travel through the water at great speed.

Canoeing

Protective helmet

Double ended paddle

A type of canoe is still used in some countries, such as Alaska, for fishing and transport. Mostly, canoes are used for sporting events, such as the slalom. Competitors have to weave their canoe in and out of a row of poles in fast flowing water, without hitting them.

Unusual boats

Gondola

Gondolas are boats used on the canals of Venice in Italy. A gondolier stands at the back of the boat, propelling it along with one long oar.

Punt

Flat bottomed boats called punts are used for pleasure. A long pole is pushed against the river bed to propel the punt along.

Reed boat

Boats made of reeds are still used in some countries round the world, such as Peru in South America. People use long poles to push the boat along.

Cargo ships

Cargo ships carry goods, or cargo, from one port to another. The cargo can be anything from oranges to steel rods or coal to wheat.

A port has roads and railways to bring cargo to the ship. It also has huge warehouses where cargo can be stored before being loaded or unloaded on to or off a ship.

Containers

Warehouses

A ship's cargo is always checked to ensure nothing is smuggled in or out of a country.

Special crane for lifting containers.

Container ship

Grain being piped down a chute.

Crane with sling unloading boxes.

▼A container ship carries cargo in large boxes called containers. These are packed before being taken to the port.

Some ships carry cargo of all shapes and sizes. It has to be tightly packed so it cannot slide about at sea ◄ and be damaged.

Some ships carry bulk food, such as sugar or wheat. It is poured down chutes into the ship and sucked out again by pipes.

Roll on/roll off ships are built so loaded trucks and trains can drive straight on and off the ship, without delay.
▼

Roll on/roll off ship

Road

Railway

Oil tankers

Very big ships that carry oil are called supertankers. They are too large for most docks so the oil is piped to storage tanks from special terminals outside the port.

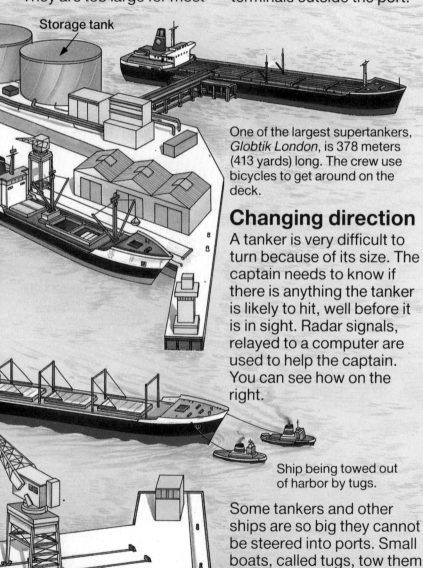

Storage tank

One of the largest supertankers, *Globtik London*, is 378 meters (413 yards) long. The crew use bicycles to get around on the deck.

Changing direction

A tanker is very difficult to turn because of its size. The captain needs to know if there is anything the tanker is likely to hit, well before it is in sight. Radar signals, relayed to a computer are used to help the captain. You can see how on the right.

Ship being towed out of harbor by tugs.

Some tankers and other ships are so big they cannot be steered into ports. Small boats, called tugs, tow them in and out of the docks, and put them into position.

Using computers

Tankers send out signals, called radar, to look for ships and rocks. Radar travels through the air until it "hits" something.

The signals bounce back to a radar screen. The tanker's computer works out how fast and in which direction the ship must go to avoid a collision.

Computer sails

Shin Aitoku Maru

The Japanese tanker, *Shin Aitoku Maru,* has special metal sails to push it along. A computer works out when the sails should be turned to catch the wind.

Things that skim

A hovercraft is a type of boat that skims above water or land supported by a cushion of air. It is sometimes called an air-cushion vehicle or ACV.

There are two other types of boats that skim above the water. They are the hydrofoil and the jetfoil. You can find out about them on the opposite page.

The hovercraft

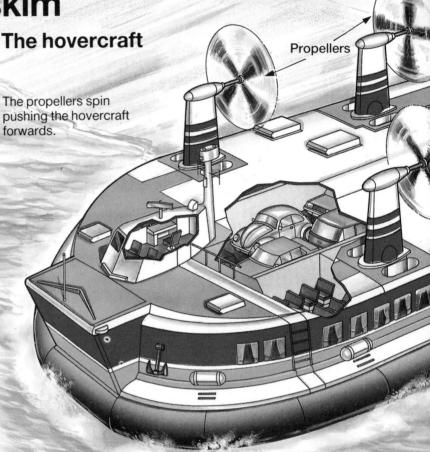

The propellers spin pushing the hovercraft forwards.

Propellers

Floating on air

Yoghurt carton

Air

Styrofoam tray

To test how a hovercraft works, cut the bottom out of a yoghurt carton. Then cut a hole in the middle of a styrofoam tray big enough to put the yoghurt carton in. If you blow into the carton, the tray will move easily on a cushion of air.

Steering the hovercraft

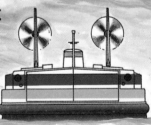

The propellers pivot to steer the hovercraft and the rudders move to one side or the other when it changes direction.

A hovercraft keeps steady in rough water as the skirt can move up and down or bulge out when the waves push the cushion about.

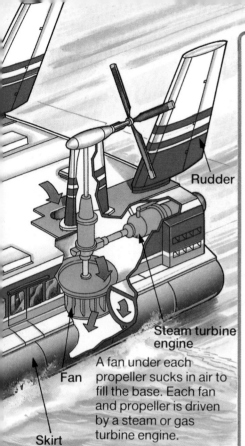

Rudder

Steam turbine engine

Fan

A fan under each propeller sucks in air to fill the base. Each fan and propeller is driven by a steam or gas turbine engine.

Skirt

A rubber skirt fitted round the base stops the cushion of air escaping.

Stopping at the port

A hovercraft comes out of the water. The engines are turned off and as no air goes into the skirt it sinks to rest on its base.

The hydrofoil

A hydrofoil is a boat that has underwater wings (called hydrofoils). The whole boat lifts out of the water as it gathers speed.

How a hydrofoil works

The top surface of the wings of a hydrofoil are smooth, so water quickly runs off them. The wings rise up, lifting the whole boat out of the water. There is then no water to push against the boat so it can go very fast.

V-foils

Some hydrofoils have V shaped wings, called V-foils. They stick out of the water on both sides of the boat as it goes faster.

Submerged foils

Submerged foils stay under the water so the hydrofoil looks as if it has legs. They can change direction to suit different weather conditions.

The Jetfoil

A jetfoil is a type of hydrofoil. It is propelled forwards by two water jets. Gas turbines work the pumps which force the water through holes under great pressure to make the jets.

Direction of water

Submarines

Submarines travel under the sea. They are powered by diesel engines or nuclear powered turbines. A nuclear submarine, like the one in this picture, has a rounder hull than a submarine with a diesel engine. Nuclear submarines can work for years without needing to be refuelled and can stay under water for as long as two years without coming to the surface.

Radio antennae
The radio antennae pick up satellite messages.

The periscope
A periscope is a tube with a mirror at both ends. When it is raised a sailor in the submarine can see what is happening above the water while the rest of the submarine is below the water.

Hydroplanes

Conning tower
The submarine is steered from the conning tower.

Sonar detector
The sonar detector picks up sound waves (see opposite page).

Double hull

Ballast tanks

Control room

Sleeping quarters

Diving

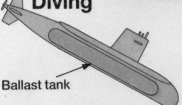

Ballast tank

Before the submarine dives, shutters are opened so the sea floods into the ballast tanks and the submarine sinks.

Underwater

Once under the water, the level of water in the ballast tanks is adjusted so the submarine stays at a chosen depth.

Surfacing

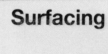

To surface, air is forced into the ballast tanks under great pressure. This forces out the water and the submarine rises.

Propeller

The propeller make the submarine go forwards.

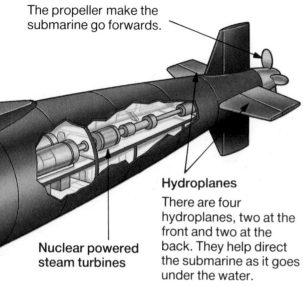

Hydroplanes

There are four hydroplanes, two at the front and two at the back. They help direct the submarine as it goes under the water.

Nuclear powered steam turbines

Submarines have a double hull. Between its two walls are ballast tanks – tanks that are filled with water to make the submarine sink.

Sonar

Sonar is a way of finding out where other ships and submarines are from the sounds they make. There are two kinds of sonar, Active and Passive.

Active sonar

The submarine sends out sound waves. When they hit something they "ping" and an echo bounces back to the submarine.

Passive sonar

Passive sonar picks up the smallest sound using electronic equipment. It makes no sound so the submarine's presence is secret.

The *Turtle*

The first submarine was built by an American in the late 18th century. It was shaped like an egg and had no engines.

Nautilus

In 1958, an American submarine, *Nautilus,* was the first vessel to reach the North Pole. It travelled there under the ice.

The Bathyscaphe

The Bathyscaphe is a submersible (small submarine) designed specially for very deep underwater research.

Lifeboats

Bad weather at sea often causes accidents and shipwrecks. Lifeboats are designed to go out in strong winds and rough seas, and their crews are trained to rescue people in danger of drowning.

Padded jacket
Waterproof padded jacket is worn for warmth. It is brightly colored to show up against the sea.

Waterproof trousers

Lifejacket
Lifejacket, filled with air, keeps a person afloat in the sea.

Bump cap
The bump cap and hood protects the head.

Inflatables

Inflatable lifeboats rescue people close to the shore.

Getting the right way up

1

Superstructure

2

The superstructure has watertight doors.

3

If a lifeboat capsizes, it can come back up again within a few seconds. This is called self-righting. A lifeboat does not sink because air is trapped inside the superstructure (the top of the boat). The weight of the heavy engines in the bottom of the boat then pulls the hull back into the water, so the boat is the right way up again.

Fishing boats

Fishing boats, called trawlers, have enormous nets, called trawls. This trawler is called a purse seiner. Its net circles the fish and is drawn in by a rope before being winched aboard.

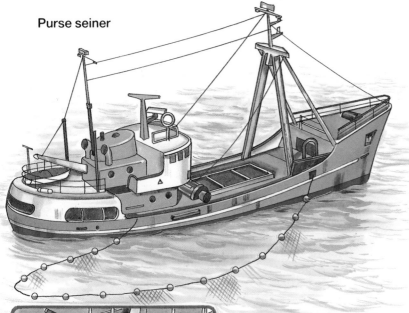

Purse seiner

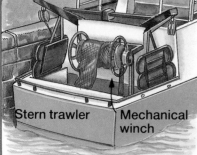

Stern trawler   Mechanical winch

Stern trawlers haul their nets in from the stern (back of the boat). They are hauled in by mechanical winch.

On board

Once on board, the fish are either packed with ice in boxes or put in huge freezers. Ships with freezers can stay at sea for a long time, without the fish going bad.

Some ships even have fish factories on board. You can find out about them on the right.

Factory ships have factories on board where the fish are cleaned and prepared for sale. Often smaller fishing boats off-load their haul onto factory ships at sea.

The fish are sent along big square pipes to huge, square trays. Here, a factory worker cleans and prepares the fish.

Some prepared fish are stored in barrels and then stacked on the ship's deck. Others are packed in trays and frozen.

Biggest and fastest

On this page you can find out about some of the world's biggest and fastest ships. Many of them are naval ships. Some are so big that they have runways on deck where aeroplanes can land and take off.

The biggest

Apart from some tankers, the biggest ships to have been built are three United States' Navy aircraft carriers called *Nimitz*, *Dwight D. Eisenhower* and *Carl Vinson*. Each weighs 92,869 tonnes (91,374 tons).

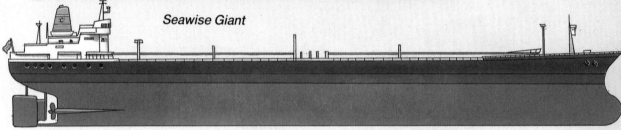

Nimitz

Seawise Giant

The flight deck is 1090 feet (333 meters) long and 252 feet (77 meters) wide.

The biggest oil tanker is called *Seawise Giant*. It is owned by Liberia, though it was built in Japan. It weighs 564,733 tonnes (555,697 tons) and is 1,504 feet (458 meters) long. It is so long that *Nimitz* is only two thirds its length.

The fastest

SS United States

Le Terrible

In 1967 an updated *Bluebird* overturned having reached a speed of 527 km/h (327 mph).

Bluebird

The fastest passenger liner was the *SS United States*. On its first voyage in 1952, it crossed the Atlantic at a speed of 35.59 knots (66 km/h, 41 mph).

A French destroyer (a light, fast warship), called *Le Terrible*, built in 1935 could travel as fast as 45.25 knots (83.9 km/h, 52.1 mph).

The jet-propelled *Bluebird* overturned in 1967, having reached 527 km/h (327 mph). The official record is 511 km/h (319 mph) by "Spirit of Australia" in 1978.

Sea-way code

At sea, there are rules that ships and boats have to obey, just as cars have to obey rules when on the road. Sailors learn to read signs and signals from other ships, lighthouses and buoys. Even though nowadays ships send messages by radio, sailors still learn all the old rules of the sea.

Lighthouse

Lighthouses

Lighthouses are built on rocky headlands. Their lights warn ships and boats to keep clear. They are also built at sea, to mark rocks and reefs.

Lightships

A lightship is used in an area where it is impossible to build a lighthouse, for instance on a sandbank.

Lightship

When standing on the deck of a ship facing its bow (front), port is to the left and starboard to the right.

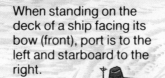

Starboard

Port

Port

Starboard

Buoys

Buoys mark areas that might be dangerous for boats, such as hidden rocks, channels or even wrecks of ships. Their positions are also marked on charts of the sea.

Buoy

Keep to the right

One of the international rules of the sea is to keep to the right. This rule stops ships and boats crashing into each other. These two ships are both going to the right, otherwise they would collide.

Both ships must also give one short blast on a siren.

Sea signals

Nowadays most ships send out radio signals to tell other ships of their whereabouts. They can also make strong blasts on a siren when it is foggy.

THINGS THAT FLY

What makes a helicopter fly?
What is a seaplane?
How does a plane fly?
What were the first planes like?
How can an airship be lighter
than air?

All about aircraft

This part of the book is about many different types of aircraft. It tells you how they fly and what powers them, pushing or pulling them through the air.

You can also find out what happens at an airport, how planes take off and land, and about the special spacecraft which fly in Space.

▲ A helicopter can hover in one place in the air. Find out how on page 60.

This is a bi-plane. You can see what the first bi-plane looked like on page 66.
▼

▲ This hot-air balloon is known as a lighter-than-air craft. See why on page 62.

Page 68 shows you what sort of engine a rocket has and how it works.

On pages 54 and 55 you ▶ can see what the inside of this Jumbo jet looks like.

Plane power

A glider stays in the air only when there are rising air currents to keep it up.

Powerful jet engines have increased the flying speed of many airliners to over 900km/h (569mph).

Rocket engines are like jet engines and push the rocket very fast out into space.

This plane is solar powered. Its engine gets its energy from the sun.

Parts of a plane

The ailerons, flaps, elevators, spoilers and rudder are all moving parts on the wings and tail of a plane which make it fly in different directions.

The flaps and spoilers help lift the plane into the air on take-off and also when coming down to land.

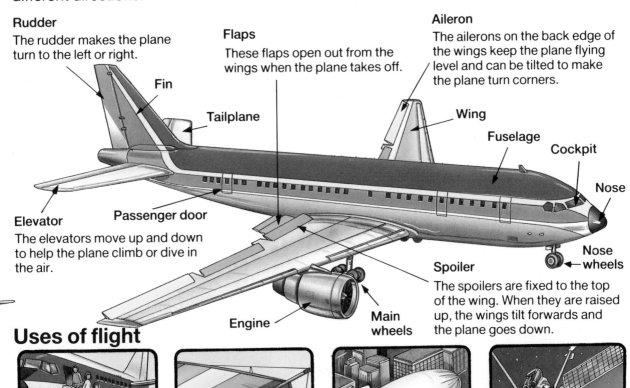

Rudder
The rudder makes the plane turn to the left or right.

Fin

Tailplane

Flaps
These flaps open out from the wings when the plane takes off.

Aileron
The ailerons on the back edge of the wings keep the plane flying level and can be tilted to make the plane turn corners.

Wing

Fuselage

Cockpit

Nose

Nose wheels

Elevator
The elevators move up and down to help the plane climb or dive in the air.

Passenger door

Engine

Main wheels

Spoiler
The spoilers are fixed to the top of the wing. When they are raised up, the wings tilt forwards and the plane goes down.

Uses of flight

Nowadays, many people travel by air. This Airbus can carry 200 passengers.

Hang gliding is a very popular sport. Experienced pilots can stay up in the air for hours.

Some airships are used for advertising, because they can fly very slowly.

Satellites above the Earth send back information about the weather, and relay television signals.

51

How planes fly

How does a plane lift off the ground? You need to know about the air to understand how this happens. Air moves around us all the time. It presses against us and has weight. You feel the weight of the air when the wind blows on your face. A plane stays up in the air because of the air rushing past its wings.

Wing experiment

To see how a wing lifts up, hold a thin strip of paper to your lips and blow hard over the top of it. It rises because there is less air on top and the air underneath pushes up.

Aerofoil

Plane wings are curved on top and flat underneath. This is an aerofoil shape. When a plane flies, air flows faster over the top of the wing, so there is less air pressure there. Stronger air pressure underneath pushes the wings up.

Forces on a plane

When a plane is flying, four forces keep it flying straight and level. These are lift and weight and thrust and drag.

Lift
Air rushing over the top of the wings and pushing from below lifts the plane.

Drag
The force of the air pushing against the plane when it is flying forwards is called drag.

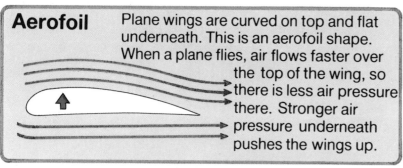

Lift

Drag

Thrust

Weight

Thrust
The propeller pulls the plane forwards through the air. This force is called thrust.

Weight
The weight of the plane pulls it down to balance against the lift.

How planes move about

A plane has to be able to turn, climb and dive. To do this, most planes are fitted with special hinged surfaces on the edges of the wings, tailplane and fins. The pilot uses special controls on the flight deck to move these.

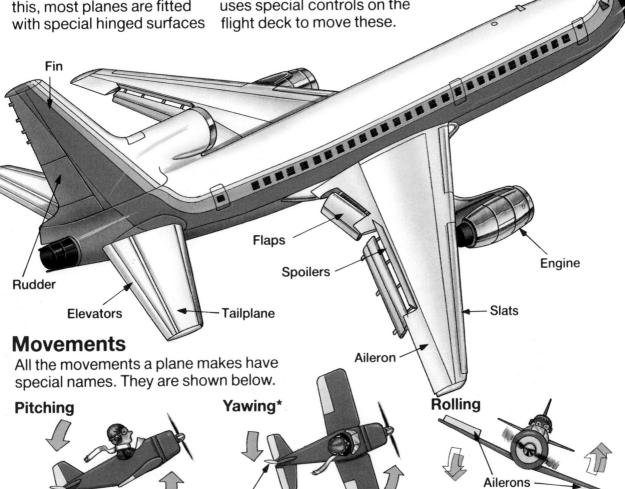

Fin

Rudder

Elevators

Tailplane

Flaps

Spoilers

Aileron

Engine

Slats

Movements

All the movements a plane makes have special names. They are shown below.

Pitching

Elevator

This is when the nose of the plane moves up or down. Moving the elevators on the tailplane makes the plane climb or dive.

Yawing*

Rudder

This is when the nose of the plane moves to the left or right. To make the plane yaw, the pilot moves the rudder.

Rolling

Ailerons

Moving the ailerons up and down on the trailing edge of the wings makes the plane roll from side to side.

*The plane in this picture is seen from above.

Airliners

Large airliners such as the Boeing 747 are designed to carry lots of passengers. The American Boeing 747 is the largest airliner in use today. It is called a Jumbo jet because of its size. It can carry up to 500 people, travel at 978km/h (608mph) at a height of 15km (9.3 miles), for 10,424km (6,477 miles).

Parts

Over 4.5 million separate parts make up one complete 747 airliner.

Boeing 747

Rudder

Elevator

Aluminium body

Seats

The 747 has room for 500 passengers, but usually carries 400 to give passengers extra room and comfort.

Seats

Body frame

Main landing wheels

Flaps

Turbofan engine

Landing wheels

On the ground, the 747 stands on two nose wheels and 16 main wheels. They all fold away after take-off.

The engines of a Jumbo jet burn more than 11,000kg (24,250lbs) of fuel every hour.

Cargo 747

This 747 has been adapted to carry only cargo. The nose of the plane swings upwards so large boxes can be loaded at the front. It can carry up to 130 tonnes (127 tons).

The 747 has a wing span of 59.6m (195ft 9in) and is 70.7m (232ft) long and 19.3m (63ft 4in) high. It is a wide-bodied airliner and ten seats can be put side by side across the cabin. With passengers and cargo, the 747 weighs nearly 406 tonnes (400 tons).

Engines and fuel

A 747 has four engines fixed beneath its wings. It carries a spare engine in case one should fail. The engines run on special aviation fuel which is stored in tanks inside the wings of the plane.

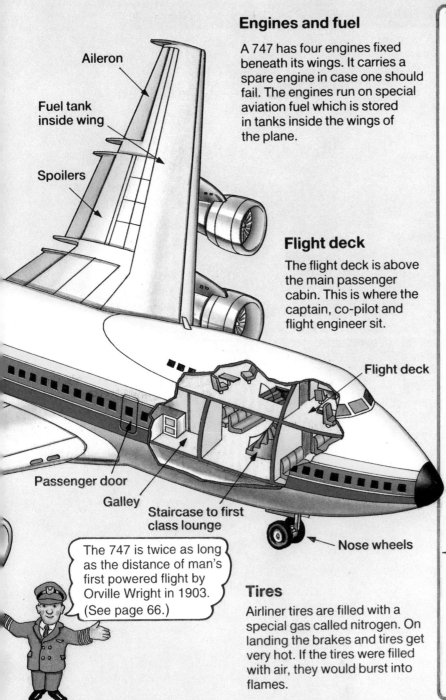

Aileron

Fuel tank inside wing

Spoilers

Flight deck

The flight deck is above the main passenger cabin. This is where the captain, co-pilot and flight engineer sit.

Flight deck

Passenger door

Galley

Staircase to first class lounge

Nose wheels

The 747 is twice as long as the distance of man's first powered flight by Orville Wright in 1903. (See page 66.)

Tires

Airliner tires are filled with a special gas called nitrogen. On landing the brakes and tires get very hot. If the tires were filled with air, they would burst into flames.

Wing shapes

Planes have different shaped wings. The shape is important because it changes how fast the plane can fly.

Swept wings

Most airliners like the 747 have a swept wing formation. This gives them greater speed.

Straight wings

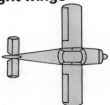

Small, light aircraft have straight, thick wings. They fly at low speeds for short distances.

Delta wings

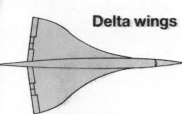

Concorde has delta-shaped wings so it can travel at twice the speed of sound. It has a top speed of 2,032km/h (1,300mph).

Aircraft engines

All modern airliners are powered by jet engines. Early planes had piston engines like the engine in a car. They ran on gas and the engine turned a propeller which pulled the plane through the air. A jet engine sucks in air at the front and pushes it out faster at the back. This moves the plane forwards.

The jet engine

Jet engines burn a kerosene based fuel. This produces hot gases which are thrust out of the exhaust at great speed, pushing the plane forwards.

Jet powered balloon

To see how a jet engine works, blow up a balloon and hold it at the neck. Air is held inside, pushing out on all sides. If you let go, the air will rush out of the neck and the balloon will shoot forwards.

Compressor

The compressor is a number of blades shaped like aerofoils. These blades turn round quickly and suck air into the engine.

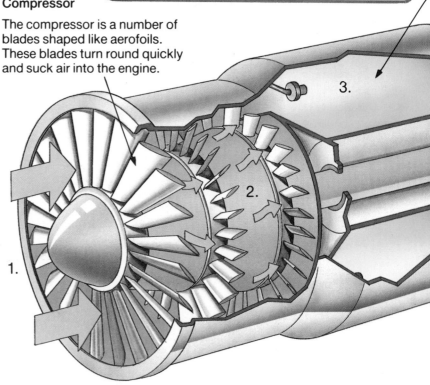

The first jet

The Heinkel He 178 was designed by a German, Ernst Heinkel, in 1939. It was the first plane to fly powered by a jet engine.

1. When the engine is on the blades turn round very fast and pull air into the engine.

2. The air gets very hot travelling fast along this tube before it goes into the combustion chamber.

Combustion chamber

This is where the air and fuel burns explosively to produce hot gases.

Turbine

The hot gases from the combustion chamber turn the turbine blades round. The turbine turns the compressor which sucks in more air to keep the engine running.

Exhaust tail-pipe

This is where the exhaust gases are pushed out of the engine.

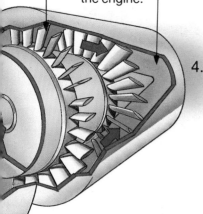

4.

3. Kerosene is sprayed into the combustion chamber and mixes with air. The mixture is lit by a spark and explodes, producing very hot gases.

4. The hot gases are pushed past the turbine wheel and rush out of the exhaust tail-pipe very fast.

Types of jets

Below are four different types of jet engines. They all power different types of aircraft.

Turbojet

Turbojets are very noisy ▶ because the exhaust gases rush out of the tail-pipe very fast. Concorde has turbojet engines.

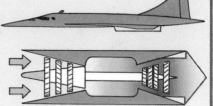

Turbofan

◀ A Jumbo jet has turbofan engines. They are less noisy and use less fuel than turbojets. A turbofan has two compressors. The front one, called a fan, also acts as a propeller pulling the plane forwards.

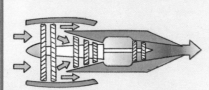

Turboprop

A turboprop is designed to ▶ turn propellers to pull the plane through the air. Slower flying planes use these engines.

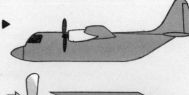

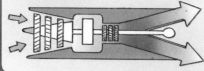

Turboshaft

◀ Turboshaft engines are usually fitted to helicopters. The engine turns both the main and tail rotor blades.

At the airport

The first airports were open fields with tents for travellers and hangars for the planes. Today, most international airports are as big as a small city. Thousands of people are needed to keep the airport running. They work in shops and restaurants, as baggage handlers, cleaners, engineers and customs officers.

Control tower

◄ The control tower overlooks the runways. Inside, air traffic controllers direct planes when they are landing, taking off and moving about on the apron. They have to know where each plane is to avoid a crash.

Passenger terminal

Baggage truck

Apron
Around the airport terminals is the apron, where the planes are loaded, unloaded and refuelled.

Luggage is loaded on to a baggage truck.

Passenger terminal

This is where everyone comes to check in for their flight and send luggage ahead to the plane. There are shops, banks and restaurants and information about aircraft arrivals and departures.

Fuel tanker
The plane is refuelled from a tanker

Ground services

Once a plane has landed, the ground services move in quickly to prepare the plane for its next flight.

Landing

Planes coming in to land must have permission from the approach controller in the tower. Pilots radio in many miles before reaching the runway.

Runway

Stacking

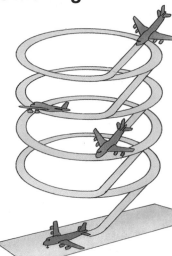

When there are several planes waiting to land, they form a stack in the air. The planes circle one above the other, about 305m (1,000ft) apart.

Taxiway

Take-off

Before take-off, the pilot gives his flight plan to the air departure controller.

The taxiways are clearly marked with lines to show the pilot exactly where he must position the plane on approaching the runway.

Runway

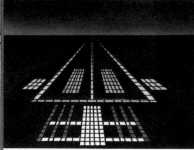

At night, bright lights and white markers on the runways and taxiways guide the pilots in to land and before take-off.

The flight plan

The flight plan gives details of the plane's destination and the height and speed it will travel at. The controller checks the plan carefully to make sure the plane flies well clear of other planes.

Helicopters

Helicopters are VTOL (vertical take-off and landing) aircraft. This means they can take off and land in a small space. Helicopters can hover in the air, fly forwards, backwards and sideways.

The rotor blades on a helicopter are aerofoil shaped, like the wings of a plane. (See page 52). When they spin round fast, the helicopter lifts off the ground.

Rotor blades

These controls tilt the rotor blades forwards and backwards. This lets the helicopter fly in any direction.

Rudder pedals

The rudder pedals control the tail rotor blades.

Rotor blades

Engine

Landing skid

Flying a helicopter

Hovering

When the rotor blades are spinning round fast and are kept level, the helicopter will hover in one spot in the air.

Going forwards

To fly forwards the pilot tilts the rotor blades down at the front. The air is pushed back and the helicopter moves forwards.

Going backwards

To fly backwards the pilot tilts the rotor blades back. Air is pulled in front of the helicopter, moving it backwards.

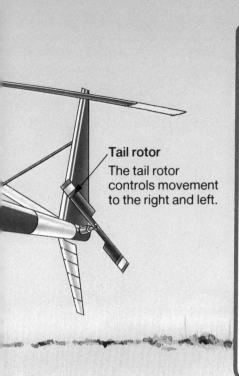

Tail rotor
The tail rotor controls movement to the right and left.

Jump jets

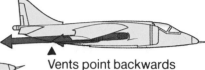

Vents point downwards on take-off and landing. ▼

▲ Vents point backwards for normal flight.

Air vents

The Harrier jump jet can also take-off and land vertically. Its powerful engine forces its exhaust gases out through air vents. On take-off, the vents point downwards. The downward force of the exhaust gases pushes the plane off the ground. The vents then swivel round and the gases are thrust backwards, shooting the jet forwards.

Useful helicopters

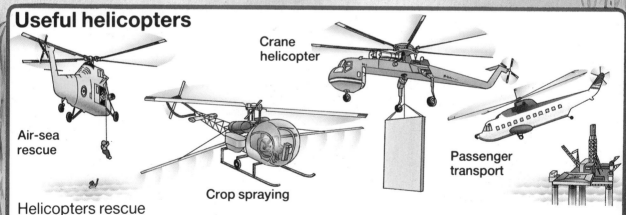

Crane helicopter

Air-sea rescue

Crop spraying

Passenger transport

Helicopters rescue people at sea. They have winches and strong steel cables joined to harnesses, to lift people out of the water.

Some farmers spray their crops using specially adapted helicopters. They can fly slowly over the fields.

This helicopter is carrying a heavy load to a building site that cannot be reached in any other way.

Workers on oil rigs out at sea have to be taken to work by helicopter. An oil rig has a small landing pad for helicopters.

Lighter-than-air

The flying things on these pages are not like normal aircraft. They are known as lighter-than-air craft. They do not have wings, but are filled with gas or hot air to lift them off the ground.

The first balloon

Their first passengers were a duck, a rooster and a sheep.

The Montgolfiers, two French brothers, invented the first hot-air balloon in 1783. They watched smoke rising from a fire and decided they could make other things rise in smoke.

Hot-air balloons

Balloons were the first aircraft that people flew in. The first ones were filled with hot air. Later, they were filled with gas that was lighter than air to make them fly.

Nylon Material

Ropes

Gas burner

Basket

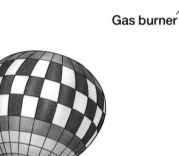

How hot-air balloons fly

The balloon is inflated by blowing hot air into the bag using a gas burner. Hot air is lighter than cool air, so the balloon will rise.

To keep the balloon in the air, the air inside it is kept hot with short bursts of flame. Balloons cannot be steered. They go where the wind blows them.

To descend, the pilot lets the air inside the balloon cool. It gets heavier, so the balloon drops. On the ground, the pilot lets the last of the hot air out.

Airships

The first airships were shaped balloons with steam engines fitted to them. The engine turned a propeller which pulled the airship through the air. They were filled with a gas which was lighter than air, called hydrogen.

A Zeppelin airship

Upper and lower rudders

Rigid airships like this one were over 200m (656 ft) long.

Gas bags inside the framework were filled with hydrogen gas.

Steel framework

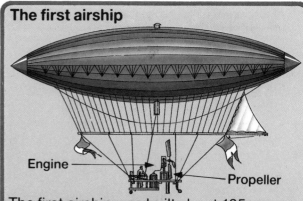

Engine

Propeller

The first airship was built about 125 years ago by a Frenchman called Henri Giffard. It was 43.5m (143 feet) long and was powered by a small steam engine. It could be steered through light winds.

The airship was fixed to a mooring mast by steel wires attached to the nose.

Propeller

This airship had five propellers.

Engine and propeller

Passenger cabin

The outside skin was made of linen material.

Fuel and water tanks

Navigation and control cabin (gondola)

Blimps

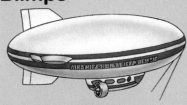

This blimp is the sort of airship you see today. They sometimes carry television cameras to film football matches, other sports and news events.

Rigid airships

Count Zeppelin, a German, was a famous inventor of rigid airships from 1900. His airships had metal frames. Inside these were bags of hydrogen. Many of the airships carried people from Germany to America. They stopped flying because the hydrogen gas often caught fire.

63

Wind power

The flying things on these pages do not have engines. When people first tried to fly, they fixed wings to their arms and jumped from steep hills. From this idea, the first gliders were designed and built. People were only able to travel a very short way. Modern gliders can fly for hours if there are plenty of air currents to keep them up.

The first glider

A German called Otto Lilienthal was flying the first gliders about 100 years ago. His gliders were made from wood and fabric.

Modern gliders

Modern gliders are made of very light materials like plywood and fibreglass.

Tailplane

Rudder

Cockpit

The body is narrow to cut through the air easily. The wings are long and thin to give plenty of lift. A glider needs more lift from the aerofoil wings because it has no engine.

Launching a glider

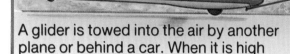

Tow cable

A glider is towed into the air by another plane or behind a car. When it is high enough, the tow cable is released and the glider flies on its own.

Flying a glider

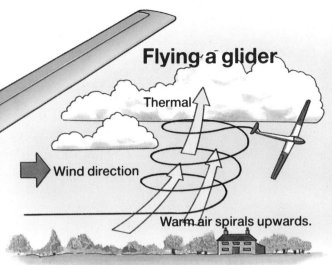

Thermal

Wind direction

Warm air spirals upwards.

To stay up in the air, the pilot has to find places where warm air rises. Rising warm air currents are called thermals. A skilled pilot will know where to find thermals and can spiral upwards with the air currents.

Hang gliders

Steel wires

Nylon sail

Aluminium frame

Hang gliders are launched by running into the wind from a hill top and catching air currents.

Harness

Crash helmet

A hang glider is like a large kite which supports the weight of a person. It is made from a nylon sail and a light aluminium frame. The pilot hangs from the frame in a harness and steers by swinging his body about under the sail.

Parachutes

Today, parachute jumping is a very popular sport. This square-rig parachute can move forwards at about 40km/h (25mph) and can be steered so the jumper can land on a target.

Parachute descent

The jumper leaps from a plane with a parachute pack on his back. He pulls a cord and the canopy ▶ comes out.

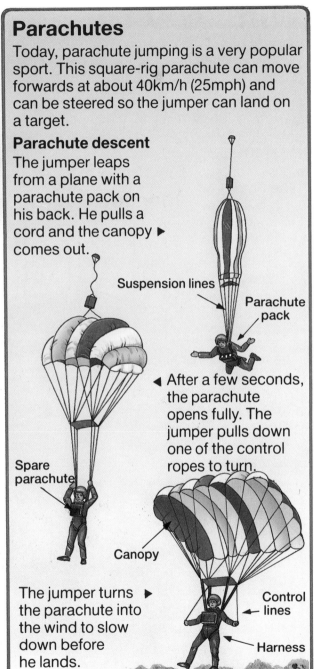

Suspension lines

Parachute pack

◀ After a few seconds, the parachute opens fully. The jumper pulls down one of the control ropes to turn.

Spare parachute

Canopy

The jumper turns ▶ the parachute into the wind to slow down before he lands.

Control lines

Harness

First flyers

Less than 100 years ago no one had ever flown in a powered plane and only very few people had flown in a glider (see page 64). This page tells you about the first planes and what made them fly. On the opposite page you can find out about some famous first flights.

(see page 64)

First off the ground

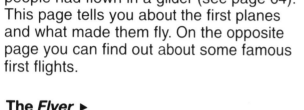

Bat-like wings

Very light steam engine

Eole was too heavy to fly. It only managed a "hop".

Enclosed cabin

In 1890 Clément Ader was the first person to rise off the ground in a self-propelled flying machine, called *Eole*.

The *Flyer* ▶

The pilot worked control wires by moving his body from side to side.

Wings covered by muslin material.

First to fly

The first powered flight was in 1903, in an engine-driven plane built by Wilbur and Orville Wright. Their machine had two sets of wings, one above the other and was called a bi-plane.

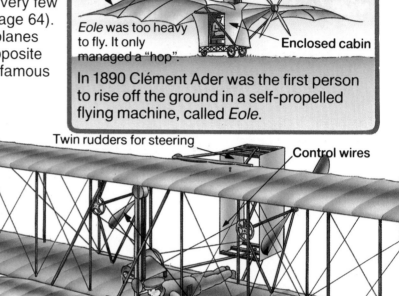

Twin rudders for steering

Control wires

Control lever operated by hand.

The two propellers turned in opposite directions to push the plane through the air.

The Wright Brothers' *Flyer* had no cabin. Instead the pilot controlled the machine from a lying down position on the lower wing.

Unlike the Wright Brothers, many early experimenters were killed because they did not know how to control their flying machines.

Float-sea planes

Henri Fabre's float-sea plane

Glenn Curtiss' seaplane

A float-sea plane takes off and lands on water. The first one was flown by a Frenchman, Henri Fabre, in 1910. The next year an

American, Glenn Curtiss, flew a plane with floats as well as wheels. Nowadays, seaplanes are used all over the world.

Famous flights

First across water

Blériot flew his own plane, *Blériot XI.*

One of the most daring first flights was across the English Channel. A Frenchman, Louis Blériot, achieved this in 1909.

To the moon

◄ In 1969, the first men landed on the Moon. The American crew travelled there in the *Apollo XI* spacecraft.

Crossing the Atlantic

In 1927, an American, Charles Lindbergh, made the first non-stop solo flight across the Atlantic, in 33 hours and 39 minutes.

Round the World

Wiley Post, an American, ► was the first person ever to fly round the world. He did this between 15-22 July 1933.

Into space

◄ The first space journey was in 1961. A Russian cosmonaut, Yuri Gagarin, travelled in the spacecraft, *Vostok 1.*

To Australia

The first solo flight from ► England to Australia was made by a woman pilot, Amy Johnson in 1930. She flew a de Havilland Gypsy Moth.

67

Space flight

Where is Space?

The Earth is surrounded by a layer of air, called the atmosphere. The further you go from the Earth, the thinner the atmosphere becomes, until it finally disappears. This is where Space begins.

Flying in space

An ordinary plane cannot fly in Space because its engines need air. A rocket carries all its fuel and oxidizer (to produce oxygen to make the fuel burn) with it into Space.

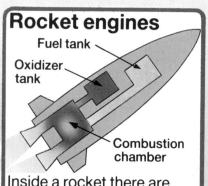

Rocket engines

Fuel tank

Oxidizer tank

Combustion chamber

Inside a rocket there are separate tanks of fuel and oxidizer. These mix together and burn, producing hot gases which rush out of the exhaust, thrusting the rocket up.

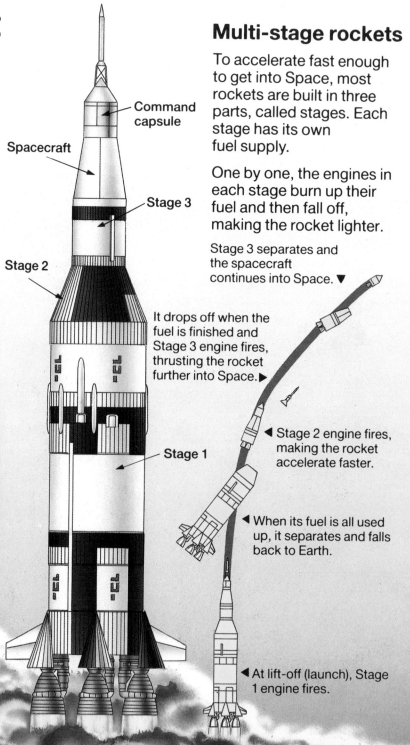

Command capsule

Spacecraft

Stage 3

Stage 2

Stage 1

Multi-stage rockets

To accelerate fast enough to get into Space, most rockets are built in three parts, called stages. Each stage has its own fuel supply.

One by one, the engines in each stage burn up their fuel and then fall off, making the rocket lighter.

Stage 3 separates and the spacecraft continues into Space. ▼

It drops off when the fuel is finished and Stage 3 engine fires, thrusting the rocket further into Space.▶

◀ Stage 2 engine fires, making the rocket accelerate faster.

◀ When its fuel is all used up, it separates and falls back to Earth.

◀ At lift-off (launch), Stage 1 engine fires.

Satellites

A satellite is an object which flies round (orbits) a larger object, like a planet.

Satellites are launched into orbit from rockets.

Communications satellite

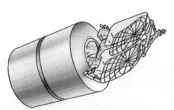

This type of satellite enables you to telephone across the world.

Weather satellite

Weather satellites collect information which is used to forecast the weather.

The Space Shuttle

The American Space Shuttle is different from an ordinary rocket because it can be used again. When it returns to Earth, it lands on a runway like a plane.

Into Space and into orbit

There is a force all around Earth called gravity which keeps things on the ground. When you throw a ball into the air, it comes down again. Gravity pulls it back to Earth. Getting past gravity is the hardest part of a space journey. A rocket must travel very fast to get into Space and launch a satellite into orbit.

A rocket travelling faster than 40,000km/h (24,856mph) will shoot out into Space.

A satellite launched from a rocket at about 29,000km/h (18,020mph) will go into orbit around the Earth.

A rocket flying at less than 29,000km/h (18.020mph) cannot escape Earth's gravity and it will fall back to Earth.

Biggest and fastest

On this page are some of the world's biggest and fastest planes. The biggest commercial airliner is the Jumbo jet which you can see on pages 54 and 55. In 1974 a Jumbo carried 674 passengers to safety from a cyclone in Australia.

The biggest

Lockheed C-5A Galaxy (America)

This is the biggest transport plane in the world. It can carry two tanks, 270 soldiers and lots of machinery.

Mil Mi-12 (Russia)

This is the world's largest helicopter. It has four engines and it weighs 105 tonnes (103.3 tons).

Graf Zeppelin II (Germany)

This was the biggest rigid airship ever built. It was 245m (803.8 feet) long. This is about the same length as three and a half Jumbo jets standing nose to tail.

The fastest

Concorde

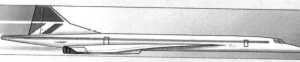

Concorde is the fastest airliner in the world. It flies at 2,333km/h (1,450mph) which is over twice the speed of sound.

Lockheed SR-71

This United States Air Force jet, flew at 3,529.5km/h (2,193.2mph). This is about 13 times faster than the fastest car on the road.

Air sports

At most air shows today you will see displays of aerobatics, or stunt flying. Pilots turn and twist their planes about in the sky.

Aerobatics

The pilots wear strong harnesses to hold them in their seats.

Famous Flyer

In 1934, Geoffrey Tyson, a famous barnstormer, flew across the English Channel upside down.

Aerobatics began after the First World War. Pilots travelled in flying circuses performing daring stunts in the sky. In America, they were called barnstormers.

Air racing

Air racing is one of the fastest sports. In a race, eight planes fly around a course marked by pylons. The race includes take-off and landing.

Formation flying

Some groups, like the French Air Force's *Patrouille de France,* fly in formation at air shows all over Europe. The team of nine fly close together and cross flight paths at great speed, trailing streams of colored smoke. They are very skilled pilots.

71

OUR EARTH

What's under the sea?
How did the Earth begin?
How much does the Earth weigh?
What are clouds made of?
Why do the stars come out
at night?

What is the Earth like?

The Earth is a huge ball of rock spinning round in space. It is one of nine planets which travel round a star called the Sun. Together they are known as the Solar System. Our Sun is just one of many millions of other stars in the Universe. It has a special force called gravity, which keeps the planets travelling round it, and stops them floating into space.

Earth facts

★ The Earth is not perfectly round. It bulges slightly round the middle and is flat at the ends. These are called the North and South Poles. There is a line round the middle called the Equator.

★ The Earth is divided in half at the Equator. The top half is called the northern hemisphere. The bottom half is called the southern hemisphere.

★ Little more than a quarter of the Earth's surface is land. Most of it is in the northern hemisphere, which you can see here. The land is divided into seven blocks called continents.

Water covers nearly ¾ of the Earth's surface. There are four main oceans, which are all linked together.

Nearly 1/8 of the land on Earth is dry desert. Only certain animals and plants can live there.

The Earth is always spinning like a top. It spins on its axis, which is an imaginary line between the Poles.

The Moon is a ball of rock which travels round the Earth. It is 384,000km (230,400mi) away. This is about 20 times as far as from England to Australia. Other planets have their own moons.

The further you are from the Equator, the colder it is. The coldest places on Earth are the North and South Poles. They are always covered with ice.

The Earth is about 40,000km (nearly 25,000mi) all the way round. In a car, it would take about a month to travel round it, without stopping.

Near the Equator, it is hot all year round. In many places, there are thick, jungly forests. The trees sometimes grow as high as a 20-storey building.

Nearly 1/5 of the land on Earth is mountainous. Few people live on mountains. It is often too steep to build on them, and too cold for many things to grow.

The Earth weighs about 6,000 million, million, million tonnes.

The hottest part of the world is an area on each side of the Equator, called the Tropics.

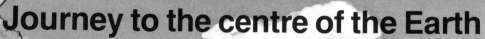

Journey to the centre of the Earth

Imagine you are going on a journey down through the Earth. First you have to travel through the rocky, outer layer called the crust.

The top layer of soil is made of tiny specks of crushed rock and the rotting remains of plants. Beneath the soil is a layer of small stones. Beneath that are layers of rock.

Inside the rock you may find an underground stream or river.

Inside the Earth

Here a piece has been cut out of the Earth, so you can see what it looks like inside. It is about 6,300km (3,900mi) to the centre.

Under the crust is a layer of softer rock, called the mantle. At the top of the mantle the rock is hot and liquid. It is moving around all the time.

The centre of the Earth is called the core. The outer core is made of hot, liquid metals – mostly iron and nickel. The inner core is solid metal.

The temperature in the centre could be as high as 4000°C.

The Earth is covered with a hard crust. It varies from about five to 64km thick. No-one has ever dug below the crust. But scientists know roughly what it is like inside.

Caves are often found in limestone, which is worn away easily by water. Rainwater makes cracks and holes in the ground. These get bigger and eventually make caves and tunnels.

76

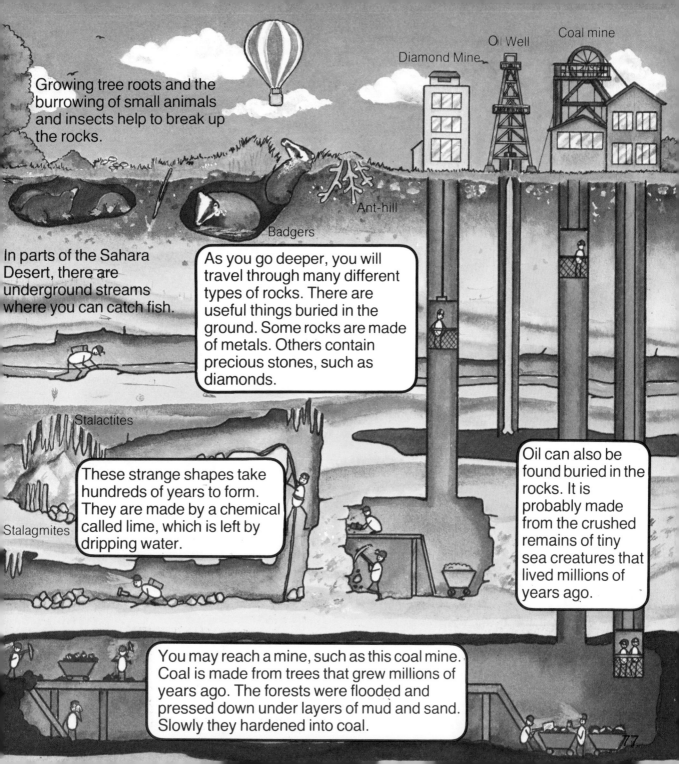

Growing tree roots and the burrowing of small animals and insects help to break up the rocks.

Diamond Mine

Oil Well

Coal mine

Ant-hill

Badgers

In parts of the Sahara Desert, there are underground streams where you can catch fish.

As you go deeper, you will travel through many different types of rocks. There are useful things buried in the ground. Some rocks are made of metals. Others contain precious stones, such as diamonds.

Stalactites

Stalagmites

These strange shapes take hundreds of years to form. They are made by a chemical called lime, which is left by dripping water.

Oil can also be found buried in the rocks. It is probably made from the crushed remains of tiny sea creatures that lived millions of years ago.

You may reach a mine, such as this coal mine. Coal is made from trees that grew millions of years ago. The forests were flooded and pressed down under layers of mud and sand. Slowly they hardened into coal.

87

Why are there hills and valleys?

Some parts of the Earth are flat. Others are hilly and mountainous. The Earth's surface is always changing. But the changes are usually so slow, you are not likely to notice many in your lifetime. Sometimes hot, liquid rock in the mantle squeezes the crust or pushes against it. This makes bumps in the surface. Over millions of years, the bumps turn into mountains.

Glaciers are slow moving rivers of ice, which carry rocks, soil and stones with them. About a million years ago, in the Ice Age, there were lots of glaciers. Most of them have melted now. But you can still see the steep-sided, flat-bottomed valleys which they carved out.

Sometimes liquid rock from the mantle bursts through the crust. It cools and hardens, leaving a cone-shaped mountain, called a volcano. When hot rock, called lava, bursts out of the top, the volcano is erupting.

Cone-shaped mountains are often extinct volcanoes, which do not erupt any more.

New mountains are often steep and high, with pointed peaks.

Waves fling sand and pebbles against the rocks. This can carve strange shapes along the coastline.

Blow hole

A block mountain is made when there is a crack in the Earth's crust.

Sea stacks

Sometimes, when a road or railway cuts through a mountain, you can see different layers of rock.

Sea arch

Just as mountains are being pushed up from below, the land is being shaped from above too. It is slowly worn away by rivers and glaciers, and by rain, wind, ice and sun. Rain and wind carry sand and grit with them. These are thrown against the rocks and rub them, rather like sandpaper. Some rocks are softer than others and wear away more quickly.

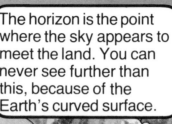

The horizon is the point where the sky appears to meet the land. You can never see further than this, because of the Earth's curved surface.

Most people live in valleys, on low land, called plains, or on flat highland areas, called plateaux.

Sometimes, moving rock in the mantle makes the rocks on the surface split and shake. This is called an earthquake.

Look out for rocks that have been worn away into strange shapes.

Old mountains are lower and smoother, because they have been worn away.

Fold mountains are made when the crust is pushed or squeezed. All mountain ranges (groups of mountains) are made like this.

A gorge is a narrow, steep-sided valley, made when a river cuts through hard rock.

79

Water

Earth is the only planet in our Solar System which has water. The amount of water doesn't change. It is reused over and over again. This process is called the "water cycle". Follow boxes 1 to 4 to see how it works.

3 When it is colder, the moisture turns back to water and rain falls from the clouds.

2 The specks of moisture join together to make clouds.

4 When it rains, water sinks into the ground and collects in underground streams and springs. These join rivers and eventually flow back to the sea.

1 The Sun heats the water on the surface of rivers and seas, and turns it into moisture in the air. This is called evaporation.

A river often starts from a spring on a hillside. The place where it starts is called its source.

At first, a river usually flows straight and fast. Then it becomes slower and wider and swings from side to side, to avoid the harder rock.

When a river flows over hard rock onto a softer one, it wears away the soft rock more quickly. This makes a step in the river, called a waterfall.

Meanders

1 **2** **3**

Ox-bow lake

The bends in a river are called meanders. Over many years, they gradually get wider and wider. After a flood, a river may break over its banks and flow straight on. The loop it leaves behind is called an ox-bow lake.

Rivers help shape the landscape. They carve out the land and carry rocks and soil to the sea. After hundreds of years, steep-sided valleys and gorges form.

The place where a river joins the sea is called the mouth.

A small river flowing into a bigger one is called a tributary.

Sometimes a river drops a lot of mud and stones at the mouth. If the sea does not wash it away, it builds up into a delta, like this.

The parts of the hill that jut out into the river are called spurs.

Lakes are made when water fills big dips in the ground.

Some shallow lakes dry up if there is not enough rain.

A geyser is a spring of hot water which shoots up through the ground. It is heated by hot rocks in the crust.

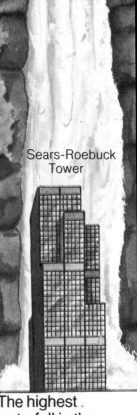

Sears-Roebuck Tower

The highest waterfall in the world is Angel Falls in Venezuela, which is nearly 1km (over half a mile) high. It is over twice as tall as the tallest building in the world, which has 110 storeys.

81

What's in the sea?

Seas and oceans cover nearly ¾ of the Earth's surface. They are full of all kinds of different plants and animals. Sea water has lots of useful chemicals and minerals in it, including salt. The chemicals are washed from the soil and brought to the sea by rivers. The sea is never still. The water is always moving.

Tsunami are giant waves made by earthquakes.

Flying fish

Jellyfish

Sea snake

Most animals and plants live near the surface. The water is warmer there because it is heated by the Sun. The bottom of the sea is very cold and dark.

If you put a message in a bottle and throw it out to sea, it may end up in another part of the world. This is because there are rivers of water in the oceans, called currents. They move in huge circles between hot and cold regions. Currents are caused by the wind and by the Earth's spin.

Corals are small, jelly-like animals, which live in warm, shallow seas. Each coral makes a case of limestone round its body for protection. The case is left behind when it dies. New corals grow on top. Gradually a wall is built up, called a coral reef.

The bottom of the sea is not flat. It is full of mountains and valleys, just like the land. Sea mountains that stick up above the surface are called islands.

Seas can be hot or cold. The hottest sea is the Persian Gulf. It is sometimes as hot as 35°C. The coldest sea, the Arctic Ocean, is frozen in many places.

Sometimes the reef sticks up above the sea to form an island. A circle of coral islands is called an atoll.

Waves

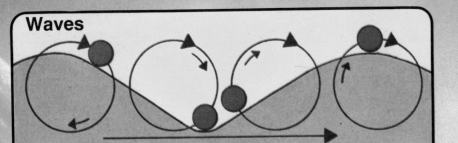

Waves are made by the wind. They look as though they are moving along the surface, but really the water is just going round in circles. If you throw something in the sea, it will go up and down, like this.

Fish can breathe under water because they have gills which strain the oxygen from the water.

Seahorse

Shark

Octopus

Seaweed and small shellfish live near the shore.

Mauna Kea mountain in Hawaii measures 10km (6mi) from the bottom of the sea to its peak. This is higher than the world's highest "land" mountain, Mount Everest.

The saltiest sea in the world is the Dead Sea. It has so much salt that nothing lives in it. You can float in it easily, without swimming.

The deepest part of the sea is Challenger Deep in the Pacific Ocean. It is over 11km (over 7mi) deep. If you dropped a steel ball into it, it would take over an hour to reach the bottom.

High tide

Low tide

On most seashores, the height of the water rises and falls twice a day. These are called high and low tides. Tides are caused by the gravity, or pull, of the Moon and the Sun. This makes two bulges in the oceans on opposite sides of the Earth. As the Earth spins, the bulges move round, producing the different tides.

What's in the sky?

The Earth is wrapped in a layer of air, called the atmosphere. It contains several different gases. One of them is oxygen, which we need in order to live. Another is carbon dioxide, which plants need. The air protects us from dangerous rays from the Sun, called ultra-violet rays. It also acts as a blanket, stopping the Sun's heat from escaping at night. Air is kept in place by the Earth's gravity.

You cannot see air – only the tiny bits of dust floating in it. You can only feel it when it is blowing against you. Wind is moving air.

Air is heavy, but our bodies are made so that we cannot feel it. It gets lighter, the higher you go. By the sea, the air pressing down on your thumbnail weighs about a kilo.

84   *These layers are not to scale.

The atmosphere is divided into four main layers. It gets thinner gradually and disappears at about 9,500km (6,000mi) from Earth.

1046 km
In the ionosphere, the air is very thin and hot and full of electricity. It gets hotter the higher you go.

Space rocket

Noctilucent clouds are the highest known clouds. They appear after sunset and are probably made of meteor dust.

Meteors are specks of dust from space. Sometimes they fall into the Earth's atmosphere and burn up.

64 km
The next layer is the stratosphere. Most planes fly at this level because the air is calmer.

10 km
The first layer is called the troposphere. It is the narrowest layer*, but contains 90% of the air. Most of our weather happens here. The air gets colder as you go higher.

Clouds are made of tiny drops of water or ice. You find different types of clouds at different heights.

What makes the stars twinkle?

The outer layer of atmosphere is called the exosphere. It merges with space where there is no air at all.

Weather satellite

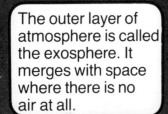

In relation to the size of the Earth, the air is as thin as an apple skin.

These are streams of glowing lights, called auroras. You can sometimes see them from countries near the Poles.

Jet streams are high speed winds, which usually blow from the west. Pilots flying east use them to speed up their flight.

Radio waves bounce off the ionosphere and are reflected back to different parts of the Earth.

Some birds can fly as high as about 8km (about 5mi).

On high mountains the air is very thin. Climbers take extra supplies of oxygen with them.

Stars appear to twinkle because light bends as it passes through air. The angle changes with the density and temperature of the air. The light passes through both warm and cold and thick and thin air, so it shines from different directions at once. This looks like twinkling.

What makes the sky change colour?

The Sun's rays contain all the colours of the rainbow. But you cannot see them all. The colour of the sky depends on the position of the Sun. When it is overhead, the sky looks blue. When it is low, the sky may look red, orange or violet.

Days and nights

The Sun is about 1,300,000 times as big as Earth. It does not look it, because it is so far away.

The Sun is about 150 million km (93 million mi) away. It would take over 1000 years to get there on a bike.

The Earth spins round at a speed of about 1600km (1000mi) an hour.

The Sun is a huge ball of burning gases, which gives out heat and light. You cannot always see it because of the Earth's spin. When your part of the Earth is turned away from the Sun, you have night, and when it is turned towards the Sun, you have day.

The Earth takes 24 hours to do a complete spin. For about half of this time, your part of the Earth is on the side facing the Sun. During this time, it looks as though the Sun is moving across the sky. In fact it is the Earth that is moving in front of the Sun.

Time changes

It is not the same time all over the world. When you are having midday, people on the other side of Earth have their midnight. The world is divided up into 24 time zones. When it is 1 o'clock in one zone it is 2 o'clock in the one to the east of it and 12 o'clock in the one to the west. When you travel across time zones you have to adjust your watch. The date changes from one day to the next day at a place called the International Date-line.

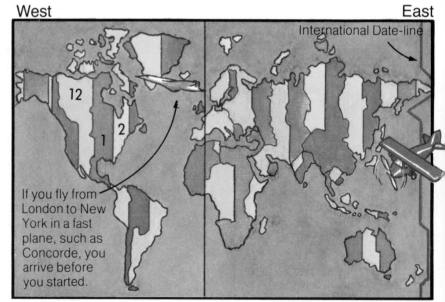

West

East

International Date-line

If you fly from London to New York in a fast plane, such as Concorde, you arrive before you started.

If you go right round the world, you cross the International Date-line. Then you lose or gain a whole day.

Shadows

Morning

The Shadows point in the opposite direction to the Sun.

Evening

Midday

The Sun's light travels in straight lines. It cannot go round things. So there are dark shadows behind anything which stands in its way. In the early mornings and evenings, the sun is low and makes long shadows. At midday, the sun is overhead and the shadows are very short. You can use the shadows on a sun dial to help tell the time.

Night

At night you may see the Moon and the stars. Stars are suns too, though they are so far away they look smaller than our Sun. During the day we cannot see them, because our Sun's light is so much stronger than theirs.

The Moon is a ball of rock which goes round, or orbits, the Earth. It takes about a month to go round. The Moon has no light of its own. You can only see it because the Sun shines on it and it reflects sunlight down to the Earth.

The Moon does not really change shape. It just looks as if it does. At each stage in its orbit round the Earth, a different part of it is lit up. This is how much you would see, if it were in the position shown in the previous picture.

The seasons

The Earth spins on its axis and travels round the Sun at the same time. It takes 365¼ days to make a complete trip. We make a year 365 days long. Every four years, we add an extra day to February, to make up for it.

The Earth does not stand upright on its axis. It is always leaning over to one side, so that part of the Earth is tilted towards the Sun. This part gets the most direct heat and light. As the Earth moves round the Sun, the part that is tilted towards it changes. This gives us the seasons.

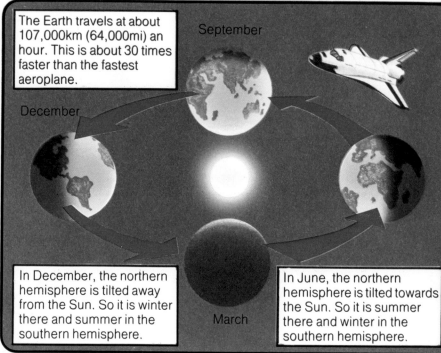

The Earth travels at about 107,000km (64,000mi) an hour. This is about 30 times faster than the fastest aeroplane.

September

December

In December, the northern hemisphere is tilted away from the Sun. So it is winter there and summer in the southern hemisphere.

March

In June, the northern hemisphere is tilted towards the Sun. So it is summer there and winter in the southern hemisphere.

Hot and cold places

As the Earth is a ball its surface is curved. When the Sun's rays reach the curved surface of the Earth they get spread out. They have to spread over more surface at the Poles than they do at the Equator. This is why it is always cold at the Poles and always hot at the Equator.

Summers are hotter than winters because when the Earth is tilted towards the Sun the rays are less spread out.

The Sun's rays are always spread out at the Poles, so it is always cold there.

In this picture it is summer in the northern hemisphere.

The Equator is never tilted away from the Sun. That is why it is always hot there, and there are no seasons.

It is winter in the southern hemisphere. The seasons are always the opposite of those in the northern hemisphere.

Why are days different lengths?

In summer, it is not only hotter, but there is more daylight. This is because the part of the Earth that is tilted towards the Sun stays in the Sun's light for longer. The closer you get to the Poles, the greater the difference in daylight between summer and winter.

This diagram shows summer in the southern hemisphere. The red lines stand for daytime. The white lines stand for night. The dotted lines show the part of the Earth you cannot see.

In the far north of countries such as Norway, there is darkness for almost 24 hours in winter.

In summer, there is daylight for almost 24 hours.

At the Equator, days and nights are always 12 hours long.

Eclipses

Sometimes the Moon seems to pass right in front of the Sun. As the Moon and the Sun look the same size in the sky, the Moon covers up the Sun. It gets dark for a short time in a few places on Earth.

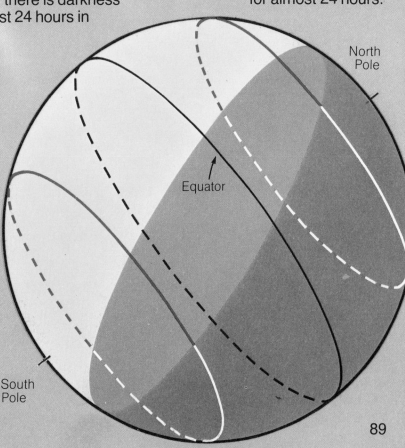

North Pole

Equator

South Pole

Weather

Weather is a combination of air, sun and water. When the air moves, it makes the wind. The Sun gives us warmth. Water makes the clouds, rain and snow.

What makes the wind blow?

Warm air rises, because it is lighter than cold air. As it does so, cold air moves in to take its place. Air is always moving between hot and cold regions. This makes the winds. They do not blow straight between the Poles and the Equator, because the Earth's spin makes them change direction slightly.

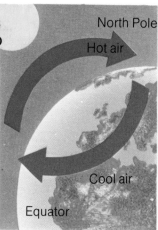

North Pole

Hot air

Cool air

Equator

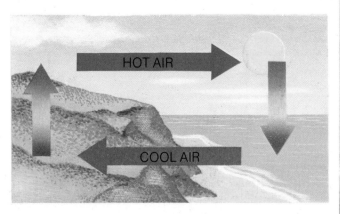

HOT AIR

COOL AIR

Land heats up and cools down faster than the sea, so they are always different temperatures. During the day, cold winds blow in from the sea. At night, warm winds blow out to sea from the land.

Clouds

Warm air can carry more moisture than cold air. When it rises, it gets cooler. Some of the moisture turns to water droplets, or ice crystals (if it is very cold). These join together as clouds. Look at the shapes of clouds. Sometimes they can tell you what kind of weather to expect.

Cirrus are high, wispy clouds, made of ice crystals. Warmer weather coming.

Cirrocumulus are like ripples. Rain soon.

Altocumulus are small and puffy. Water in the clouds sometimes bends the light to make a rainbow ring round the Sun. This is called a corona.

Cirrostratus. You may get a ''halo'' round the Sun or Moon, because the light is reflected by ice crystals in the clouds.

Flat cumulus clouds. Warm, sunny day.

Cumulonimbus is a huge thundercloud.

Nimbostratus is a grey clo[ud] Rain and drizzle soon.

Stratus makes a thick blanket near the ground. When it is ver[y] low, it is called fog.

What makes the rain?

As it gets colder, more and more moisture in the air is turned into water droplets. These water droplets bump into each other in the clouds and form bigger drops.

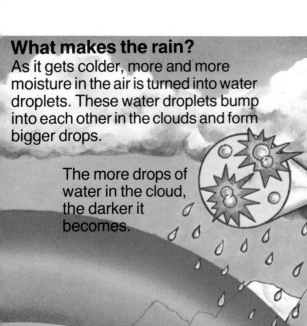

The more drops of water in the cloud, the darker it becomes.

Finally, the water drops become so heavy, the cloud cannot hold them. Then they fall as rain.

It often rains in mountains. Clouds have to rise to get over them. As they rise, they get colder and rain falls.

When the Sun shines through the rain, you may see a rainbow. Sunlight is made of many colours. Normally you do not see them all. The raindrops bend the light, so that you see each colour separately.

They are always in the same order – red, orange, yellow, green, blue, indigo and violet.

When you see a rainbow, it looks like an arch. From high in the sky, you would see it as a complete circle.

Cold Weather

When it is freezing, the water in the clouds turns to specks of ice. The specks get bigger and turn into crystals, which join together to make snowflakes.

Ice specks

Ice crystals

Snowflakes always have six sides.

Snowflakes

If the temperature at ground level is below freezing, the snow melts and falls as rain or sleet.

Frost

At night, the air cools. Some of the moisture in it turns to dew on the ground. If it is very cold, the dew turns to frost.

Storms

Lightning

Thunder

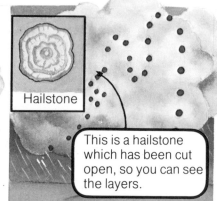

Hailstone

This is a hailstone which has been cut open, so you can see the layers.

In a storm, strong winds make the water droplets in clouds rub against each other. This produces a spark of electricity, called lightning, which shoots out of the cloud. Lightning heats the air around it. The hot air pushes against the cooler air. This makes a loud noise, called thunder. Thunder and lightning happen at the same time. You see the lightning first, because light travels faster than sound.

Hailstones are frozen raindrops. The wind blows them up and down through layers of freezing air, before they fall. Each time, the hailstone gets covered with another layer of ice.

Winds are measured in forces. The strongest, force 12, is a hurricane. They can do a lot of damage. Hurricanes happen in warm, sea areas, where the air is very hot and damp. In some parts of the world, they are called typhoons or cyclones.

A tornado is a fast-moving funnel of twisting air. As it moves, it sucks up everything in its path. Tornadoes happen in very hot, flat places. The wind inside a tornado can move at over 600km (400mi) an hour. A waterspout is a tornado over the sea.

What is your climate like?

The climate is the weather that is usual for your part of the Earth. It depends mainly on your latitude – which means how far you are from the Equator. But other things affect the climate too, such as winds, currents, the height of the land and the distance from the sea.

There are warm and cold currents in the oceans. A warm current called the Gulf Stream warms the coasts of North West Europe.

The climate of the North Atlantic coast is colder, even though it is at the same latitude. This is because of a cold current, the Labrador Current.

In the middle of continents, the climate is often extreme. The summers are very hot and the winters are very cold. At Verkhoyansk in Siberia, the temperature can vary from −70°C to 36°C.

Mountainous regions tend to have more rain.

Inland areas tend to be dry. This is because the wet winds from the sea have lost most of their moisture by the time they reach them.

The higher you are above sea level, the colder it is. Mount Kilimanjaro has snow on its peaks all year round, even though it is on the Equator.

The sea makes the climate milder. If you live near the coast, or on an island, you probably have cooler summers and warmer winters than inland.

The story of the Earth

The Earth is about 4,600 million years old. It looked very different when it first began. The shape of the land and the climate slowly changed. Certain types of plants and animals appeared. Others died out because they were not so well suited to the conditions. This process is called evolution. Follow this path to see what happened.

The Earth probably began as a huge swirling cloud of dust and gases. Gradually it grew hotter and hotter and turned into a ball of liquid rock.

4,600 million years ago

Then the surface began to cool into a hard crust. Hot, liquid rock burst through the crust in many places. When this cooled, it hardened too.

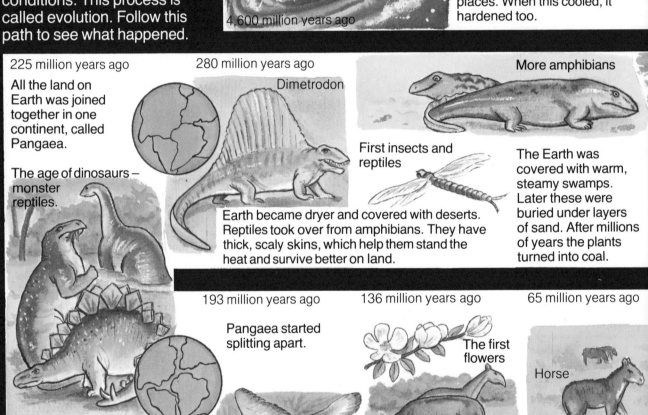

225 million years ago

All the land on Earth was joined together in one continent, called Pangaea.

The age of dinosaurs – monster reptiles.

280 million years ago

Dimetrodon

First insects and reptiles

Earth became dryer and covered with deserts. Reptiles took over from amphibians. They have thick, scaly skins, which help them stand the heat and survive better on land.

More amphibians

The Earth was covered with warm, steamy swamps. Later these were buried under layers of sand. After millions of years the plants turned into coal.

193 million years ago

Pangaea started splitting apart.

Pterodactyl

Archaeopteryx – the first bird.

136 million years ago

The first flowers

The first mammals – animals with fur, that feed their young with milk.

65 million years ago

Horse

Dinosaurs died out. Mammals, trees and plants increased.

3,800 million years ago

As the Earth cooled, it gave off clouds of steam and gases. The moisture in the clouds cooled into water drops and heavy rain poured down. This flooded the Earth and made the first seas.

2,500 million years ago

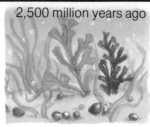

The first living things grew in the sea. They were neither plants nor animals and were very tiny. Then plants developed.

Mountains began forming

570 million years ago

As the plants grew, they made oxygen. This made it possible for animals to grow. The first animals were very small and lived in the sea.

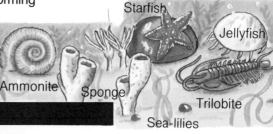

Starfish

Jellyfish

Ammonite

Sponge

Trilobite

Sea-lilies

300 million years ago

400 million years ago

Fish developed. They were the first animals with backbones.

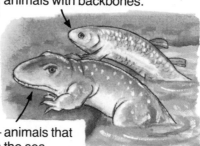

The first amphibians – animals that can live on land and in the sea.

500 million years ago

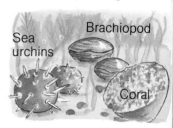

Sea urchins

Brachiopod

Coral

Ferns grew in swamps. There were still no plants or animals on the dry land.

40 million years ago

Sabre-tooth tiger

Ape

Deer

2 million years ago

Mammoth

The Ice Age. The climate got much colder. Furry animals developed, which could survive well in the cold.

1 million years ago

The early ancestors of people appeared. They lived in caves and made tools from stone. They knew how to use fire, to cook and keep warm.

5,000 million years in the future

Scientists think that in about 5,000 million years, the Earth will end. The Sun will increase its size about 100 times and the Earth will be swallowed up.

95

Earth words

Here are some of the special Earth words which have been used.

Crust, Mantle and Core

The thin, rocky surface of the Earth is called the crust. The layer of softer rock beneath it is the mantle. Some of this rock is hot and liquid and moves around. This causes mountains, volcanoes and earthquakes. The centre of the Earth is called the core.

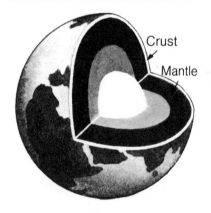

Crust

Mantle

Volcano

A volcano is a mountain or hill with a hole which goes right through the Earth's crust. Sometimes the volcano erupts and lava, steam and gases pour out of the hole. Some volcanoes get blocked up and become extinct. This means they do not erupt anymore.

Gravity

Gravity is a special magnetic force which attracts things. The Sun's gravity keeps the planets in orbit. Earth's gravity keeps the Moon spinning round it and stops us from floating around.

Latitude and Longitude

Lines of latitude and longitude are lines invented by scientists to divide up the Earth. Lines of latitude are rings round the Earth, such as the Equator, which goes round the middle. Lines of longitude run between the North and South Poles.

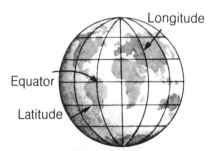

Longitude

Equator

Latitude

Tides

The tides are the rise and fall of the height of the sea. They are caused by the gravity of the Sun and Moon pulling against the Earth. The highest tides happen when the Sun and Moon are pulling in the same direction.

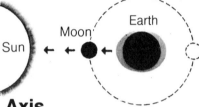

Sun

Moon

Earth

Axis

The axis is the line which the Earth spins round. It runs between the North and South Poles. There isn't really a line there.

Atmosphere

Atmosphere is the thin blanket of gases which surrounds a planet. Earth's atmosphere contains the gases which people, animals and plants need to live. No other planet in our Solar System has the right atmosphere for us to live on.

THINGS OUTDOORS

Why do seasons change?
Where do rivers come from?
How old is a tree?
What are rainbows made of?

Why does it rain?

Every day millions of tiny drops of water rise up into the air, from rivers and seas.

When lots of these tiny drops of water float in the same part of the sky, they make a cloud.

If tiny drops bump into each other, they mix together and become bigger drops.

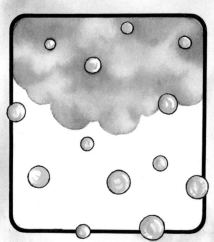

When these drops become heavy enough, they fall back to Earth. We call this rain.

In the country, rain soaks into the ground. In towns it goes down drains.

Eventually the rain runs back into the rivers and seas. It then rises again to the sky to make clouds.

Rainbows

Make your own rainbow

The best way to understand rainbows is to make one yourself.

Put a glass of water on a flat sheet of white paper in front of a sunny window. You will see colored light on the paper.

Inside a rain drop

Sunlight

Raindrops in the sky can act like the water in your glass. Sunlight divides into seven colors inside a raindrop.

Why you see the colors

When there is a rainbow, the raindrops reflect the sunlight. White light from the Sun is made up of different colors.

Each color is bent by a different amount, so you can see them separately. Red light is bent the least, so it appears on the outside of the rainbow.

To see a rainbow, you have to stand in between the sunlight and the rain.

Sunlight

raindrops

This is how the light reaches your eyes.

The colors of a rainbow are always in the same order— red, orange, yellow, green, blue, indigo and violet.

Thunder and lightning

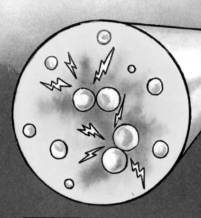

1 In the circle, you can see what happens in a cloud during a storm. Lots of tiny drops of water bump and rub against each other. This makes electricity in the cloud.

2 When the electricity leaves the cloud, it makes a spark that shoots towards the ground.
This is what we call a flash of lightning.

3 Lightning sometimes strikes tall trees or buildings. This is because electricity travels better down a wet tree or building than through the air.

4 During a storm, you should stay away from anything that might be hit by lightning.
The electricity in a flash of lightning is very dangerous.

5 The lightning shown here is forked lightning. If lightning jumps from one cloud to another cloud, it lights up the bottom of the clouds. This is called sheet lightning.

What is thunder?

A flash of lightning is very hot. When it goes through the air, it heats up the air around it.

As the air gets hot it takes up more room. It pushes away the air near the flash of lightning.

As the air is pushed away very quickly, it makes a loud sound. We call it thunder.

Why do you see the lightning before you hear the thunder?

Lightning and thunder happen at the same time, but light travels faster than sound through air.

You can find out how far away a storm is. Count the seconds between the lightning and the thunder.

Divide the number of seconds by three. This tells you how far away the storm is in kilometers.

101

Snow and ice

The air in a cloud is mixed with lots of tiny drops of water. When the drops get very cold, they turn into ice.

1 Water droplet

Ice crystal

Ice particles

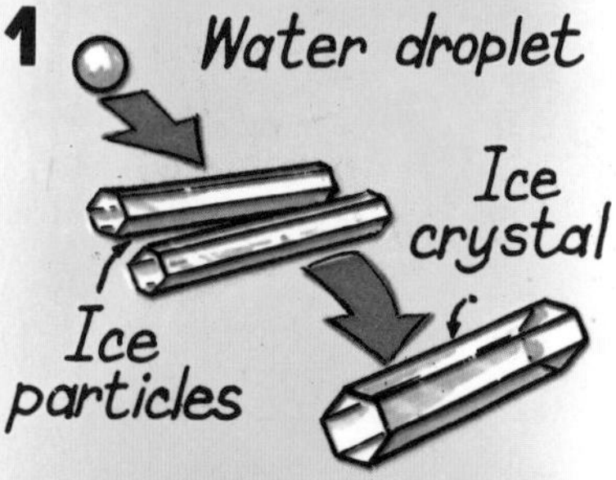

The pieces of ice start very small. As they go through the air, more water freezes on them and they become bigger.

When the ice crystals are big enough, they join together and make snow flakes. If the snow flakes are heavy enough, they fall to the ground.

The North Pole and the South Pole are very cold. They are covered by ice and snow all through the year. At the North Pole there is no land—only very thick ice floating on the Arctic Ocean.

The Arctic   North Pole

South Pole   Antarctic

2 Boiling point   Steam

Water   Freezing point   Ice

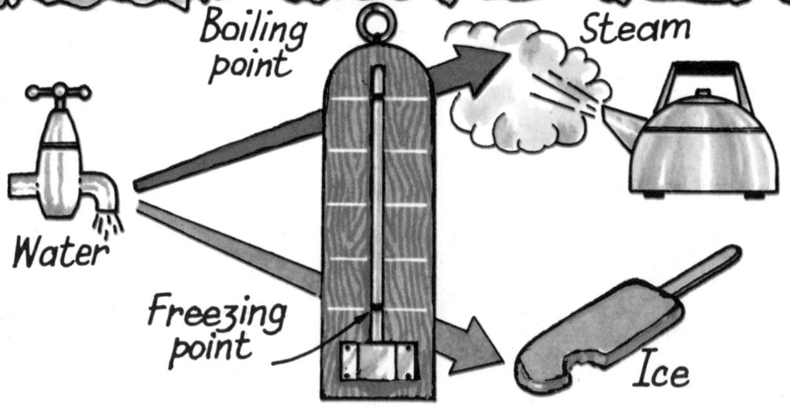

Ice and steam are made of the same stuff as water. Water turns into ice when it gets colder than freezing point. When it is hotter than boiling point, water turns to steam.

Icebergs are huge chunks of ice that have broken away from the edges of icy places. They float in the sea until they melt in warm water.

Nine tenths of an iceberg are below the water.

6

In the winter we put a liquid called anti-freeze into car radiators. This does not freeze as easily as water and stops the pipes cracking.

3

On very cold nights, when damp air touches cold things such as leaves, it makes ice on them. This ice is called frost.

4

Icicles are made when water that is dripping freezes one drop at a time. Some icicles are very heavy and their points are very sharp.

5

This much water makes this much ice.

water   ice

If water in a pipe freezes, the pipe can crack. This is because the ice takes up more space than the water.

The Seasons

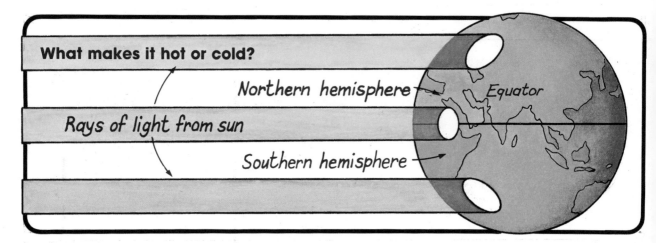

What makes it hot or cold?

Rays of light from sun

Northern hemisphere

Equator

Southern hemisphere

The Equator is an invisible line around the center of the Earth. It is usually hotter near the Equator. It gets colder the nearer you get to the Poles. This is because the sunrays that heat up the Earth are more spread out away from the Equator.

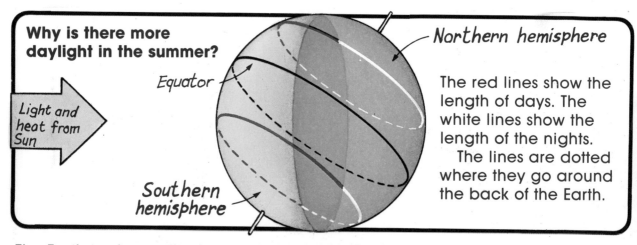

Why is there more daylight in the summer?

Light and heat from Sun

Equator

Northern hemisphere

Southern hemisphere

The red lines show the length of days. The white lines show the length of the nights.

The lines are dotted where they go around the back of the Earth.

The Earth is always tilted to one side. As the Earth moves around the Sun, this tilt means that sometimes the Northern Hemisphere is leaning towards the Sun and sometimes the Southern Hemisphere is. When a hemisphere is leaning towards the Sun, it is summer there.

Why do the seasons change?

The changing seasons are caused by the changing position of the Earth in relation to the Sun. Each season lasts about three months. There are changes in weather, temperature and length of daylight.

1 Winter

2 Spring

In winter, the Sun's rays are spread out over a wider area of the Earth's surface. This is why it is colder.

By springtime, the Earth has moved around the Sun. That is why the days are longer and the Sun's rays make it warmer.

4 Autumn

3 Summer

In autumn, the Earth has moved around and the weather begins to get colder and the days get shorter.

In summer, the Sun's rays can be hot, because the Earth is leaning towards the Sun. Parts of the Earth now nearest the Sun become warm.

Volcanoes

1

The Earth is made of three sections. The outside is called the crust. It is thin and brittle. The inside is made of soft rock. This is called the mantle.

The center of the Earth is the core. Scientists believe that the rock there is so hot that it is liquid.

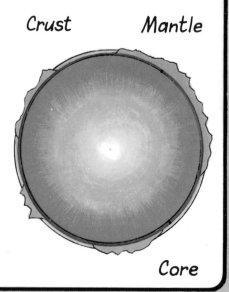

Crust   Mantle

Core

2

Crust

Mantle

The Earth's crust is very thin compared with the rest of the Earth. It varies in thickness from 8 kilometers to 64 kilometers.

3

Earth's crust

The mantle under the crust of the Earth is made of hot soft rock. This moves around all the time.

4

Magma

This soft rock is called magma. It can be hot enough to melt the rock above it.

5

Sometimes the hot magma breaks through a thin weak part of the crust. This is the start of a volcano.

6 Some volcanoes do nothing for hundreds of years. Then suddenly the hot magma shoots out of the crater. This is called erupting.

7 The magma cools as it comes to the top. It flows out of the crust and is called lava. It flows down the sides of the volcano and becomes hard like rock.

8 Some of the lava is full of bubbles of gas. This becomes rock called pumice. Because of the gas bubbles, it can float.

9 Many volcanic eruptions can be heard for hundreds of kilometers. In 1883, a volcano called Krakatoa exploded in Indonesia.
The noise could be heard 4,700 kilometers away in Australia.

10 The hole which is made by the hot magma breaking through the crust is called a crater.

11 During each eruption lava builds up in layers on the sides of the volcano. This is how the cone shape is formed.

Close to the ground

Look carefully under stones, inside flowers and between the grass. You will find lots of creatures close to the ground.

Worms eat rotting plants. The remains of the plants pass through their bodies into the soil. This improves the soil and helps the plants grow.

This is a side view of the ground, just below the top of the soil.

Worms sometimes pull leaves down into the ground to eat.

Soil is made of lots of tiny pieces of powdered rocks and rotting plants. Good soil has gaps of air between the particles to allow plant roots to grow.

Worm watching

Put a piece of board over a patch of grass. Leave it for a few weeks and then look underneath.

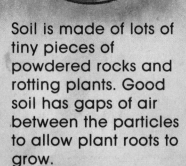

You will probably find worms and other little creatures. They like being in cool, dark places.

108

Slugs and snails love to eat young plants. The best time to see slugs and snails is at night when it is cool and dark.

Slug   Snail

You can often find woodlice on the bark of old twigs. They eat the rotting wood.

The top of a toadstool carries its seeds, called spores. Under the ground, a toadstool is made of lots of fine white strands.

Woodlouse

The roots of some trees send out runners that go up to the top of the ground to start another tree.

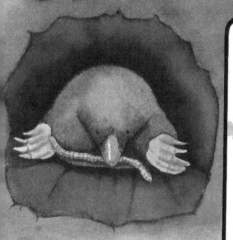

Ants

Ant nest

This ant is about ten times bigger than lifesize.

Moles live in nests of grass under the ground. They build tunnels and catch worms to eat.

Ants live in large groups underground. They sometimes build small mounds of earth above their nests and bring their eggs up to the mounds to be warmed by the sunshine.

Fruits

Buttercup

How flowers grow

These pages show you how a buttercup grows. Most plants grow in the same way. All flowers make seeds from which new plants grow.

Flowers need pollen from other flowers of the same kind before they can make new seeds. Pollen is carried by insects or by the wind.

Buttercup seeds are inside the fruits. The fruit is only as big as a pinhead.

How seeds are spread

The wind blows some fruits.

Some fruits hook onto animal fur.

Some fruits burst open to throw out seeds.

Birds eat some fruits. Seeds may be passed out in their droppings.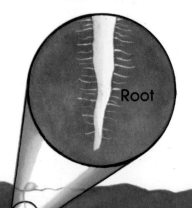

The seed is in here.

Root

Before it can turn into a new plant, the seed needs water. Rain makes the seed swell. It starts to grow.

The seed puts out a tiny root with little hairs. The root grows down into the ground.

Watch a seed grow

Roll up a piece of blotting paper. Put it in a jam jar so it presses out against the sides. Put a bean half way down the jar between the glass and the paper.

Now fill the bottom third of the jar with water. After a day or two look at the roots through a magnifying glass. Beans grow fast, so a shoot will soon grow out of the jar.

Caterpillars, slugs and snails like to eat young shoots. Young plants can also be damaged by bad weather.

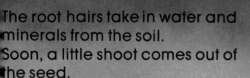

The root hairs take in water and minerals from the soil. Soon, a little shoot comes out of the seed.

The leaves grow. The light helps the plant to make food.

Later, flowers grow on top of the stalks. They start to make seeds that will grow into other plants.

111

Trees

Trees are the biggest living things in the world, and they also live longest.

Leaves

The leaves make the food for the tree. They need light to make food from water and a gas in the air called carbon dioxide.

One year's growth
Summer growth
Spring growth

Bark

The thick stem of a tree is called the trunk. This is covered by bark. The bark stops a tree from getting too hot or too cold.

Growth rings

When a tree is cut down, you can see rings on the inside. The dark wood has grown each summer. The lighter wood grew each spring. Count the darker rings and you will see roughly how old the tree is.

Roots

The roots of a tree go a long way down into the ground. This helps the tree to stand up. The roots absorb water from the soil so that the tree can grow.

Flowers

Many trees have flowers but some are hard to see.

Insects or wind carry pollen from one flower to another. This makes the seeds for new trees.

Fruit and seeds

Some trees have fruits like apples and oranges. The seeds are inside these fruits. Nuts are large seeds which have hard outsides.

Bark rubbing

Tape a piece of thin paper to the trunk of a tree. Rub gently over the paper with a wax crayon. Be careful not to tear the paper.

You can learn to recognize different trees by looking at their bark carefully. If you make bark rubbings, you can keep the different patterns in a book.

113

Rivers

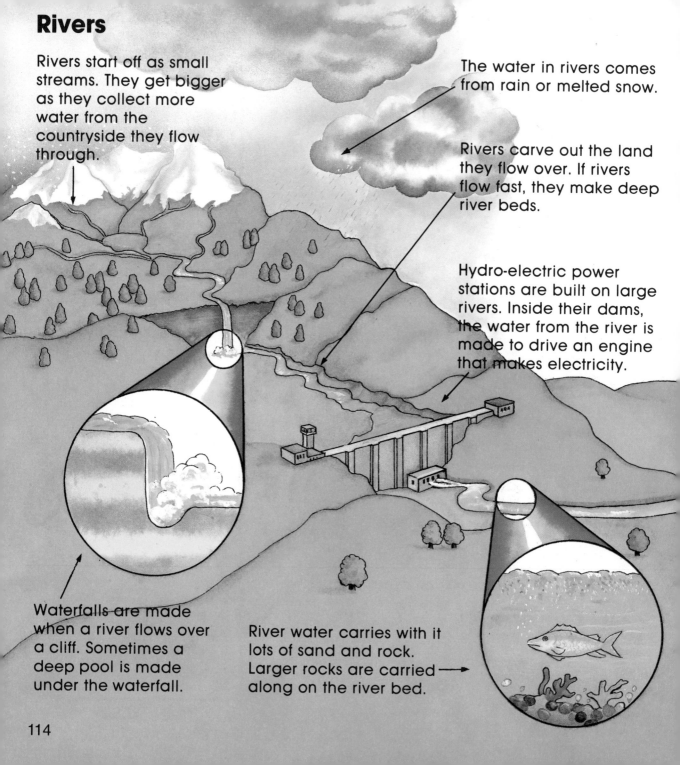

Rivers start off as small streams. They get bigger as they collect more water from the countryside they flow through.

The water in rivers comes from rain or melted snow.

Rivers carve out the land they flow over. If rivers flow fast, they make deep river beds.

Hydro-electric power stations are built on large rivers. Inside their dams, the water from the river is made to drive an engine that makes electricity.

Waterfalls are made when a river flows over a cliff. Sometimes a deep pool is made under the waterfall.

River water carries with it lots of sand and rock. Larger rocks are carried along on the river bed.

Dirty rivers

Some rivers that flow through towns are very dirty. Some people put dangerous and dirty rubbish into the water. This can pollute the river.

Plants that live in these rivers soon die. The fish cannot live if the water becomes poisoned by chemicals.

People have built a rubbish tip that is overflowing into this river.

Factories sometimes put dirty water into rivers.

Here a tanker has crashed and oil is going into the water.

Poison weedkillers are sometimes washed by the rain into the river.

Scientists check how dirty the water is. There are now laws to try and stop people polluting rivers.

When a river is flowing slowly, it can not carry the pieces of sand and rock that float in the water.

When the river meets the sea, it sometimes drops its load and makes a group of islands called a delta.

You can tell a canal from a river because its sides are straight. Canals are built to carry ships over land if there is no suitable river.

Under the sea

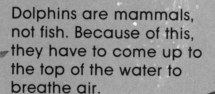

More than half the Earth's surface is covered with water. Thousands of different animals live under the sea.

Dolphins are mammals, not fish. Because of this, they have to come up to the top of the water to breathe air.

There are millions of tiny plants and animals living in the sea. They are called plankton. You cannot see most of them unless you look through a microscope. Many of the fish eat these plants and animals.

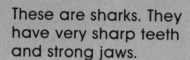

These are sharks. They have very sharp teeth and strong jaws.

Whales are the largest animals alive today. They can be up to 33 metres long and they can weigh as much as 200 tonnes. That is as heavy as 200 small cars.

An octopus has eight legs. The legs have suction pads on them, which the octopus uses to catch crabs and small fish.

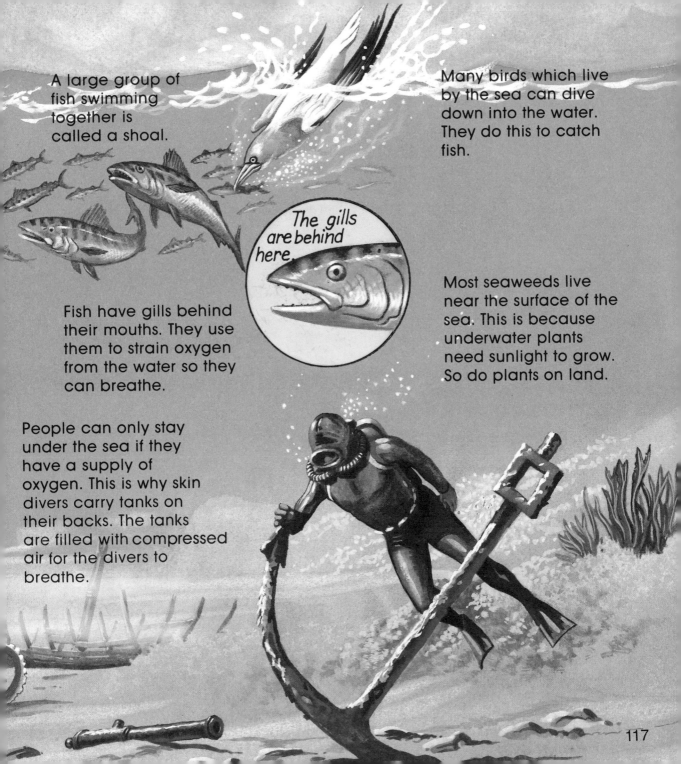

A large group of fish swimming together is called a shoal.

Many birds which live by the sea can dive down into the water. They do this to catch fish.

The gills are behind here.

Fish have gills behind their mouths. They use them to strain oxygen from the water so they can breathe.

Most seaweeds live near the surface of the sea. This is because underwater plants need sunlight to grow. So do plants on land.

People can only stay under the sea if they have a supply of oxygen. This is why skin divers carry tanks on their backs. The tanks are filled with compressed air for the divers to breathe.

117

Measuring things

How to measure exactly

If you want to measure things exactly you will need a ruler or a tape measure. We usually use the metric system to measure.

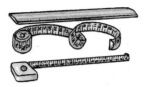

A millimeter is very small, only as long as this line⊙. There are ten millimeters in one centimeter. The ruler on this page is divided into centimeters. There are 100 centimeters in one meter.

The tail of the kite goes round this page. The distance between each bow of ribbon is five centimeters. How long is the tail?

The answer is on page 120.

Using your feet

If you do not have a ruler or a tape measure you cannot measure things exactly, but you can measure them roughly. Try using your own feet. Make certain the toe of one foot always touches the heel of the other. If you measure your shoe you can work out exact distances this way.

Using your hands

Stretch out your hand and measure the distance between the tip of your thumb and your little finger. You can then always use your hand to measure distances roughly.

Measure across your hand from thumb to little finger

Using your arms

Stretch out your arm and measure from the tip of your nose to the tip of your longest finger. When you know this distance, you can measure cloth or a length of string.

Measure from your nose to the tip of your middle finger

Using string to measure things

If things are a difficult shape to measure, try using a piece of string.

Find the shortest road through the park on this map.

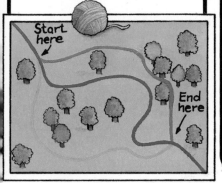

Answer on page 120.

Using a twig to measure a tree

With a tape measure, mark off one metre on a tree trunk. Start on the ground. Walk away from the tree until you can see all of it. Find a straight twig. Hold this out in front of you.

One meter mark

Move your thumb up the twig until it is in line with the mark on the tree. Mark the twig where your thumb is. Then see how many times the length of the twig above the thumb goes into the height of the tree. This will tell you roughly the height of the tree in meters.

Kite Puzzle

Will the kite fit into the box? You can use a ruler to help you check.

The answer is on page 120.

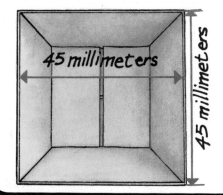

45 millimeters

45 millimeters

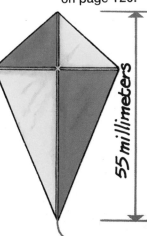

55 millimeters

Outdoor Quiz

1 What are clouds made of?
(1) Air (2) Water (3) Air and water.
2 Light and sound both take time to travel through the air. Which travels faster?
3 Why do water pipes crack in the winter sometimes?
4 What is the middle of the Earth called?
5 Why do ants sometimes build mounds of Earth above their nests?

6 What are the largest animals alive today?
7 How many legs does an octopus have?
8 Why does a fish have gills?
9 What is the name of a large group of fish?
10 Why do dolphins have to come to the top of the sea to breathe air?

Answers to questions about Measuring things:

The tail of the kite is one metre long.

The shortest road on the map of the park is the orange road.

Yes, the kite will fit into the box, like this:

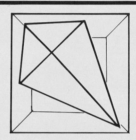

ROCKETS AND SPACEFLIGHT

What is a satellite?
Can people live in space?
How do rockets work?
How do people land on the Moon?
Why do astronauts wear space suits?

About spaceflight

You live on the planet called Earth. This picture shows where the Earth is in space.

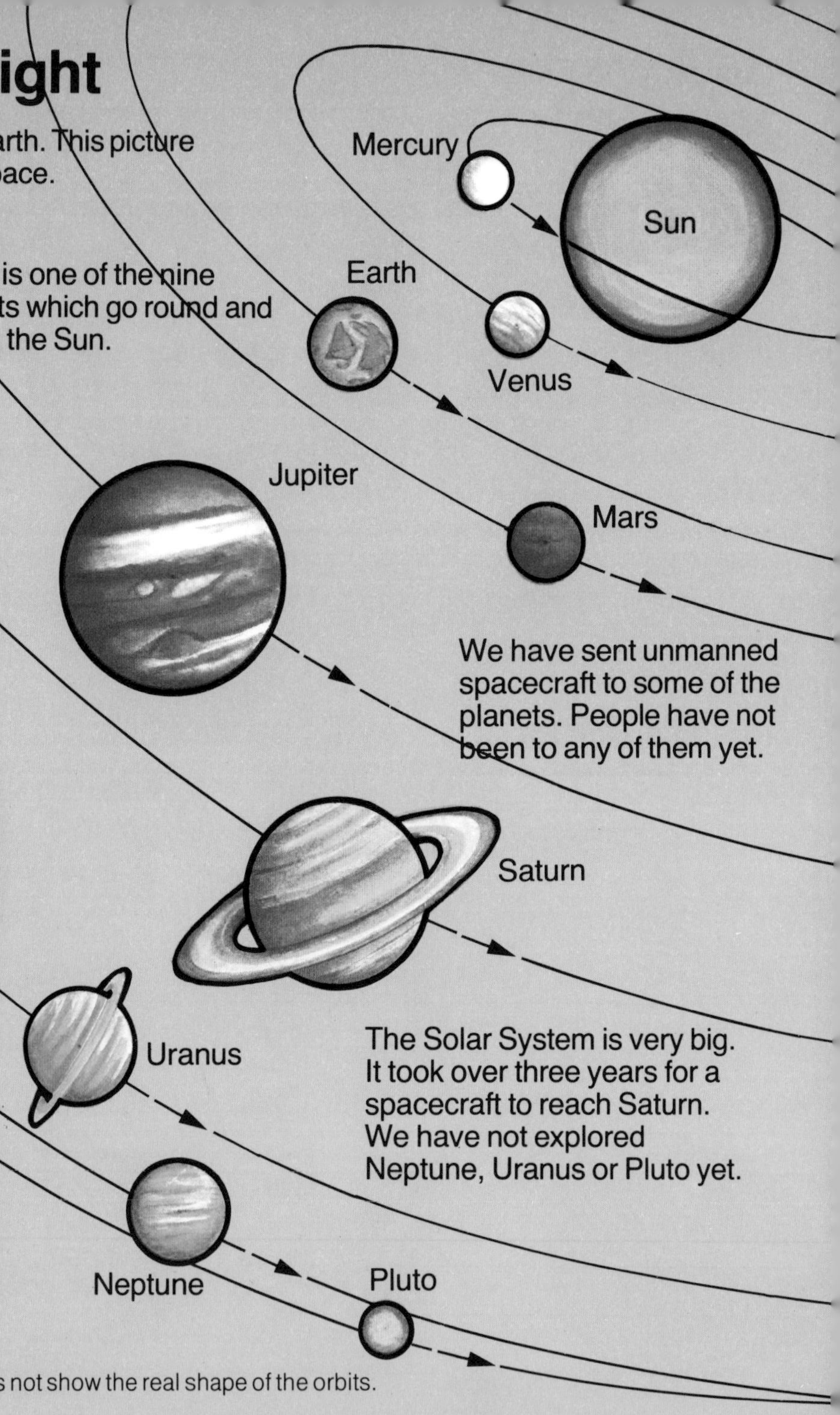

Earth is one of the nine planets which go round and round the Sun.

The Sun and the nine planets together are called the Solar System.

Our Sun is a star. It is the only one in the Solar System. All of the other stars are much further away in space.

Mercury

Sun

Earth

Venus

Jupiter

Mars

We have sent unmanned spacecraft to some of the planets. People have not been to any of them yet.

Saturn

Our Moon

Moon's orbit

The Moon is the Earth's closest neighbour in space. It is a big ball of rock. The Moon circles round the Earth.

Uranus

Neptune

Pluto

The Solar System is very big. It took over three years for a spacecraft to reach Saturn. We have not explored Neptune, Uranus or Pluto yet.

This picture is not to scale. It does not show the real shape of the orbits.

Leaving the Earth

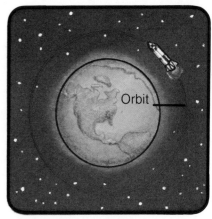

Getting off the Earth is the hardest part of a space journey. A strong force called gravity tries to pull the spacecraft back down.

Gravity is what makes things fall to the ground. It is gravity which keeps things on the Earth and stops them flying out to space.

Gravity even affects spacecraft close to the Earth. It makes them circle round and round the Earth. This is called orbiting.

Planning space journeys

Sending a spacecraft to the Moon or a planet is hard because the Earth, Moon and planets are moving all the time. A space journey has to be very carefully planned. It is controlled by lots of people and computers.

A space journey takes so long that a planet will have moved before the spacecraft gets to it. The spacecraft has to be aimed at the place where the planet will be at the end of its journey.

Rockets

A rocket is a very strong kind of engine. It is the only kind powerful enough to fight gravity and launch a spacecraft into space.

The picture below shows a spacecraft and its big launching rockets.

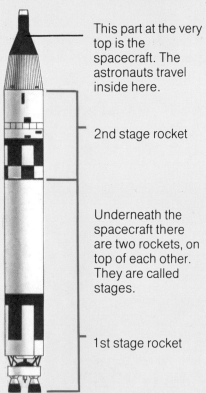

This part at the very top is the spacecraft. The astronauts travel inside here.

2nd stage rocket

Underneath the spacecraft there are two rockets, on top of each other. They are called stages.

1st stage rocket

The stages work one at a time. They fall off when they have used up all their fuel. This makes the load lighter for the next rocket to carry.

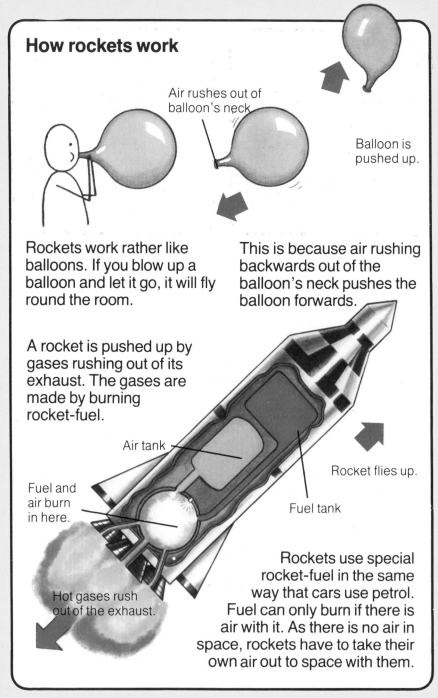

How rockets work

Air rushes out of balloon's neck

Balloon is pushed up.

Rockets work rather like balloons. If you blow up a balloon and let it go, it will fly round the room.

This is because air rushing backwards out of the balloon's neck pushes the balloon forwards.

A rocket is pushed up by gases rushing out of its exhaust. The gases are made by burning rocket-fuel.

Air tank

Rocket flies up.

Fuel and air burn in here.

Fuel tank

Hot gases rush out of the exhaust.

Rockets use special rocket-fuel in the same way that cars use petrol. Fuel can only burn if there is air with it. As there is no air in space, rockets have to take their own air out to space with them.

Rocketing into space

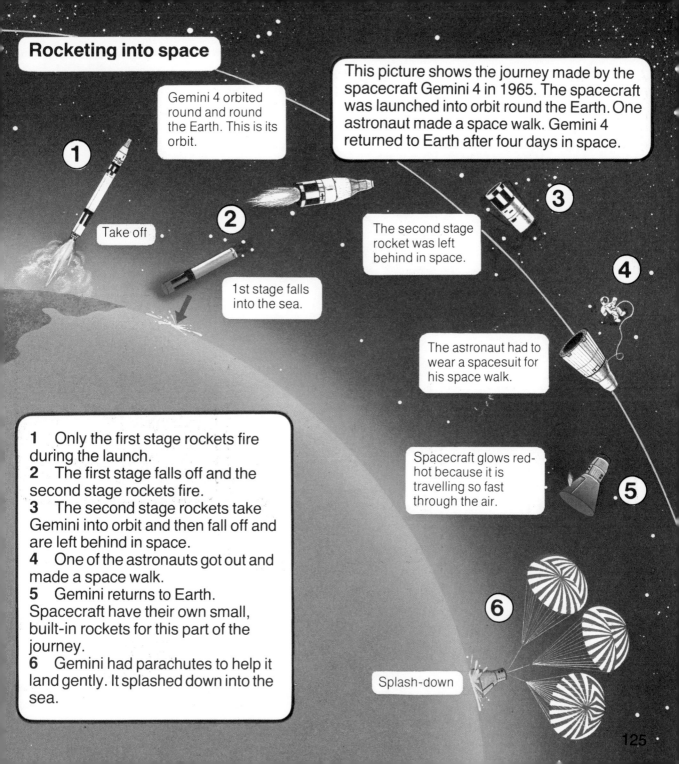

1

Gemini 4 orbited round and round the Earth. This is its orbit.

Take off

This picture shows the journey made by the spacecraft Gemini 4 in 1965. The spacecraft was launched into orbit round the Earth. One astronaut made a space walk. Gemini 4 returned to Earth after four days in space.

2

1st stage falls into the sea.

3

The second stage rocket was left behind in space.

4

The astronaut had to wear a spacesuit for his space walk.

Spacecraft glows red-hot because it is travelling so fast through the air.

5

1   Only the first stage rockets fire during the launch.
2   The first stage falls off and the second stage rockets fire.
3   The second stage rockets take Gemini into orbit and then fall off and are left behind in space.
4   One of the astronauts got out and made a space walk.
5   Gemini returns to Earth. Spacecraft have their own small, built-in rockets for this part of the journey.
6   Gemini had parachutes to help it land gently. It splashed down into the sea.

6

Splash-down

Mission to the Moon

One of the most exciting space missions was the first manned landing on the Moon. It took place in 1969. This gigantic, three stage rocket took the three astronauts in the Apollo spacecraft to the Moon. Since then, five other manned Apollo spacecraft have landed on the Moon.

1st stage rocket

2nd stage rocket

The Lunar Module

The astronauts travelled in the Apollo Command Module. This orbited round the Moon, but did not land on it. A special, small spacecraft, called the Lunar Module, landed the astronauts on the Moon. The Lunar Module was stored behind the Apollo Command Module.

The trip to the Moon took about three days. On the way, the astronauts took the Lunar Module out of storage. The third stage of the Saturn rocket and the Lunar Module storage compartment are left behind in space.

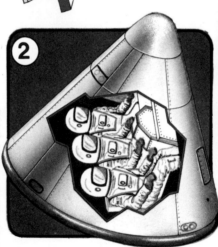

The Apollo spacecraft was launched by a huge three stage rocket, called a Saturn 5.

This picture shows the three astronauts inside the tiny Apollo Command Module. It is the only part which returned to Earth.

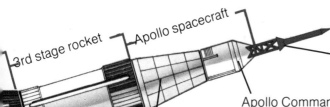

3rd stage rocket

Apollo spacecraft

Apollo Command Module

This launch escape rocket takes the Command Module to safety if there is an accident at take-off.

The Lunar Module is stored inside here.

4

Two of the astronauts got into the Lunar Module and flew it to the Moon. Here it is landing. It has its own small, built-in rockets.

5

After exploring on the Moon the astronauts returned to the Command Module. It had stayed in orbit above the Moon with one astronaut on board.

The bottom part of the Lunar Module was left behind on the Moon. Only the top part took off and flew back to the Apollo Command Module.

6

The Lunar Module was left behind in space. The three astronauts flew home in the Command Module. It had small rockets of its own too.

On the Moon

The fourth Apollo Moon mission took a moon-buggy, so that the astronauts could explore further.

The astronauts had to wear spacesuits when they were on the Moon. Look on the next page to find out about spacesuits.

Lunar Module

Astronaut

Moon buggy

Spacesuits

Astronauts do not have to wear special spacesuits when they are on board their spacecraft. They have to put them on if they go outside into space or on the Moon or another planet. There is no air to breathe in space. It is hotter than an oven in the Sun's light, but colder than a freezer in the shade. This picture shows two astronauts in space.

Astronauts sometimes have to leave their spacecraft to do repairs or set up experiments.

They wear spacesuits and are connected to their spacecraft by long cables.

The spacesuit has air tanks. It also keeps the astronaut at the right temperature.

Putting on a spacesuit

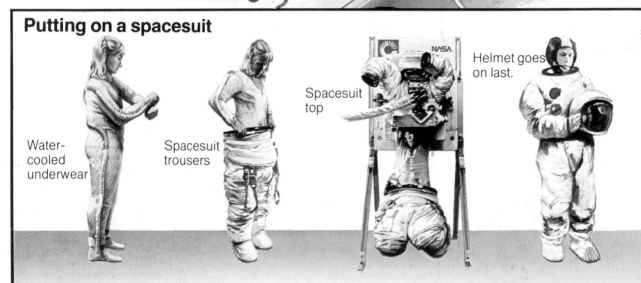

Water-cooled underwear

Spacesuit trousers

Spacesuit top

Helmet goes on last.

Astronauts wear special underwear under their spacesuits. There are tubes going through the material. These carry water round to keep the temperature steady.

Spacesuits are rather bulky and hard to put on. The astronaut puts the trousers on first and then climbs into the top while it is still hanging up.

This is the spacesuit worn by the Shuttle astronauts. Look on the next page to find out about the Shuttle.

Flight cap

Ear-phones

Microphone

Bubble helmet

Outer helmet

Gold layer

This outer helmet goes on top of the bubble helmet. The front is covered with a thin layer of real gold which acts like sunglasses.

The airtanks and radio are inside this big backpack. It is fixed to the suit top. It has enough air for seven hours.

Backpack

Astronauts wearing spacesuits talk to each other by radio. Their caps have a microphone and earphones. A clear bubble helmet goes over the head and joins up to the suit. It fills with air for the astronaut to breathe.

Glove

The backpack also pumps the water round the underwear.

The suit has a tiny computer which makes sure that everything is working. It tells the astronaut if anything breaks down and shows how to mend the fault.

Astronauts can even go to the toilet as the spacesuit has a kind of nappy inside.

Shoes

Spacesuits are made from very tough materials, so they do not tear easily.

Floating in space like this is a very strange feeling. Astronauts have said that it feels a bit like swimming in deep, still water.

Cable

This cable keeps the astronaut attached to the spacecraft. It is covered in thin gold.

Space Shuttle

The Shuttle is the newest kind of spacecraft. It is the first one which can be used more than once. It will fly out to space and back to Earth many times.

These are the Shuttle's three main engines. It has other smaller ones.

The Shuttle is the first spacecraft to have wings. They help it to glide back to Earth.

These doors open when the Shuttle is out in space. This helps to keep the spacecraft cool and exposes the special equipment inside.

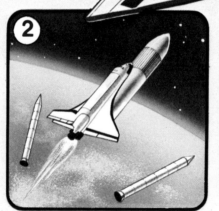

Rocket exhaust

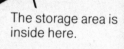
United States

The storage area is inside here.

Wing

Flying the Shuttle

1

The Shuttle has its own rockets but needs two big booster rockets and an extra fuel tank to launch it into space.

2

The booster rockets and fuel tank fall off when they run out of fuel. The boosters can be used more than once too.

3

The Shuttle has a large storage area for taking things up into space. It can open up when the Shuttle is in orbit.

This picture shows parts of the Shuttle cut away, so that you can see inside.

The living-quarters and flight-deck are inside the small nose part of the Shuttle.

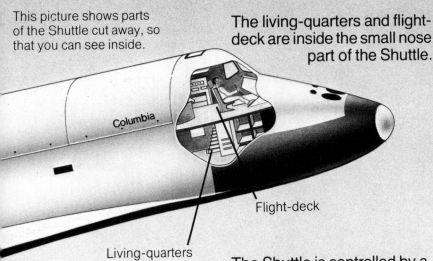

Columbia

Flight-deck

Living-quarters

The Shuttle is controlled by a pilot, a co-pilot and five computers on board, and many people at mission-control on Earth.

Special tiles on the outside help to keep the Shuttle cool.

The Shuttle returns to Earth like a glider. It falls though the air glowing red-hot because it is going at high speed.

It lands like an ordinary plane, on a very long runway. The Shuttle takes only one hour to come to Earth from space.

Shuttle missions

The Shuttle will be used to put new satellites into orbit and bring old or broken ones to Earth.

The Shuttle is planned to take this big telescope into orbit round the Earth. It will be used to study the stars and is controlled from Earth.

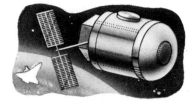

The Shuttle is also booked to take scientists and a laboratory out to orbit and back again. They will do lots of experiments in space.

On board a spacecraft

One of the strangest things about being in space is that everything becomes completely weightless because there is no gravity. There is no "up" or "down". Things will just float in mid-air unless they are fixed to something.

Control instruments

The instruments are all one way up. The crew try to stay the same way up too.

Astronauts sleep in sleeping bags fixed to the "walls". They cannot lie down as they are weightless.

Weightlessness makes the muscles weak. The astronauts use exercise machines to keep fit and healthy.

Astronauts have to hold the special handles when they are doing things, otherwise they push themselves into mid-air.

The spacecraft is controlled most of the time by people at mission control on Earth. The astronauts can take over if necessary.

Space travel makes some astronauts feel sick at first. This may be because they are weightless.

This is a storage area for equipment. Things have to be put away inside cupboards, otherwise they will float around in the spacecraft.

Handles

Astronauts eat ordinary food packed in cans which they heat up in a tray. They have to be careful that the food does not float away.

Food tray

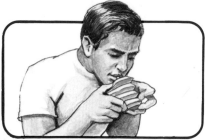

Even liquids float in space. Astronauts have to suck their drinks out of tubes as they cannot use cups.

Baths are a problem. The astronauts shower inside a big bag which stops the water flying about.

The weightless astronauts move by pushing against the walls and using handles. They seem to be flying.

Space station Skylab

A space station is a spacecraft big enough for a crew to live and work in for several weeks. This is the space station Skylab. It was launched into orbit round Earth in 1973.

Space stations stay in orbit all of the time, even when there is no crew on board. Three crews visited Skylab. Each one stayed in space for 56 days.

This is a telescope for studying the Sun.

Skylab was the biggest spacecraft ever made. Inside it was as large as a three-storey house.

The Skylab crews did lots of scientific experiments. The most important was to show that people could live in space for a long time.

These solar panels powered the telescope.

Sunshade

Skylab was damaged when it was launched. One of the solar panels and part of the protective outer skin were torn off.

This solar panel powered electrical equipment inside Skylab. There should have been another one on the other side.

Solar panel

The first crew had to repair Skylab. They put up a sunshade over the damaged outer skin, to stop Skylab overheating.

The second crew put up this gold foil sunshade.

The astronauts and equipment are inside this part of Skylab.

Going to Skylab

The astronauts got into Skylab through doors here.

Skylab

Apollo spacecraft

Skylab was launched without a crew. The astronauts went up to it and back again in Apollo spacecraft, like the ones which went to the Moon.

The Apollo had to be joined to Skylab. This is called docking. The astronauts crawled into Skylab through special doors in the Apollo and Skylab.

Skylab's end

Skylab was in a low orbit close to Earth. Gravity was able to pull it back to Earth in 1979 after six years in space. The spacecraft broke into

pieces as it fell through the air. Most of the pieces burnt up before reaching Earth. A few fell into the sea and some landed in Australia.

Working on Skylab

The crews did lots of work in Skylab. Here are some of the experiments and studies they did.

One crew studied the comet Kohoutek which passed close to Earth in 1973.

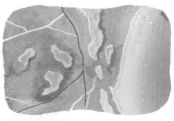

This picture shows a view of Earth from Skylab. The crews took thousands of photographs of the Earth and Sun.

One crew took a spider into space to see if it could spin a web while weightless. The first one was not very good, but later ones were better.

Satellites

There are many small, unmanned spacecraft in orbit close to the Earth. They are called satellites. Satellites carry instruments and do lots of useful jobs. This picture shows a satellite called Landsat. It studies the Earth.

Solar panel

Landsat takes pictures of the Earth and sends them down to special television sets on the ground.

These pictures help us to make maps. They also help us to find new supplies of things like oil and gas.

Landsat's cameras and instruments point down towards Earth.

Weather satellites

Other satellites watch the weather. They help scientists to make the weather forecasts.

Satellites have solar panels to provide power for their instruments. The solar panels make electricity from sunlight.

Television by satellite

(1) Several satellites are used to send television pictures from one part of the world to another. The pictures are sent as radio signals.

(2) These signals are beamed up through space to the satellite. They bounce off the satellite and back to Earth, but to a different place.

(3) The signals are picked up on Earth by big dish-shaped aerials like the one above. The satellite has dish-shaped aerials as well.

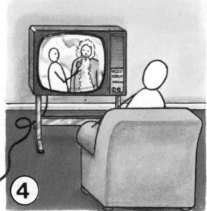

(4) The signals are then sent to your television set and turned back into pictures. The whole journey takes just a few seconds.

Going round the Earth

The Earth spins round once every day.

Television satellites move in time with the Earth. This means that they stay above the same place all the time.

Satellites which study the Earth orbit much faster. They see the whole world once every few hours.

Visiting the planets

People have travelled in space only as far as our Moon. Unmanned spacecraft, called probes, are used to explore the planets, as these are very far away.

This is Voyager 2, a probe that went to Jupiter in 1979 and Saturn in 1981.

Probes are launched into space by rockets.

Aerial for sending radio signals back to Earth.

TV cameras

These television cameras took pictures of Saturn. These were then beamed back to Earth as radio signals.

Messages from Mars

This picture shows the Viking lander probe on the planet Mars. It is sending pictures and information to Earth.

Mars

Earth

The information and pictures travel across space as radio signals. They take 20 minutes to reach Earth from Mars.

Here are scientists studying the pictures and information from the probe on Mars. They are using a computer.

More probes

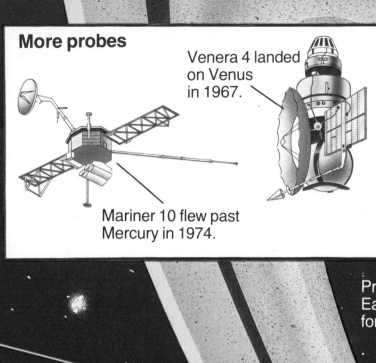

Venera 4 landed on Venus in 1967.

Mariner 10 flew past Mercury in 1974.

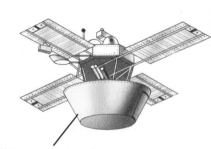

Viking 1 landed on Mars in 1976.

Probes do not return to Earth but stay in space forever.

This is the planet Saturn.

These are Saturn's rings.

Shadow of the rings cast by the Sun.

Some probes land on the planets they visit. Others, like Voyager, just fly close by, without landing.

The future in space

One day people may live and work in huge space cities like the one pictured here. It is about as big as New York and not at all like a spacecraft. The space city has artificial gravity and is full of air in the parts where people live. There are houses, parks, farms, offices, schools, factories, shops and even sports centres – in fact, everything that people want.

The space city would have solar panels to make electricity from sunlight.

Satellites would be used for sending messages between the Earth and the space city.

Shuttles would be used to ferry people and supplies between the Earth and the space city.

In the future, we may put large solar panels into space. These would make electricity from sunlight and beam it down to Earth.

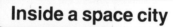

Inside a space city

This picture shows what it could be like inside a space city. This is the ring-shaped part where people live. It has gravity, air, plants, buildings and even a river. There are big windows to let in sunlight and heat.

The sky would look slightly different from a space city. You would be able to see Earth and would have a different view of the Moon.

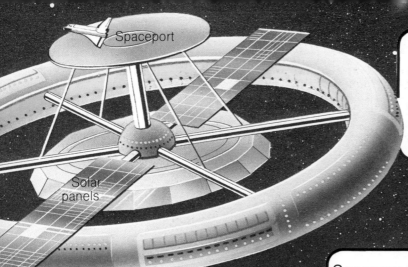

Spaceport

Solar panels

People would live and work inside this ring-shaped tube. The middle part of the space city is an industrial area and spaceport, where there is no gravity.

Space would be a good place to build spacecraft. There would be no need to build the huge rockets needed to launch them from Earth.

The space city would be made in space. It could be built from metals and other things mined on the Moon and planets.

Living on Mars

People would have to wear spacesuits if they went outside the city.

This picture shows what a city on Mars might be like. It is built under domes that are filled with air and kept warm. There is little air on Mars and it gets very cold. A colony on the Moon could be similar to this one.

Star travel fantasy

This picture shows what a spacecraft of the future might be like. It has left our Solar System and is travelling to another star. Scientists think that there could be a planet rather like Earth there.

At the moment star travel seems to be impossible. This is because the stars are so very far away. It would take much longer than a person's lifetime to travel to them in the spacecraft which we have today.

Even the nearest star is too far away to visit. If stone age people had been able to make a spacecraft and set out on a journey to the nearest star, they would be only about half way there by now, 50,000 years later.

Perhaps the crew of a star ship could be frozen or put into a deep sleep for the long journey to the stars. Computers and robots might look after the spacecraft and wake up the crew when they arrived.

Going through a space warp

People who write stories about space and some scientists have thought about the problems of star travel. They have imagined new ways of travelling through space. This picture shows one idea – a space warp.

The space warp is like a hole in space. The star ship goes into the hole in one part of space, but comes out again in a completely different place. The whole journey could take just a few seconds.

Travelling space city

Perhaps people will go to other stars in huge travelling space cities. Many people would be born, have children and die before arriving.

Beaming through space

Another idea is to beam people through space. They would be broken down into tiny specks for the journey and joined together at the other end.

Spaceflight words

Here are some of the special spaceflight words which have been used in this part of the book.

Solar System

The Solar System is made up of our Sun and the nine planets which orbit round it. We have sent unmanned spacecraft to explore some of the Solar System.

Planets

A planet is a big ball of rocks and gases which orbits the Sun. Earth is a planet. People have not been to any other planets.

Moon

Our Moon is a ball of rock which orbits the Earth. There have been six manned missions which landed on the Moon. Some other planets have moons of their own too.

Stars

The stars are gigantic balls of hot burning gases. Our Sun is a star. The other stars are very far away. They are too far to visit by spacecraft.

Spacecraft

A spacecraft is a vehicle which travels in space. Some spacecraft have people on board. Others, such as satellites, are unmanned.

Rockets

Rockets are a very strong kind of engine. They are used to launch and power spacecraft. Rockets are very large.

Probes

Probes are unmanned spacecraft which are sent to study other planets. They have special equipment on board, which sends back to Earth lots of pictures and information.

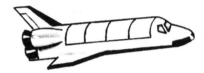

Shuttle

The Shuttle is the first spacecraft which can be used more than once. It made its first spaceflight in 1981.

Solar panels

Solar panels are used to power the equipment on board spacecraft such as probes and satellites. They make electricity out of sunlight.

Finding Out About

SUN, MOON AND PLANETS

Why do some planets have rings?
What is the Solar System?
Which planet is closest to the Sun?
What is a comet made of?
What makes the Sun shine?

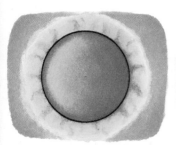

Our part of space

Our part of space is called the Solar System. It is made up of the Sun, nine planets which go round it, 43 moons which go round the planets and a band of space rocks called the Asteroid Belt. The Sun is so big we can show only part of it on this page. It is a huge ball of burning gases. The planets are much smaller balls of rocks and gases or liquids and gases. All of the moons and asteroids are rocky.

Jupiter

Jupiter is the biggest planet.

Jupiter's rings

Sun

Mercury

Venus

Earth

Mars

Mercury, Venus, Earth and Mars are the planets made of rock and gases. Earth is the biggest of them.

Asteroid Belt

Planets' years

Mercury's year lasts for 88 Earth days.

Saturn's year is 10,800 Earth days long.

The planets all travel round and round the Sun. This is called orbiting. They each take a certain length of time to go round once. This time is the planet's "year". Earth's year is 365¼ days long. Planets close to the Sun have shorter years than those further away from the Sun.

Moons

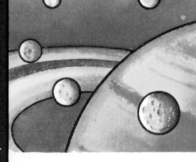

Mercury and Venus are the only planets which do not have moons. Earth has only one. Jupiter has 16 and Saturn has 18.

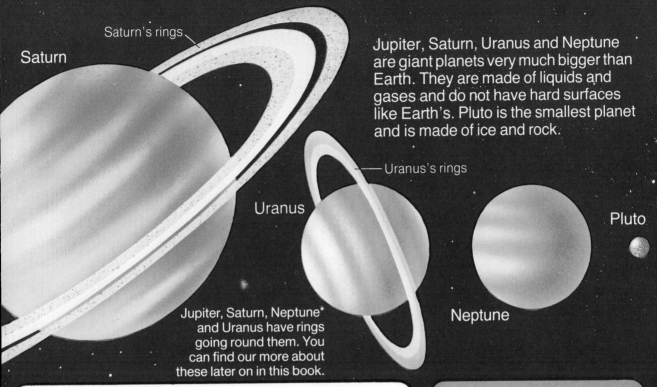

Saturn

Saturn's rings

Jupiter, Saturn, Uranus and Neptune are giant planets very much bigger than Earth. They are made of liquids and gases and do not have hard surfaces like Earth's. Pluto is the smallest planet and is made of ice and rock.

Uranus's rings

Uranus

Pluto

Neptune

Jupiter, Saturn, Neptune* and Uranus have rings going round them. You can find our more about these later on in this book.

Why are there days and nights?

Sunlit side is day.

Dark side is night.

The Sun lights up half of the planet.

Here it is evening.

The planets spin like tops as they orbit round the Sun. Different parts of their surfaces are lit by the Sun as they spin. This gives them day and night. They all spin at different speeds and so have different length days. Earth spins once every 24 hours.

The planets are all a very long way away from the Sun. If the pictures above were made into a scale model of the Solar System, this is how far from the model Sun some planets would have to be.
Mercury – 12.5m (38 ft) about the length of a room.
Earth – 98m (321ft) about as long as a football pitch.
Jupiter – 506m (1,660ft) about as long as five football pitches.
Pluto – 3,835m (2.3mi) about 45 minutes walk.

*Neptune's rings are smaller and cannot be seen from Earth, even with a powerful telescope. They were only discovered in 1989. (See page 161.)

147

The Sun

The Sun is the most important part of the Solar System. It holds all the planets in their positions in space and gives them their light and heat. Without the Sun, the Solar System would be dark and cold.

This picture shows the Sun as if a slice had been cut out of it so that you can see inside. The Sun is not solid like Earth. It is a huge ball of fiery gases.

The Sun is made of the gases hydrogen and helium. It does not burn like an ordinary fire on Earth. The Sun burns by turning hydrogen into helium.

The Sun is the hottest thing in the Solar System. It reaches an incredible 15 million °C in the centre. A pin head as hot as this could kill someone standing 150km (90mi) away.

Our nearest star

This is how our Sun may look from Triton, one of Neptune's moons.

Our Sun is actually a star, like the stars you can see at night. It looks different to us on Earth because we are closer to the Sun than to other stars. From more distant planets, the Sun probably looks like a big bright star in the sky.

The surface of the Sun is much cooler than the inside. It reaches about 6,000°C which is 60 times hotter than boiling water.

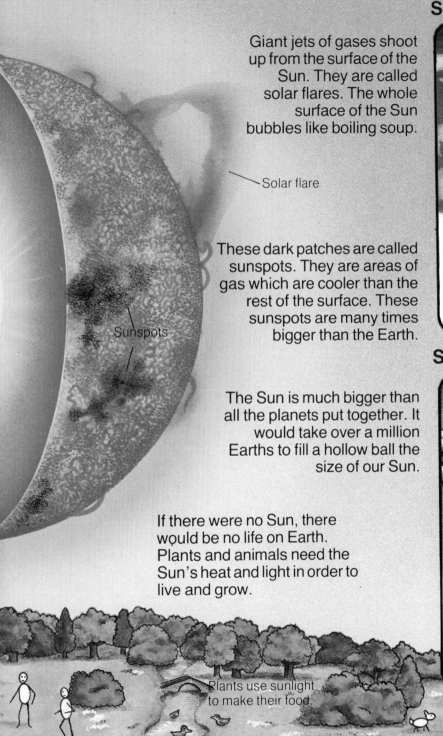

Solar flares

Giant jets of gases shoot up from the surface of the Sun. They are called solar flares. The whole surface of the Sun bubbles like boiling soup.

Solar flare

Earth's size

This gigantic solar flare was studied by astronauts on the spacecraft Skylab. It is many times bigger than the Earth.

These dark patches are called sunspots. They are areas of gas which are cooler than the rest of the surface. These sunspots are many times bigger than the Earth.

Sunspots

Studying the Sun

Telescope

Paper

Image of the Sun

It is dangerous to look at the Sun. Astronomers focus a telescope so that it makes a picture of the Sun on a sheet of paper.

The Sun is much bigger than all the planets put together. It would take over a million Earths to fill a hollow ball the size of our Sun.

If there were no Sun, there would be no life on Earth. Plants and animals need the Sun's heat and light in order to live and grow.

Plants use sunlight to make their food.

159

The Moon

Moon reflects the Sun's light.

The Moon is the biggest and brightest thing in the sky at night. It shines but it does not make its own light. The Moon just reflects light from the Sun. The Moon is Earth's closest neighbour in space but it is still a long way away. The journey to the Moon is as long as going round the Earth about ten times.

The Moon is much smaller than Earth. It would take 81 Moons to weigh as much as one Earth and 50 Moons to fill a hollow ball the size of Earth.

The Man in the Moon

The Moon is said to look like a face from Earth. The "face" is made of areas of dark rocks.

Farside of the Moon

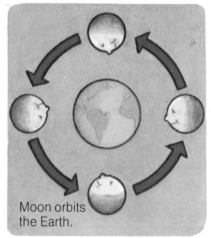

Moon orbits the Earth.

Spacecraft orbiting the Moon.

The Moon orbits round the Earth once every 27⅓ days. It always keeps the same half facing the Earth. No-one had seen the farside of the Moon until 1959 when the Luna 3 probe orbited the Moon and sent back pictures.

Why does the Moon change shape?

From Earth the Moon seems to change its shape. It grows from a thin sliver into a bigger crescent. Then it becomes a Half-Moon which swells until it is a whole Full-Moon. It slowly shrinks back to a half, to a crescent and down to a sliver. The whole process takes about a month and is shown in the picture below. The different shapes are called phases.

You cannot see all these phases of the Moon at the same time.

The Moon is not really changing shape. It just looks as if it is from Earth. This is because we see different parts of the Moon's lit up side as it orbits round the Earth. Look at the pictures below and follow the Moon on its journey round Earth.

New-Moon

Crescent

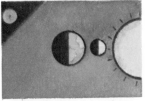

Half-Moon

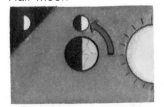

Gibbous Moon

Full-Moon

Gibbous Moon

Half-Moon

Crescent

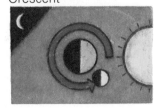

When the Moon is directly between the Earth and the Sun we cannot see any of the lit up side at all. Strangely, this phase is called a New-Moon. The lit up side becomes visible as the Moon moves round. We can see a Half-Moon when it is a quarter of the way round its orbit. When Earth is between the Sun and the Moon we can see all of the lit up side as a Full-Moon. After this, less and less of lit up side is visible from Earth.

On the Moon

Things are very different on the Moon than on the Earth. We know a lot about what it is like on the Moon because astronauts have been there. This picture shows two of them on the Moon.

Earth can be seen in the sky, just as the Moon can be seen from Earth. The Earth seems to change its shape and go through phases from the Moon.

The sky is always black, even in the daytime.

Spacecraft and astronaut

The Moon has mountains, flat areas, hilly areas, crevices, craters and dead volcanoes. It is a bare, dead world, where nothing lives or grows.

Moon craters

There are millions of holes called craters on the Moon.

The astronauts had to wear spacesuits and use airtanks on the Moon as there is no air there. They carried out lots of experiments.

Craters vary in size from tiny specks to holes bigger than cities. Some are so big they can be seen from Earth.

This machine measured moonquakes.

The craters were probably made by stray space rocks, called meteorites, which crashed into the Moon, millions of years ago.

The surface of the Moon is bare greyish rock. It is all bumpy and stoney and covered with a layer of fine dust. It is very dry as there is no water at all on the Moon.

Moon days and nights

The Moon has days and nights that are each 14 Earth days long. The Sun shines all the time during the long day and makes the Moon hotter than boiling water. At night the Moon is dark and freezing – much colder than ice.

Moon walk

Everything weighs less on the Moon than on Earth.

Astronauts could jump higher on the Moon than they could on Earth.

Astronauts walking on the Moon moved with big, swaying strides, bouncing up and down as they walked. They moved in this funny way as they weighed much less on the Moon than they did on Earth. On Earth an astronaut in his spacesuit weighed 135kg (300lb) but on the Moon he weighed only 23kg (50lb). This is because the Moon has less gravity than Earth. Gravity is the force which pulls things to the ground.

Moon soil and Moon weather

Things cannot live on the Moon because there is no air or water there. The astronauts brought Moon soil and rocks back to Earth for scientists to study.

They found that with air and water, plants could grow in Moon soil on Earth.

Footprint in Moon dust

There is no wind or rain or any other weather on the Moon. This means the astronauts' footprints will never be blown or washed away.

The Moon is a completely silent place. Noises cannot be heard as there is no air to carry sounds from one place to another.

The planet Mercury

This picture shows Mercury, the closest planet to the Sun. Being close to the Sun makes Mercury very hot during the day. It is very cold at night.

Mercury is a small planet, only slightly bigger than our Moon. Photographs of Mercury were taken by spacecraft which flew very close. These show that it looks like our Moon.

The surface of Mercury is covered in craters and dusty stoney soil. There is no air or water on Mercury. It is a dry, dead, desert of a world.

Mercury's craters are like the Moon's.

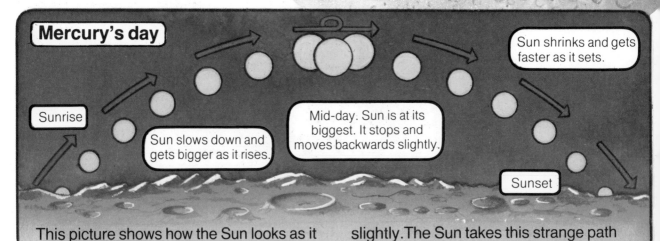

Mercury's day

Sunrise

Sun slows down and gets bigger as it rises.

Mid-day. Sun is at its biggest. It stops and moves backwards slightly.

Sun shrinks and gets faster as it sets.

Sunset

This picture shows how the Sun looks as it moves across the sky from some parts of Mercury. It seems to change its size and speed as the day goes by. At mid-day the Sun even stops and goes backwards slightly. The Sun takes this strange path through the sky because the distance between it and Mercury changes during the day. The Sun seems to grow bigger because Mercury is moving closer to it.

A visit to Venus

Venus is the hottest planet in the Solar System. It reaches a scorching 480°C which is hot enough to make things glow a dull red.

Venus is covered in thick clouds of poisonous sulphuric acid. These clouds never clear to let sunshine through and so it is always dull and dreary.

Why Venus is hot

Heat bounces off the clouds.

The thick clouds make Venus hot as they trap the Sun's heat. It can go through the clouds down to the surface but cannot get out again.

Backward planet

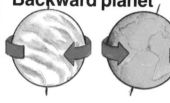

Venus spins in the opposite direction to the other planets. It is very slow and takes 243 Earth days to spin once. This is longer than the time Venus takes to orbit the Sun, which is 225 Earth days. So, a day on Venus is longer than a year.

It would be impossible for people to visit Venus. They would be roasted by the heat, pushed over by the winds, crushed and suffocated by the thick air and poisoned by the acid clouds.

Lightning

Crevice

Boulder

The air on Venus is made of carbon dioxide gas. It is 60 times thicker than the air on Earth.

The surface of Venus is dry, rocky and very hot. There are deep cracks called crevices and volcanoes.

What it is like on Mars

This picture shows what it is like on Mars. Mars is sometimes called the Red Planet because it is made of red rocks. The rocks are coloured by rust. Even the sky is pink on Mars. It is coloured by dust from the rocks.

The surface of Mars is like a rocky desert. There are many boulders and craters, high mountains, deep canyons and dusty sand dunes.

A Martian year is almost two Earth years long. A day on Mars is only half an hour longer than an Earth day.

The air on Mars is very thin and made of carbon dioxide gas. The winds are strong enough to whip up dust storms that cover the whole planet. Mars is about half the size of Earth.

Mars is further from the Sun than Earth is. This makes it cold. The temperature is always below freezing point.

Dust storm

Crater

Rocks

Dunes

Viking spacecraft on Mars

Ice caps

Mars has ice caps at the North and South poles. This is the only water left on Mars. They melt slightly in the summer and shrink in size.

Mars moons

Deimos

Phobos

Mars has two tiny moons, called Deimos and Phobos. Phobos orbits Mars three times a day and goes through most of its phases in each orbit.

Mars has the largest volcano in the Solar System. It is called Olympus Mons. All the volcanoes on Mars are dead and do not erupt anymore.

Volcano ———

Wispy clouds

Scientists think that there may have been lots of water on Mars millions of years ago. There are dried up river beds and rocks which look as if they were worn down by water.

We know a lot about Mars because spacecraft have landed there and sent pictures back to Earth.

The Asteroid Belt

There are thousands of rocks going round the Sun in the space between Mars and Jupiter. They are called the asteroids.

Most asteroids are pebble-sized but some are as big as skyscrapers and a few even larger than cities.

Asteroids are very knobbly and cratered.

The asteroids may be the shattered remains of a planet which exploded millions of years ago. Or they may be left over rocks which did not form into a planet when the other planets formed.

Jupiter and Saturn, the giant planets

Jupiter and Saturn are quite alike. They do not have rocky surfaces like Earth. They are made of gases and liquids. This picture shows the vast, swirling clouds of gases on Jupiter.

This is Io, one of Jupiter's 16 moons. It is the only place in the Solar System, apart from Earth and Venus, which has live volcanoes.

The clouds of gases rise up and fall like waves. They make bands of different colours as they contain different chemicals.

The cloud layer is about 1,000km (625mi) thick. Below this is liquid hydrogen which does not exist naturally on Earth.

Fierce winds blow all the time, swirling the clouds into bands and whirling storms, which look like spots in the cloud tops.

Huge streaks of lightning flash between the clouds.

Jupiter and Saturn spin faster than any of the other planets, although they are the biggest. They each turn once in about 11 Earth hours.

Jupiter and Saturn are a long way from the Sun and so take a long time to orbit it. Jupiter's year is 12 Earth years long, Saturn's is 29½.

Jupiter is the giant of the Solar System. It would take 1,300 Earths to fill a ball the size of Jupiter.

It is impossible to land on Jupiter as it does not have a rocky surface.

Bulging planets

Jupiter and Saturn are not as round as the rocky planets. They are rather flattened at the top and bottom and bulge out round their middles.

The floating planet

Saturn is made of chemicals which are lighter than water. This means that the planet could float, if there was a sea big enough to put it in.

The Giant Red Spot

Two Earths could fit into Jupiter's Giant Red Spot.

A huge storm has been blowing on Jupiter for many hundreds of years. It is called the Giant Red Spot because of its size and colour.

Saturn's rings

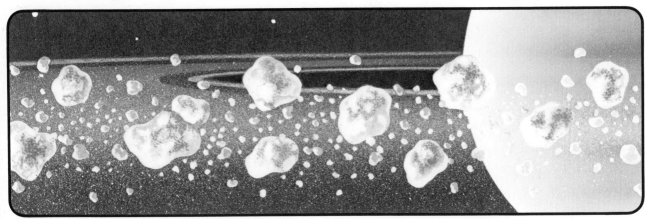

Saturn is circled by a series of rings. They orbit round the middle of the planet. The rings are not solid but made of pieces of rock and ice. Most of the pieces are pebble-sized, though some are like dust and others like boulders. The rings are thin and flat. They stretch out for about the same distance as our Moon is from Earth. Jupiter, Neptune and Uranus have rings too but they are smaller than Saturn's.

Uranus, Neptune and Pluto

Uranus, Neptune and Pluto are the three outer planets of the Solar System. They are dark frozen worlds because they are a long way from the Sun and get little of its heat and light.

Uranus and Neptune are giant gas planets, like Jupiter and Saturn but smaller. They look greeny blue in colour because of the chemicals they are made of.

Uranus's rings

This is Uranus. It is circled by nine rings. The rings are smaller than Saturn's. They are probably made of rocks and ice.

— This is the shadow cast by the rings.

Strange spin

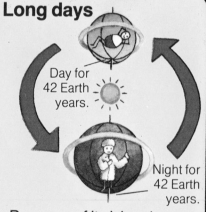

Uranus

Earth

Uranus spins round in a different way to all the other planets. It seems to be lying down, while the others stand up.

Long days

Day for 42 Earth years.

Night for 42 Earth years.

Because of its lying down spin, Uranus has very odd days. On some parts, days and nights are 42 Earth years long.

We do not know very much about these three distant planets. They are so far away they are difficult to see from Earth even with the largest telescopes. The rings around Uranus were discovered in 1977, and Neptune's were found in 1989.

Neptune

As Uranus and Neptune are far from the Sun they have long years. Uranus takes 84 Earth years to orbit the Sun and Neptune takes 165 Earth years.

Uranus and Neptune spin quite fast. Uranus takes about 15½ Earth hours to go round once. Neptune takes about 16 hours.

A spacecraft called Voyager 2 left Earth in 1977. It reached Uranus in 1986 and Neptune in 1989, when it discovered rings around this planet too. It did not land on these planets but flew past them.

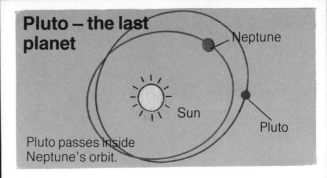

Pluto – the last planet

Neptune

Sun

Pluto

Pluto passes inside Neptune's orbit.

Tiny Pluto takes 247 Earth years to orbit right round the Sun. For most of this time it is the last planet of the Solar System. But for 20 Earth years of each orbit, it passes inside Neptune's orbit, making it the most distant planet. This last happened in 1979.

Discovering Planet X

Until about 1915, Neptune was thought to be the last planet of the Solar System. Then an astronomer, Percival Lowell, worked out that there should be another planet beyond Neptune. He named it Planet X and searched for many years but did not find it.

In 1930 another astronomer, Clyde Tombaugh, was taking photographs of stars. He noticed a stray ''star'' on the picture which he could not identify. He realised that he had photographed the mysterious Planet X. It was later named Pluto.

Comets

Comets are wandering visitors to the Solar System. About 20 come close to Earth each year but only a few are big and bright enough to be seen without telescopes. Every 10 years or so we might see a big bright comet like the one in this picture.

Comet's tail. Some have forked or double tails.

Comets are not as solid as they look. They are made of gases, ice and specks of dust.

Comets can be very large. One which appeared in 1893 had a tail that stretched out in space from the Sun to Mars.

Comet's head

Meteors

Comets leave bits of dust from their tails behind in space. Earth passes through the dusty places each year and we see a shower of bright shooting stars in the sky. They are called meteors by scientists.

Meteors are specks of comet dust which burn red hot as they fall through Earth's air. Sometimes larger pieces of stray space rock come close to Earth and burn up as they fall through the air.

Big bright comets can be seen from Earth for many weeks or even months.

Some comets can be seen regularly. They reappear after a certain number of years. One famous regular comet is Halley's comet which returns every 76 years. It was last seen in 1986.

Comet's path in space

Comets go round the Sun but have differently shaped orbits to the planets. Many come from the outer edges of the Solar System and go round the Sun getting even closer to it than Venus or Mercury do.

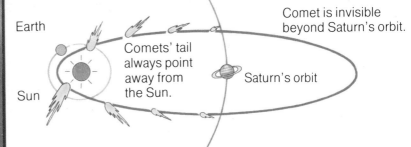

Earth

Comets' tail always point away from the Sun.

Sun

Comet is invisible beyond Saturn's orbit.

Saturn's orbit

Comets do not shine by their own light. They reflect light from the Sun. This means that they are invisible when a long way from the Sun. They start to shine when they get about as close to the Sun as Saturn is.

Meteorites

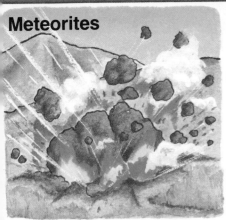

Most meteors are small and burn completely without reaching the ground. A few are big enough to survive the fall and land on Earth.

A crater in Arizona U.S.A. is over 1km (½mi) wide and 175m (575ft) deep.

It was made over 22,000 years ago.

A landed meteor is called a meteorite. Meteorites often break up as they land. They make a hole in the ground called a crater.

Most meteorites are the size of pebbles but a few are huge. One in Africa weighs 60 tonnes – as much as 12 elephants.

Life story of a star

The stars you can see at night are giant balls of hot fiery gases, like the Sun. They look smaller because they are very much further away.

Stars are not all the same. They can be different in size, colour, brightness and temperature. Our Sun is a very common kind of average-size yellow star. Stars can be blue, white, yellow, orange or red.

Stars last for thousands of millions of years but they do not stay the same forever. They change as they get older.

These pictures show the life of a star like our Sun. All stars form in huge clouds of gas and dust.

The dust and gases clump together and begin to heat up. Eventually they get so hot that the clump starts to glow and shine. It has become a star.

The Sun began as a hot blue star. As it got older it grew bigger, cooled down and turned yellow to become the star we see shining today.

Measuring with light

Stars are so far away that scientists have had to invent a new way of measuring the distances between them. They use a unit called a light year.

The nearest star is 4½ light years away. Lots of stars are hundreds of light years away.

Pluto is 6 light hours away.

The Moon is 1½ light seconds away.

The Sun is 8 light minutes away.

A light year is the distance that light can travel in one Earth year.

Light is the fastest thing in the Universe. It always travels at the same speed. Light is so fast it can go round the Earth 7½ times a second.

Scientists also use light hours, light minutes and light seconds for things which are closer in space.

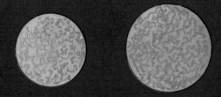

The Sun will spend most of its life as a yellow star, shining steadily for about 10,000 million years. Eventually it will swell up and turn from yellow to red and become a Red Giant Star.

Red Giants can be up to a hundred times bigger than the Sun. They are brighter but cooler than the Sun. This type of star is at the end of its life.

Stars like the Sun turn into Red Giants and then slowly cool down and shrink. They may puff off their outer layers into space, leaving behind a small, almost dead star, called a White Dwarf Star.

White Dwarf Star

Outer layers of Red Giant puff off into space.

Red Giant Star

Black Hole

The very biggest stars blow up and leave behind a Black Hole which sucks into itself anything that goes near. Not even light can escape a Black Hole in space.

Supernova

Neutron Star

Neutron Star and gas cloud.

Stars larger than the Sun also swell into Red Giants but they have a more spectacular ending. They blow up with a huge explosion called a Supernova*. Most of them leave behind a cloud of gas and dust with a tiny spinning star, called a Neutron Star, in the centre.

*However, a star does not have to be a Red Giant to become a Supernova. The most spectacular Supernova to occur since 1604 was from a Blue Giant in 1987.

165

Galaxies

Stars are not scattered about the Universe. They are gathered in huge groups, each containing hundreds of millions of stars. These groups are called galaxies. Our Sun is a star in a galaxy called the Milky Way.

Our galaxy measures about 80,000 light years across.

There are more stars in the middle of a galaxy than on the edges.

Our Sun is about here.

There are about 250 thousand million stars in our galaxy.

The Milky Way is shaped rather like a catherine wheel firework. Scientists call it a spiral shaped galaxy.
The picture above shows what the Milky Way would look like from space, seen from above or below. If seen from the side it would look the shape pictured underneath.

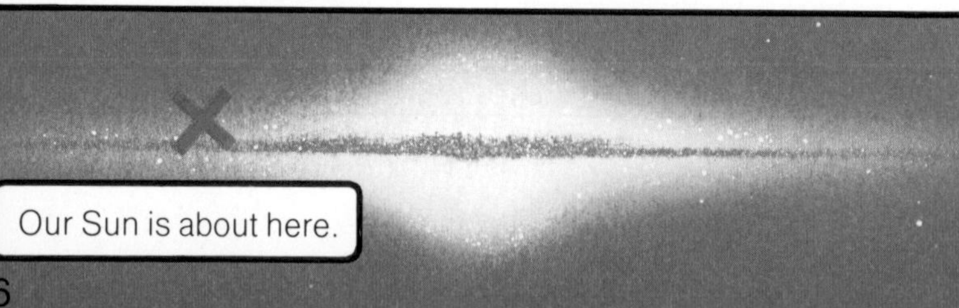

Our Sun is about here.

Galactic year

Galaxies do not sit still in space. They spin slowly round and round. One complete spin is called a galactic year. The Milky Way takes 225 million Earth years to spin once.

Other galaxies

The Milky Way is just one of many millions of galaxies that make up the Universe. The galaxies are very far away from each other. The nearest galaxy to the Milky Way is about 160 thousand light years away. Galaxies can be different sizes and shapes. Here are some of the common galactic shapes.

This galaxy is an oval shape.

This galaxy is a spiral shape like the Milky Way. There are lots of spiral shaped galaxies.

Here is another kind of spiral galaxy. It is called a barred spiral.

Some galaxies have uneven shapes. This one is almost round.

The Big Bang

Most scientists believe that the Universe began with a huge explosion about 15,000 million years ago. They call this the Big Bang. There are no words to describe what things were like before the Big Bang.

When the Big Bang explosion happened, everything which is in the Universe went flying out in all directions. Scientists say the galaxies formed from the lumps which were flung out by the Big Bang.

The galaxies are still flying away from each other today. No one knows if this will go on forever or if they will stop eventually.

Space words

Here are some of the special space words which have been used.

Years

A planet's year is the length of time it takes to go once round the Sun. Each planet has a different length year.

Days

All of the planets spin round and round. The time a planet takes to spin once is its day. The spinning moves different parts of the surface to face the Sun, giving the planet day-time and night-time.

Moons

A moon is a ball of rock which orbits round a planet. Scientists think that the rings which go round some planets may be made from a moon which broke up or did not form properly.

Asteroids

An asteroid is a piece of rock floating in space. There is a band of thousands of asteroids between the planets Mars and Jupiter.

Meteors

A meteor is a piece of space rock which gets very close to Earth (or another planet) and falls through the air. It burns up as it falls.

Meteorites

Meteors which land on a moon or planet are called meteorites. Most are made of stone but a few are made of iron or stone and iron.

Craters

A crater is the hole made by a meteorite. All of the rocky planets and moons have some craters on their surfaces.

Comets

Comets go round the Sun in long oval orbits. They have been called dirty snowballs in space because they are made of ice and dust.

Sunspots

Sunspots are dark patches on the Sun. They are areas of gas which are cooler than the surface. This makes them seem dark compared to the hotter surface.

Light years

A light year is the unit used for measuring long distances in space. It is the distance that light travels in one Earth year, which is 9½ million million km (6 million million mi).

Supernova

A Supernova is an exploding star. Since the year 1006, four exploding stars have been seen in our Galaxy. Some are so bright we can even see them in other galaxies.

Galaxies

A galaxy is a collection of millions and millions of stars. Galaxies can be different shapes and sizes. There are millions of them in the Universe.

Milky Way

We are part of a galaxy which is called the Milky Way, or sometimes just The Galaxy.

Universe

The Universe is everything that exists, all the millions of galaxies, stars, planets and moons that there are.

WHERE FOOD COMES FROM

How is food grown?
Where do bananas grow?
Which foods come from animals?
How is food kept fresh?
How are fish fingers made?

About food

You need lots of different types of food to keep you strong, fit and healthy. This book explains where each type of food comes from and what happens to it before it reaches your plate.

The story of food

Long ago, people spent most of their time searching for seeds and berries to eat.

They also hunted animals. Often they could not find any food and they had to go hungry.

Later they discovered how to tame animals. They protected them from wolves, then killed them when they needed food.

After a while, they found out how to grow plants by sprinkling seeds on the ground. They then ate these plants.

They now had all their food around them in one place. Because of this, people were much less likely to go hungry.

Famines

Some parts of the world, for example North Africa, have poor soil and hardly any rain. In a very dry year little grows. People have no money to buy food from elsewhere.

North Africa

Sometimes they have to eat seeds which should be planted for the following year. The next year they starve. This is called a famine.

Swapping food

Some food can only grow in a particular climate. For example, grapes need plenty of warm sun, and rice needs lots of rain.

Many kinds of food are sent abroad. This means people in cool places can buy grapes and people in dry places can buy rice.

Goods going into a country are called imports. Goods sent out of a country are called exports.

Rain dances

American Indians used to believe that rain was sent by rain gods. They tried to please these gods by dancing for them. They hoped this would make the gods send rain to help their crops grow.

Preserving food

Fresh food can soon go bad. Because of this, food is treated so it lasts longer and is safe to eat.

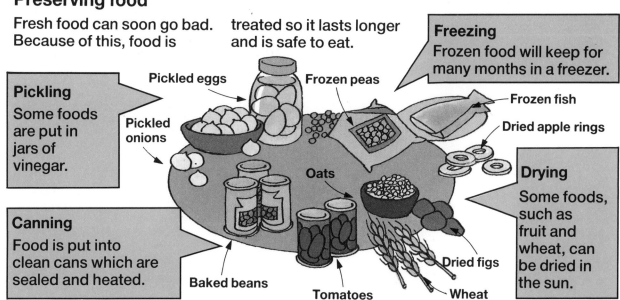

Freezing
Frozen food will keep for many months in a freezer.

Pickling
Some foods are put in jars of vinegar.

Pickled eggs

Frozen peas

Frozen fish

Dried apple rings

Pickled onions

Oats

Drying
Some foods, such as fruit and wheat, can be dried in the sun.

Canning
Food is put into clean cans which are sealed and heated.

Baked beans

Tomatoes

Dried figs

Wheat

Bread

Have you noticed how many different sorts of bread there are? Here are just a few of them.

Bread is made mostly of flour. The color and taste depends on what type of flour the baker uses.

What is flour?

Most flour comes from a type of grass known as wheat*. The seeds or grains are removed and crushed to make flour.

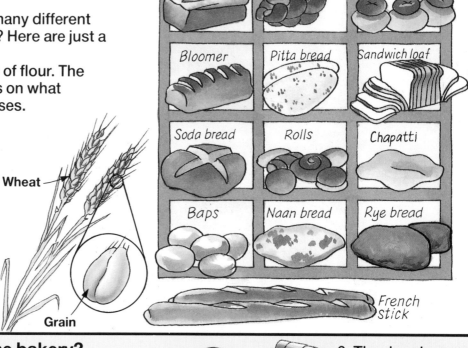

Wheat

Grain

Split loaf

Chollah

Cottage loaf

Bloomer

Pitta bread

Sandwich loaf

Soda bread

Rolls

Chapatti

Baps

Naan bread

Rye bread

French stick

What happens at the bakery?

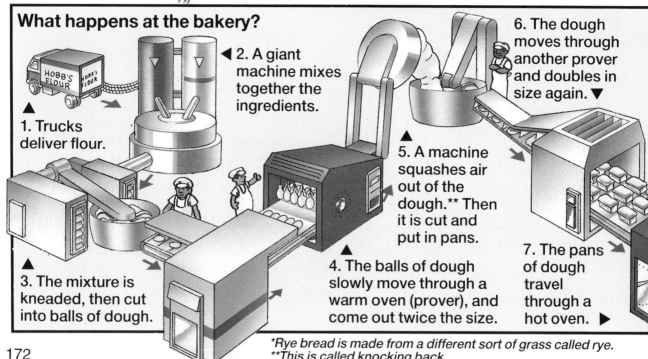

HOBB'S FLOUR

◀ 2. A giant machine mixes together the ingredients.

1. Trucks deliver flour.

3. The mixture is kneaded, then cut into balls of dough.

4. The balls of dough slowly move through a warm oven (prover), and come out twice the size.

5. A machine squashes air out of the dough.** Then it is cut and put in pans.

6. The dough moves through another prover and doubles in size again. ▼

7. The pans of dough travel through a hot oven. ▶

*Rye bread is made from a different sort of grass called rye.
**This is called knocking back.

Make your own bread

Home-made bread tastes delicious.

You will need:

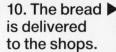

2 cups flour
2 teaspoons sugar
½ teaspoons salt
½ cup shortening
1 package/cake of yeast
½ cup warm water
1 cup warm milk

Loaf pan

1. Mix the yeast and water. Now mix everything to make dough.

2. Fold the dough towards you then push it down and away.

3. Turn it and repeat until it's no longer sticky. Put it in a pan.

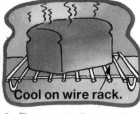

Cool on wire rack.

4. Rub oil in a plastic bag. Put the pan in it. Leave in a warm place.

5. After an hour, remove from the bag and bake in a hot oven* for half an hour.

6. Remove from the pan. Does it sound hollow when tapped underneath?**

10. The bread ▶ is delivered to the shops.

SUN BEAM

9. Some are sliced and wrapped.

8. The loaves are tipped out of their pans and cooled on racks.

What makes bread rise?

If you make your own bread, you will see that the finished loaf is bigger than the dough you started with. The ingredient which makes dough grow (rise) is the yeast.

When it is warm, yeast gives off tiny bubbles of a gas called carbon dioxide. It is the bubbles that makes the dough rise.

Look at a slice of bread. Can you see tiny holes left by the carbon dioxide?

Flat bread

Some bread is made without yeast, and is quite flat. This is unleavened bread. There are four types shown on the opposite page; can you guess which ones? (Answer on page 248.)

*Gas mark 8, or 450°F, 230°C (electric).
**If it doesn't, put it back in the pan and leave for about five minutes longer.

Milk and eggs

Most milk comes from cows. A cow cannot give us milk until she has had her first calf. After that, she produces much more than a calf could drink; about 950 gallons each year.

At the farm

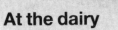

◀ 1. On large dairy farms, the cows are milked by machines linked by pipes to enormous refrigerated tanks.

2. Each day, a refrigerated tanker collects the milk and takes it to the dairy.
▼

Tank

How cream is made

Warm milk is poured into a centrifuge. This machine separates the cream by spinning the milk very quickly.

A switch on the centrifuge controls how thick the cream is.

Very thin – single

Thin – whipping

Thick – double

Very thick – clotted

You can tell how thick cream is by its name.

JOE'S DAIRY

The milk flows from the tank to the truck through this pipe.

The dairy has to be very clean and hygienic.

Tankers with milk from lots of farms in the area.

At the dairy

3. The milk is tested to make sure it is clean. Most milk is then heated for around 15 seconds, then quickly cooled down.

This is called pasteurizing. It destroys any harmful germs in the milk and keeps it fresh for longer.

4. Machines pour the milk into cartons, bottles or cans. They are then loaded on to trucks and delivered to shops.

174

Make your own yogurt

You will need:

3½ cups longlife milk

2 teaspoons fresh natural yogurt

2-3 tablespoons dried skimmed milk

chopped fruit or nuts (optional)

1. Mix a little longlife milk and the yogurt.

2. Stir in the remaining milk and the dried milk.

3. Cover with a tea-towel, and leave in a warm place.

4. After about 12 hours, add chopped fruit or nuts.

Crate of milk bottles

Milk truck

Eggs

Most of the eggs you eat come from chickens. Sometimes the egg box tells you about the lives of the chickens that laid them.

★ Free range chickens roam around a farmyard, eating whatever they find. You have to hunt for the eggs.

★ Deep litter chickens live in a warm shed with straw on the floor. The farmer gives them special food.

★ Battery chickens are kept in cages and given special food. The eggs are collected from a tray below the cage.

From the farm to the box

Every day, large farms send eggs to a packing station. Here, workers measure them, then shine a bright light on them which shows if any are bad. They then pack them into boxes.

How fresh is your egg?

Place your egg in a glass bowl full of water. Now watch to see what it does.

Fresh	Not so fresh	Bad

There is an airspace inside one end of the egg. The older the egg, the larger the space, and the more likely it is to float.

175

Cheese and butter

Butter and cheese are both made from milk. Here you can find out how they are made. You can also discover why margarine was first invented.

The story of butter

▲ Long ago, a traveller took some milk for his journey. He hung it in a leather bag around his camel's neck. It jerked around, and when he came to drink it, it had turned almost solid. This was butter.

Almost 200 ▶ years ago, people put cream in a tub with a pole in the middle (a butter churn). To make butter, they pulled the pole up and down.

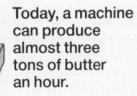

Today, a machine can produce almost three tons of butter an hour.

Cheese

There are lots of types of cheeses made all over the world. Many are named after the place where they were first made.

Most are now made in factories, and sold all around the world.

How is cheese made?

Every cheese is made differently. Here you can see how five sorts are made. If you want to find out about cheddar (letter B), for example, follow the writing with B above it.

KEY

A	Gruyère
B	Cheddar
C	Brie
D	Stilton
E	Cottage cheese

START

ABCD

1. Fresh milk is pasteurized.

E

1. Skimmed milk is pasteurized.

ABCDE

2. The milk is put into cheese vats.

ABCD

4. The milk is warmed, then rennet is added. This turns it lumpy.

ABDE

3. Bacteria is added. This makes the milk sour.

176

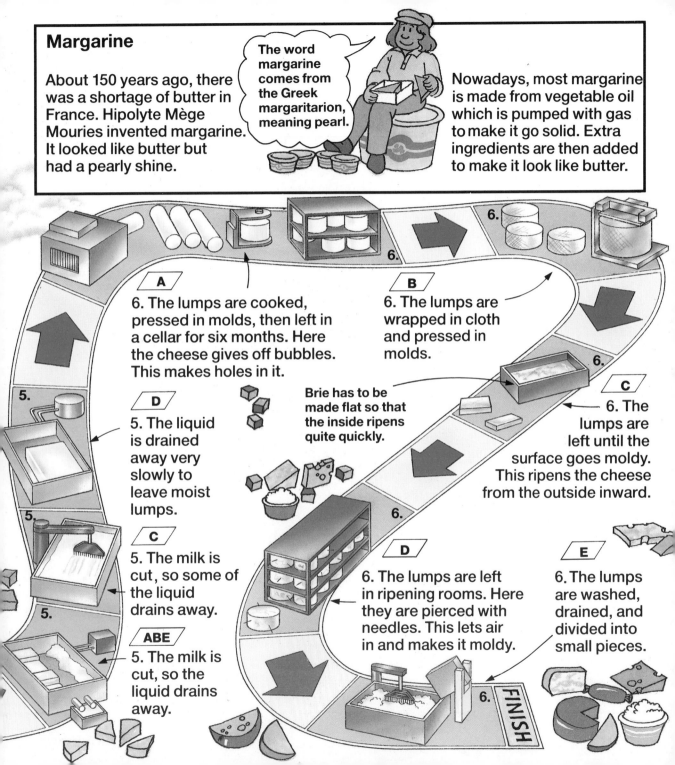

Fruit and vegetables

Some fruit and vegetables are grown in this country, but many are bought from countries which have a different climate.

They are all plants or parts of plants such as roots and stems.

You eat the center of an artichoke, and the bottom of its petals.

Celery

Asparagus

These are the leaves of plants, picked before the flower comes out.

These are the bulbs of plants.

Lettuce
Endive
Spinach
Cabbage

These are the stems of plants.

Onion

Leek

Broccoli

Spring onion

Nuts

Most nuts are fruits or seeds that come from trees. Coconuts come from a type of palm tree.

This is what the inside of a coconut looks like.

Nuts

These vegetables are the flowers of plants.

Cauliflower

These are the roots or underground stems (tubers) of plants.

Tomato

Zucchini

Carrot

Potato

These vegetables are the fruits of plants.

Pulses

Dried beans, peas and lentils are called pulses. They must be soaked before being cooked.

Chick peas

Haricot beans

Red kidney beans

Chilli

Cucumber

Pepper

How bananas get here

Banana tree

Bananas grow in hot places like the West Indies. A large red flower comes out of the middle of the trunk. When this opens up there is a stem with about 100 bananas on it.

Sweetcorn is made into cornflakes, popcorn and a type of flour (cornflour).

*See page 171 for more about importing.

Apple

Orange

Lemon

Grapefruit

Grapes grow on a plant called a vine. Some are dried to make raisins. Some are made into wine.

These are called citrus fruits. They grow on trees.

Apples and pears can be eaten raw, but some are better cooked.

Berries and soft fruit grow on bushes or plants.

Strawberry

Mango

Dates grow on palm trees.

Cherry

Most mushrooms are grown especially for eating. Wild ones can look like poisonous toadstools, so don't pick them.

Avocado
Peach

Plum

These are stone fruit (they have a stone in the middle). They grow on trees.

Making chips

Chips are made from potatoes.

First the potatoes are washed and peeled.

A machine ▶ slices them thinly. They are fried in hot oil, then drained and sprinkled with salt and flavorings.

◀ A machine weighs the chips into bags.

▲ The bananas are picked when they are still hard and green.

▲ On board ship, they are kept cool so they don't ripen too quickly.

◀ The stems are unloaded and taken to warm, damp rooms. When they are nearly ripe, they are cut into bunches called hands.

These are sent to fruit markets and shops all over ▼ the country.

TROPICO

179

Fish

Most fish are caught at sea in nets dangling from boats called fishing trawlers. The fish have to be rushed back to port very quickly, before they go bad.

Sometimes the fish are stored in freezers on the trawler instead.

Deep sea trawler

Open purse seine net

Catching fish

Deep sea trawlers catch fish from the bottom of the sea. They drag their nets along the sea-bed.

A trawler with a purse seine net catches fish which swim nearer the surface. Once the net is full, fishermen pull in the rope around the top of it.

The life of a salmon

When a salmon is about two years old it swims downstream toward the ocean.

After four years in the sea, it returns to its original river, using the sun to find its way. It knows its home by its smell.

The salmon leaps over anything in its path.

Most salmon then stay in the river until they die, but a few do the journey again.

Different sorts of fish

There are more than 30,000 different sorts of fish living in the seas, rivers, streams, lakes and ponds around the world. There are four main groups of fish: white fish, oily fish, freshwater fish and shellfish.

Oily fish, ▶ such as mackerel, mostly live in the sea.

Mackerel

White fish can ▶ be round (such as haddock), or flat (such as flounder).

Flounder

Freshwater fish, such as trout and salmon, mostly live in lakes and rivers.

Trout

Crabs ◀ Shellfish (such as crabs, prawns and mussels) mostly live on the sea-bed.

Mussels

Prawns

Preserving fish

Unless fish is eaten very soon after it is caught, it has to be treated to stop it from going bad. You can get food poisoning from bad fish.

Drying ▶
Long ago, people learned to dry fish in the sun and wind.

Smoking ▶
Hanging fish over a fire preserves it and gives it a smokey flavor.

Freezing ▶
Fish lasts for up to three months in the freezer.

Salting ▶
Ancient Egyptians used salt to preserve fish.

Pickling ▶
Soaking fish in vinegar and salt is known as pickling.

How fish sticks are made

1. The parts that make fish sticks are removed and washed.

5. They are ▶ sprinkled with breadcrumbs.

6. The sticks are quickly fried to make the coating hard.

2. They are frozen in large blocks.

3. Machines cut the blocks into sticks.

Frozen fish

4. These go through a mixture of flour, cornstarch, water and salt.

7. They are refrozen and packed. ▶

8. They are ▶ taken to shops in refrigerated trucks.

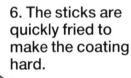

191

Meat

People have always killed animals for food. Cavemen spent their days hunting animals, and in some places there are still tribes of people who hunt animals.

Most of the meat we eat nowadays comes from farm animals.

Red and white meat

There are two main types of meat; red meat and white meat. Beef, lamb and pork are all red meat.

White meat comes from birds such as chickens, turkeys and ducks.

◀ Beef comes from cows. Most cows are killed when they are between the age of one and two. Meat from a young calf is called veal.

Pork and bacon both ▲ come from pigs. Pigs are killed when they are the right weight.

Lambs are usually killed ▲ when they are a year old. After this, the meat is called hoggett or mutton.

Chicken

Duck

Turkey

From the farmer to your plate

Here you can see what happens to the animals before they get to your plate.

Farmer

Cows and sheep mainly eat grass. In the winter, other crops such as hay and barley are also given to them.

Pigs like lots of different foods. Famers give them a special mixture called pig swill.

Auction market

Live animals are taken to market by the farmer. Cattle are sold one by one. Pigs and sheep are weighed and sold in groups.

Processing plant

The animals are killed, then stored until they are sold.

Most meat is sold direct to butchers. Some is taken to meat markets.

Cooking meat

Meat has to be cooked before we eat it, to destroy any germs in it and make it tender and tasty.

Roasting is a way of cooking the large pieces (joints) in the ▶ oven.

▲ Grilling is a good way of cooking small, tender pieces of meat such as chops.

▲ **Stewing is** the best way to cook meat which is not very tender. The meat is cooked in liquid inside, or on top of, the stove.

▲ **Frying is** cooking meat in fat in a shallow pan.

▲ **Stir-frying is** similar to normal frying. You toss thin strips of meat in a wok.

▲ **Barbecuing is** when meat is cooked on a barbecue outside.

▲ Braising means frying meat quickly, then adding liquid. The pot is then covered and put in the oven or left on top of the stove.

Meat markets
These sell meat to butchers. One famous market is Smithfield in London. Butchers often buy a whole body. This is called a carcass.

Butcher
The butcher cuts the carcass up to sell it. Other things such as sausage and hamburger are also made out of the meat.

Non meat-eaters
Some people, called vegetarians, don't eat meat or fish. They may think it is wrong to kill, or dislike the way some animals are kept. Some have religious reasons. For example, Hindus don't eat beef, and Jewish people won't eat pork.

Vegetarians eat lots of fruit and vegetables.

Sugar and chocolate

Sugar and chocolate both come from plants. Below you can find out what happens to the plants after they are picked.

Sugar

Sugar comes from sugar cane or sugar beet plants. Below you can see what is done to the plants to make brown sugar.

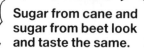

Sugar from cane and sugar from beet look and taste the same.

Sugar cane

The juice inside the thick stalks contains all the sugar.

▲
1. The tall canes are cut down and taken to a factory called a sugar mill.

▲
2. They are shredded and crushed between rollers that squeeze out the juice.

Lime

▲
3. The juice is boiled with lime. This gets rid of the unwanted bits in the juice. It is then boiled to make syrup and small lumps of sugar (crystals).

Sugar beet

Sugar beet plants look a bit like parsnips. They grow in cool places.

1. The leaves ▶ are removed, and the plants are taken to a factory.

◀ 2. Here they are washed, sliced and spun in hot water.

3. The sugar passes out into the water. This is boiled, then treated like ◀ cane juice.

4. A centrifuge* separates the brown crystals from the syrup.
▼

5. The crystals are taken to other countries to be made into white sugar. ▼

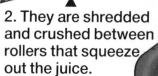

*You can find out about centrifuges on page 174.

Making white sugar

Brown sugar crystals

Brown sugar ▲ crystals are made into white sugar in a refinery.

1. The crystals are put in a pan and covered in dried molasses.

◀ 2. The molasses is melted in warm syrup. A centrifuge* separates this from the crystals.

4. The syrup is cooked in a closed pan. Crystals are then added. This makes white sugar form. It is removed and dried.

◀ 3. The crystals are dissolved in water. The unwanted parts are removed, and they turn white.

5. It is ▲ poured into packets.

Chocolate

Chocolate comes from cocoa trees which grow in South America and Africa.

Cocoa beans ▶ grow in large pods which are picked when they are ripe.

Pod

Bean

Each pod contains about 40 beans.

The beans ▶ are left under damp banana leaves for six days, to give them a nice taste.

They are dried in the sun, put in sacks and shipped to factories abroad. ▼

Here the beans are cleaned and roasted. The insides are removed and ground to a paste.

Cocoa ▶ butter is squeezed out of the paste.

Cocoa paste, cocoa butter, sugar and fat are made into liquid chocolate. This sets in molds. ▶

185

Breakfast cereal

Most breakfast cereals are made from crops which grow in fields. For example, muesli is made from oats. Below you can see how cornflakes are made.

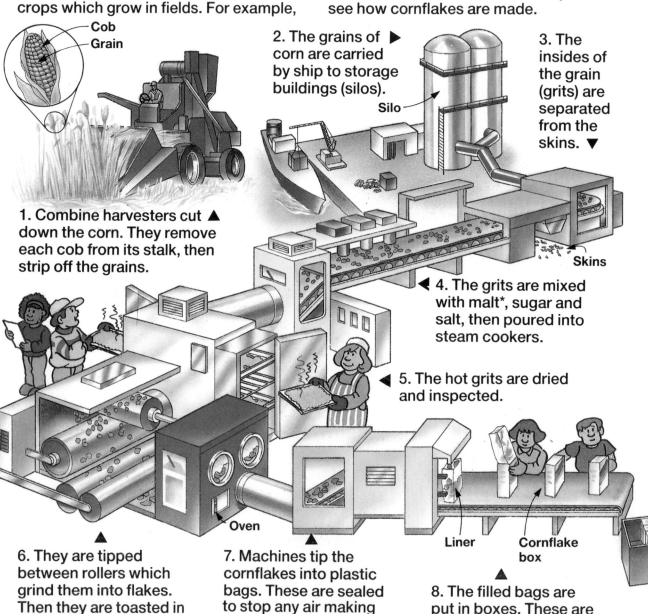

Cob
Grain

2. The grains of ▶ corn are carried by ship to storage buildings (silos).

Silo

3. The insides of the grain (grits) are separated from the skins. ▼

Skins

1. Combine harvesters cut ▲ down the corn. They remove each cob from its stalk, then strip off the grains.

4. The grits are mixed with malt*, sugar and salt, then poured into steam cookers.

5. The hot grits are dried and inspected.

Oven

6. They are tipped between rollers which grind them into flakes. Then they are toasted in turning ovens.

7. Machines tip the cornflakes into plastic bags. These are sealed to stop any air making the cornflakes stale.

Liner

Cornflake box

8. The filled bags are put in boxes. These are then delivered to shops.

*Malt is barley that has sprouted and then been dried.

Pasta

Pasta is made out of semolina. This is wheat (see page 172) which has been rolled and sieved into even grains.

Below you can see how spaghetti is made.

Semolina

Mixer

Water

Extruder

◄ 1. Semolina and water are tipped into a machine called an extruder.

2. The extruder pushes it through tiny holes which split it into long strands of wet spaghetti.

To extrude means to push out.

◄ 3. The spaghetti is now hung on rods and left to dry.

4. When the spaghetti is dry and hard, it is cut and put in packets.

Other sorts of pasta

The extruder can make pasta in all sorts of shapes and sizes. A few are shown here.

Lasagne

Rings

Rigatoni

Spaghetti

Wagon wheels

Stars

Macaroni

Macaroni

For macaroni, the extruder has larger holes than those for spaghetti. There is a pin in the middle of each hole. This makes holes in the macaroni.

Canned spaghetti

Some spaghetti is sent to factories. Here it is cooked, chopped up and put into cans with tomato sauce.

187

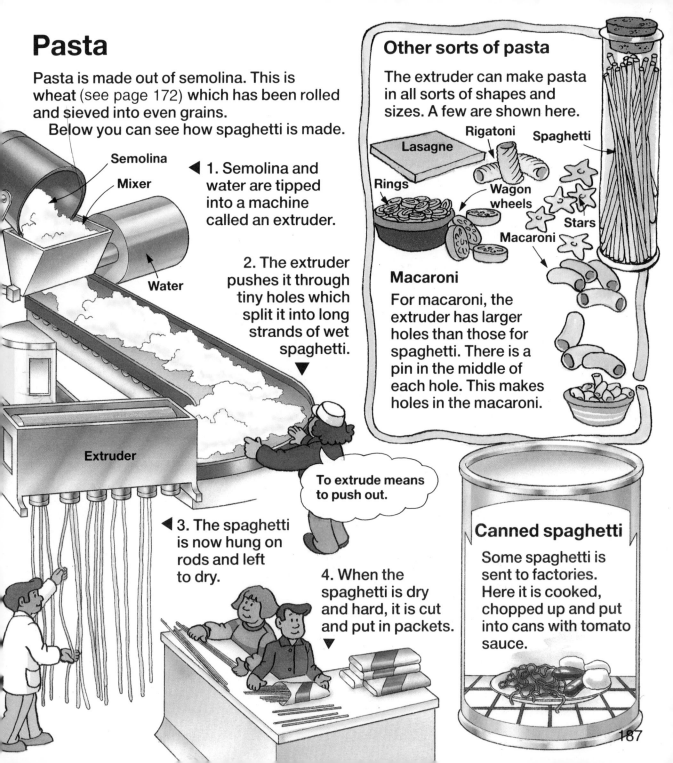

Rice

90% of the world's rice is grown and eaten in China and the Far East. The rest comes from the USA, where modern machines are used. These make rice-growing quick and efficient. In China and the Far East, rice is still grown by hand, as shown below.

1. Sacks of seeds (paddy) are put in water. They are left to sprout.

2. Sprouts are sown in a sheltered area, and looked after for a month. ▼

3. A large field is now flooded. Oxen are used to dig trenches. ▼

4. Workers place the small plants in trenches. ▼

5. When the plants are bigger, workers turn water wheels with their feet. This lets more water in.

6. Each plant is sprayed to stop rats, birds and insects eating them.

7. The fields are drained. The workers then cut down the rice with scythes (large knives).

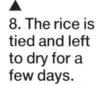

8. The rice is tied and left to dry for a few days.

9. The rice is threshed (beaten) to separate grains from the stalks.

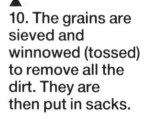

10. The grains are sieved and winnowed (tossed) to remove all the dirt. They are then put in sacks.

The first American rice

In 1694, a ship carrying rice and spices was sailing from Madagascar. A storm blew up, and the ship had to shelter in Charleston, USA.

The captain gave the people some sacks of rice seed. They planted this seed, and soon there was enough rice for everyone in South Carolina.

Different sorts of rice

There are three main sorts of rice:

★ Long grain rice is good with savory dishes such as curry.
★ Medium grain rice is used for both savory and sweet dishes.
★ Short grain rice is good for rice puddings.

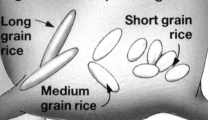

Long grain rice

Short grain rice

Medium grain rice

Make your own rice pudding

This recipe makes a thick, creamy pudding with a sugary skin on top. You will need:

⅓ cup uncooked rice

4 cups milk

¼ teaspoon salt

¼ cup sugar

2 tablespoons butter

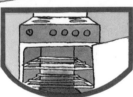

1. Heat the oven to Gas Mark 2.*

2. Heat the rice and milk in a saucepan.

3. Let the rice simmer for 10 minutes.

4. Let the rice cool. Beat the eggs in a bowl.

5. Mix everything together and put in a dish.

6. Bake in the oven for about half an hour.

*Electric ovens: 150°C or 300°F.

Drinks

Below you can find out how fizzy drinks* are made.

You can also see where coffee and tea come from.

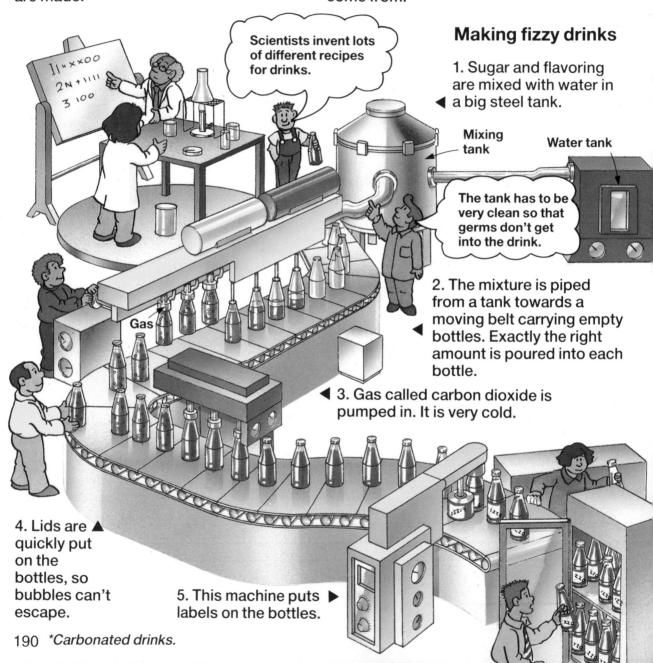

Scientists invent lots of different recipes for drinks.

Making fizzy drinks

1. Sugar and flavoring are mixed with water in a big steel tank.

Mixing tank

Water tank

The tank has to be very clean so that germs don't get into the drink.

Gas

2. The mixture is piped from a tank towards a moving belt carrying empty bottles. Exactly the right amount is poured into each bottle.

3. Gas called carbon dioxide is pumped in. It is very cold.

4. Lids are ▲ quickly put on the bottles, so bubbles can't escape.

5. This machine puts labels on the bottles. ▶

190 *Carbonated drinks.

The life of a coffee bean

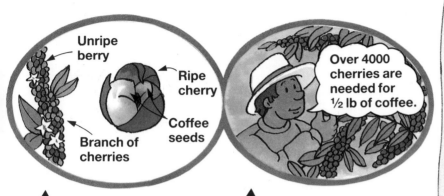

1. Berries from coffee trees are dark green at first. As they ripen they turn yellow, then they turn deep red and are called cherries.

2. The cherries are picked or left until they fall off the trees. They are then collected and sifted to remove the dust, leaves and twigs.

> Over 4000 cherries are needed for ½ lb of coffee.

Unripe berry
Ripe cherry
Coffee seeds
Branch of cherries

3. A machine removes the flesh (pulp). The outsides are washed, dried and put in a machine called a huller. The parts that are left are called beans.

Pulper

4. Sacks of beans are shipped abroad.
The beans are roasted. Some are sold whole. Others are ground into granules or powder.

60kg sacks

Where does coffee grow?

Coffee trees need plenty of warm weather. If it is too hot or cold, they will die.

TROPIC OF CANCER

North America
Europe
Africa
South America
Australia

TROPIC OF CAPRICORN

Most coffee is grown between the Tropic of Cancer and the Tropic of Capricorn.

Tea

Tea leaves grow on bushes mainly in China and India.
Before modern ships were built, tea was carried to many countries in ships called clippers.

Tea clipper

Food facts

Milk, cheese and butter

★The top five butter producers are:
(Tons per year)

USSR	1,290,000
India	730,000
France	600,000
USA	595,000
W. Germany	530,000

★87.7% of milk is water.

★The largest cheese ever made weighed 33,488lb. A tractor trailer 12ft long was made especially to carry it.

Fruit and vegetables

★The largest chip ever was 4in x 7in. It was made from a giant potato.

★The longest banana split was 23,162ft. It was made from over 35,000 bananas.

★The hottest spice is the chilli pepper.

★The record for eating baked beans with a cocktail stick is 2,780 in 30 minutes.

★The oldest method of preservation is drying. Dried fruit was found in the tombs of the ancient kings of Egypt.

Fish

★The largest Paella (a Spanish fish and rice meal) was 33ft wide and 18in deep. It fed 15,000 people.

★About 81 million tons of fish are caught every year. Japan catches most – about 12 million tons.

Rice

★Over half the people living in the world eat more rice than anything else.

Meat

★A sausage maker in Birmingham, Britain made a sausage 5·5 miles long – that's about 87,000 ordinary sausages.

★Mr Boyer made the first meat substitute (something used instead of meat that looks and tastes very much like it) from soya beans about 50 years ago.

Breakfast cereals

★The first cornflakes were made by Mr. Kellogg in Michigan, USA in 1902.

★Mr. Graham (USA) invented the first breakfast cereal. He called it Graham Crackers.

Sugar and chocolate

★More than 100 million tons of sugar are eaten every year.

★The largest chocolate model ever made was of the design for the Olympic center for the 1992 Olympics in Barcelona, Spain. It measured 33 x 16ft and was 29in high.

Drinks

★The average adult in Britain drinks about 1,650 cups of tea every year – about 4-5 cups a day.

★People in Finland drink the most coffee (28.4lb each per year). The Japanese drink least (3.6lb each).

HOW THINGS ARE MADE

How is glass made?
How is wool produced?
Where does leather come from?
What is paper made of?
How are tin cans made?

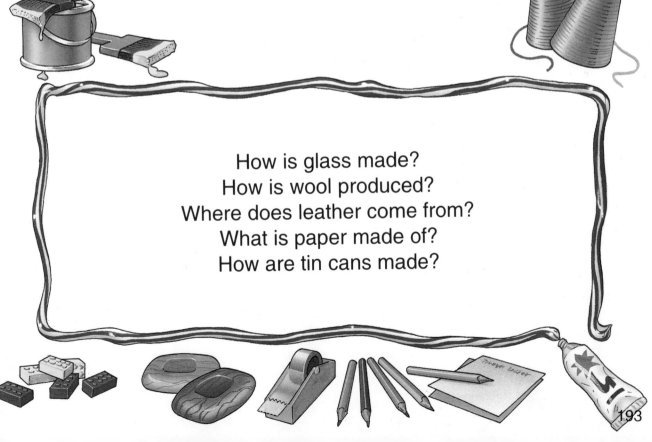

What are things made from?

Many natural things in the world around us are very useful. We can use parts of plants and animals, earth, rocks, trees, oil, gas and so on to make into the things we need. Today most things are made in factories. Lots can be made in a short time.

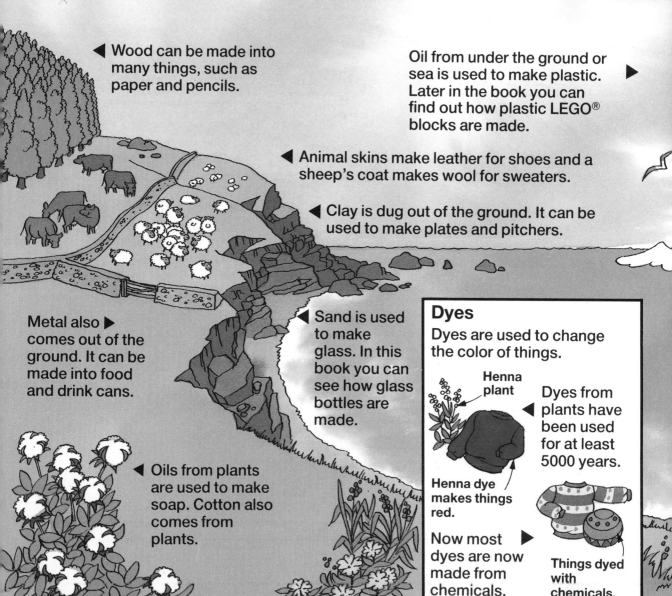

◀ Wood can be made into many things, such as paper and pencils.

Oil from under the ground or sea is used to make plastic. Later in the book you can find out how plastic LEGO® blocks are made. ▶

◀ Animal skins make leather for shoes and a sheep's coat makes wool for sweaters.

◀ Clay is dug out of the ground. It can be used to make plates and pitchers.

Metal also ▶ comes out of the ground. It can be made into food and drink cans.

◀ Sand is used to make glass. In this book you can see how glass bottles are made.

Oils from plants are used to make soap. Cotton also comes from plants.

Dyes

Dyes are used to change the color of things.

Henna plant

◀ Dyes from plants have been used for at least 5000 years.

Henna dye makes things red.

Now most dyes are now made from chemicals. ▶

Things dyed with chemicals.

People drill for oil from oil rigs far out at sea.

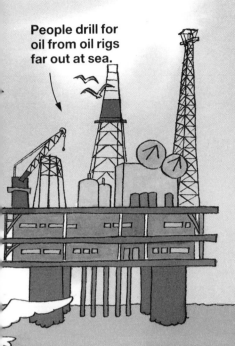

Chemicals

Everything around us is made of chemicals – land, sea, air, houses, rocks, oil and even our bodies.

Scientists can separate ▶ out the chemicals in things like oil, rocks and plants and use them to make the things we need.

Medicines, plastic, paint and glue are made from chemicals.

Smoke coming out of a chemical factory.

◀ These chemicals are made in factories. They are very useful, but the smoke from the factories can be harmful.

Running out of power

Power is needed to run machines, cars and trucks. Power comes from things like gas, oil and coal.

What would happen if we ran out of gasoline?

▲ Some scientists believe that we will run out of oil in about 100 years' time.

If we could find ways of using all the power from the waves, wind, water and sun, we would have 20 billion times more power than we need.▼

Wind turbines can make power from the wind.

Recycling

Cans, bottles and paper needn't be thrown away. They can be collected, taken to a factory and used to make new things.

Putting bottles in a bottle bank.

This is called recycling. It means we use less power, wood, chemicals and so on.

Leather shoes

Shoes can be made out of many different materials, such as leather, plastic or canvas. Leather is good because it stops feet getting too hot.

Leather is made from animal skin. The skin of a large animal like a cow is called a hide. It has to be treated in a factory to stop it from rotting.

Making leather

1. Hides are ▶ soaked in water and a chemical called lime inside a turning drum. This makes it easier to scrape off the animal hair.

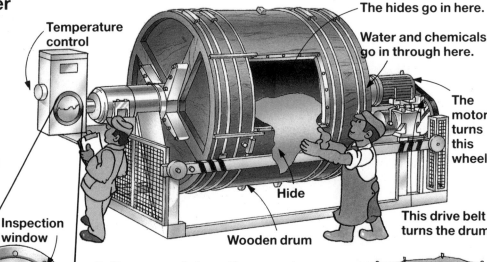

Temperature control

The hides go in here.

Water and chemicals go in through here.

The motor turns this wheel.

This drive belt turns the drum.

Hide

Wooden drum

Inspection window

2. The hides are soaked in other liquids such as acid. ▶

3. For several days they are ▲ left in the turning drum with water and chemicals called chromium salts. This turns the leather bluey-green.

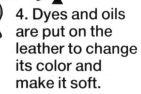

4. Dyes and oils are put on the leather to change its color and make it soft.

6. The leather is sprayed and polished. A pattern may be pressed into it. It is now ready to be made into shoes.

We stretch the leather to make it softer.

◀ 5. The leather is glued on to a sheet of glass to go through a heated tunnel. This dries it.

Making a shoe

Shoes are made on models of feet called lasts. This picture shows the parts of the shoe.

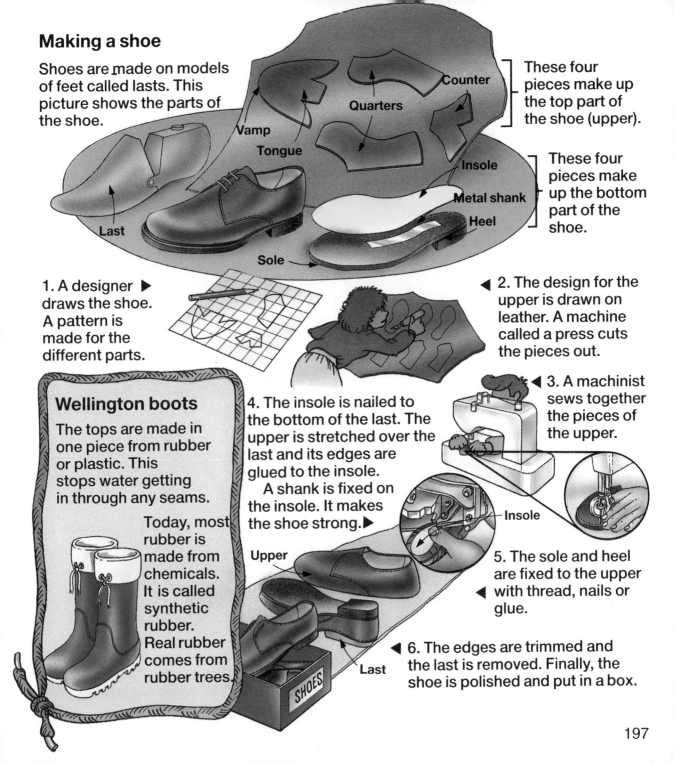

Vamp

Tongue

Quarters

Counter

These four pieces make up the top part of the shoe (upper).

Insole

Metal shank

Heel

These four pieces make up the bottom part of the shoe.

Last

Sole

1. A designer ▶ draws the shoe. A pattern is made for the different parts.

◀ 2. The design for the upper is drawn on leather. A machine called a press cuts the pieces out.

◀ 3. A machinist sews together the pieces of the upper.

Wellington boots

The tops are made in one piece from rubber or plastic. This stops water getting in through any seams.

Today, most rubber is made from chemicals. It is called synthetic rubber. Real rubber comes from rubber trees.

4. The insole is nailed to the bottom of the last. The upper is stretched over the last and its edges are glued to the insole.

A shank is fixed on the insole. It makes the shoe strong.▶

Upper

Insole

Last

SHOES

5. The sole and heel are fixed to the upper ◀ with thread, nails or glue.

◀ 6. The edges are trimmed and the last is removed. Finally, the shoe is polished and put in a box.

Clay pottery

Clay can be shaped in many different ways. To make clay hard and waterproof, it must be baked in a very hot oven called a kiln and covered in a type of glass called glaze. This is how clay pitchers are made in a factory.

◀ 1. First a picture of a pitcher is drawn and a model of it is made without a handle.

Model

2. Plaster is poured ▶ over the model. When it has set, the plaster is cut in half and the model is taken out. The shape of the pitcher is left on the inside. This is a mold.

Mold

Slip

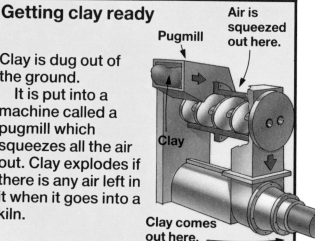

Getting clay ready

Clay is dug out of the ground.

It is put into a machine called a pugmill which squeezes all the air out. Clay explodes if there is any air left in it when it goes into a kiln.

Pugmill

Air is squeezed out here.

Clay

Clay comes out here.

3. Slip (liquid clay) is ◀ poured into the mold. The plaster soaks up some of the water in the slip.

This leaves a layer of clay in the shape of the pitcher on the inside. Extra slip is poured out.

Clay pitcher

4. The molds are opened. The pitchers are taken out and handles are stuck on with slip. The pitchers are dried.

5. The pitchers are baked (fired) in a kiln. This makes them hard.

Kiln

Glaze

6. Glaze is sprayed on ▲ the pitchers. They are fired again.

7. The pitchers are ▲ decorated. They are then fired again to stop the decorations washing off.

Making things by hand

The potter's wheel

The person who makes pots is called a potter. She can make them on a turning wheel, using her hands to make different shapes. This is called throwing.

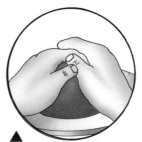

▲ Getting a ball into the center.

▲ Bringing up the sides of the pot.

▲ Shaping the neck of the pot.

Slab pots

Square pots can be made by cutting out pieces of clay and joining them together with slip. Pots made in this way are called slab pots.

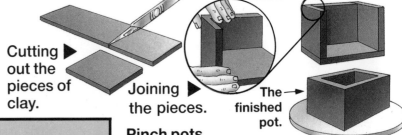

Cutting ▶ out the pieces of clay.

Joining ▶ the pieces.

The → finished pot.

Plates

Plates and flat dishes are called flatware. They can be made on a wheel, in a mold, or by 'jiggering' with a metal tool as shown here.

A pancake of clay is put on a turning mold which shapes the plate.

▼

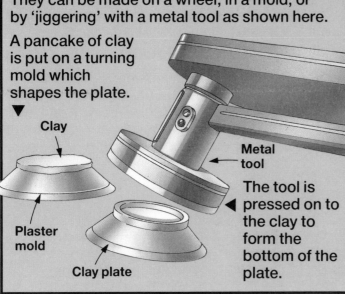

Clay

Metal tool

The tool is pressed on to the clay to form the bottom of the plate.

Plaster mold

Clay plate

Pinch pots

These are pots you can make by hand. You pinch it with your fingers.

◀ 1. Roll a ball in your hands. Make a hole in the middle with your thumb.

2. Turn the pot and ▶ squeeze the sides with your thumb and fingers.

◀ 3. Keep squeezing until the pot is the right shape and has thin sides.

Woollen sweaters

Sweaters can be made from wool or synthetic fibers (see page 211), or a mixture of both. Woollen sweaters are the warmest.

Many things have to be done to the sheep's wool before it can be made into clothes.

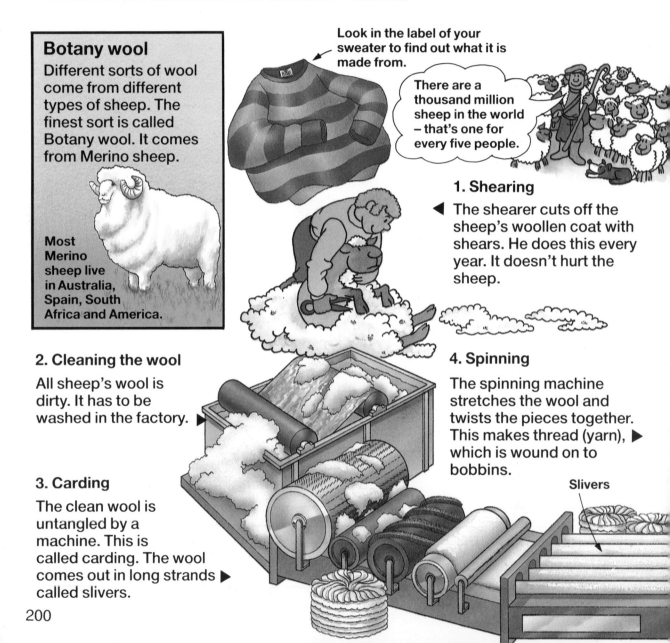

Botany wool

Different sorts of wool come from different types of sheep. The finest sort is called Botany wool. It comes from Merino sheep.

Most Merino sheep live in Australia, Spain, South Africa and America.

Look in the label of your sweater to find out what it is made from.

There are a thousand million sheep in the world – that's one for every five people.

1. Shearing

◄ The shearer cuts off the sheep's woollen coat with shears. He does this every year. It doesn't hurt the sheep.

2. Cleaning the wool

All sheep's wool is dirty. It has to be washed in the factory. ▶

3. Carding

The clean wool is untangled by a machine. This is called carding. The wool comes out in long strands ▶ called slivers.

4. Spinning

The spinning machine stretches the wool and twists the pieces together. This makes thread (yarn), ▶ which is wound on to bobbins.

Slivers

200

Woollen cloth

Other things like blankets and coats are also made from wool. Instead of being knitted, the yarn is woven into cloth on a machine called a loom.

Shuttle

Weft

Warp

Loom

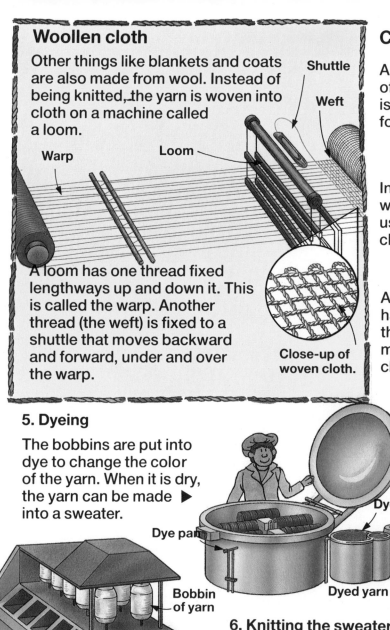

A loom has one thread fixed lengthways up and down it. This is called the warp. Another thread (the weft) is fixed to a shuttle that moves backward and forward, under and over the warp.

Close-up of woven cloth.

Clothes from other animals

A camel's hair falls ▶ off in the spring. It is made into cloth for coats.

In South America, ▶ wool from llamas is used to make clothes and ropes.

Angora rabbits ▶ have fine silky fur that can be used to make soft, furry clothes.

Knitting machine

5. Dyeing

The bobbins are put into dye to change the color of the yarn. When it is dry, the yarn can be made ▶ into a sweater.

Dye

Dye pan

Dyed yarn

Bobbin of yarn

Close-up of knitting

6. Knitting the sweater ▶

The pieces of the sweater are knitted on machines which can knit complicated patterns. They are sewn together on a sewing machine. The sweater is then pressed and packed.

Spools of cotton

Cotton plants grow in hot countries such as India, China, Egypt and America.

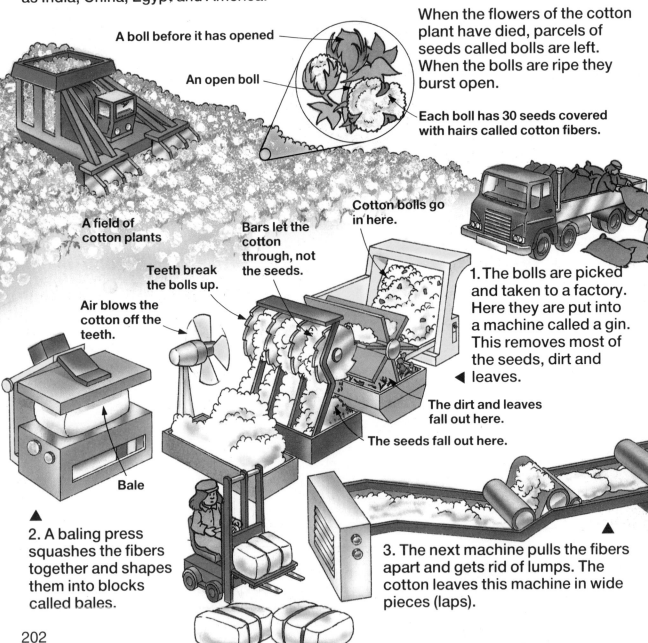

A boll before it has opened

An open boll

When the flowers of the cotton plant have died, parcels of seeds called bolls are left. When the bolls are ripe they burst open.

Each boll has 30 seeds covered with hairs called cotton fibers.

A field of cotton plants

Cotton bolls go in here.

Bars let the cotton through, not the seeds.

Teeth break the bolls up.

Air blows the cotton off the teeth.

1. The bolls are picked and taken to a factory. Here they are put into a machine called a gin. This removes most of the seeds, dirt and ◀ leaves.

The dirt and leaves fall out here.

The seeds fall out here.

Bale

▲
2. A baling press squashes the fibers together and shapes them into blocks called bales.

3. The next machine pulls the fibers apart and gets rid of lumps. The cotton leaves this machine in wide pieces (laps).

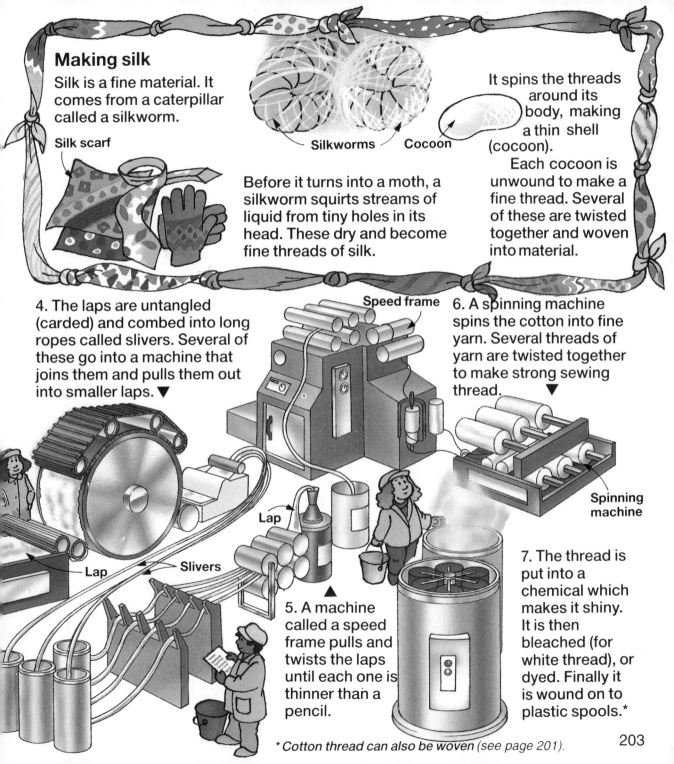

Making silk

Silk is a fine material. It comes from a caterpillar called a silkworm.

Silk scarf

Silkworms   **Cocoon**

It spins the threads around its body, making a thin shell (cocoon).

Before it turns into a moth, a silkworm squirts streams of liquid from tiny holes in its head. These dry and become fine threads of silk.

Each cocoon is unwound to make a fine thread. Several of these are twisted together and woven into material.

Speed frame

4. The laps are untangled (carded) and combed into long ropes called slivers. Several of these go into a machine that joins them and pulls them out into smaller laps. ▼

6. A spinning machine spins the cotton into fine yarn. Several threads of yarn are twisted together to make strong sewing thread. ▼

Spinning machine

Lap

Lap   **Slivers**

5. A machine called a speed frame pulls and twists the laps until each one is thinner than a pencil.

7. The thread is put into a chemical which makes it shiny. It is then bleached (for white thread), or dyed. Finally it is wound on to plastic spools.*

Cotton thread can also be woven (see page 201).

203

Paper

Most paper is made from wood. This comes from evergreen trees in North America and Scandinavia. Quick-growing gum trees in South America, Spain and Portugal are also used.

A forest the size of Wales is enough to supply the world with paper each year.

1. The trees are chopped ▶ down and the bark is taken off. A machine cuts the logs into 'chips' about 1in long.

Chip

2. The chips are ▶ cooked in water and chemicals to break them up. The wood is now pulp.

◀ 3. To get rid of dirt and lumps, the pulp is washed. Next it is put into bleach to whiten it. Then it is washed again.

Dye added here.   **Beater**

◀ 4. The pulp is beaten to break up the wood into tiny thin strands called fibers.

Paper machine

Pulp on moving belt.

◀ 5. The thick pulp is mixed with water. To make colored paper, dye can be added.

6. The paper machine spreads ▲ out the pulp on a moving belt with millions of tiny holes in it. The belt jiggles from side to side, helping the fibers to stick together.

Suction boxes suck the water away. As it begins to dry out, the pulp becomes paper.

Rollers

Paper   **Felt**

▲

7. It moves on to a layer of felt. Rollers squeeze more water out and press the fibers together.

8. Hot rollers dry the paper. It is wound on to rolls, then cut into pieces. ▶

204

Looking at paper fibers

Wood is made up of tiny strands called fibers. Cooking and adding chemicals to the wood and beating the pulp breaks the fibers up into tiny frayed pieces. When water is added and then removed, these stick together to make paper.

Beater

Pulp before beating

After some beating

After a lot of beating

Tear some paper. Can you see tiny whiskers on the edge? These are fibers.

Recycling paper

Waste paper can be dissolved in hot water to turn it back into pulp and used to make new paper or cardboard. This is called recycling. It uses less power and chemicals and fewer trees.

Half the pulp for new paper is made from used paper and cardboard.

Paper with wax or plastic on it cannot be recycled.

Boxes, magazines and newspapers can be recycled.

Making money

The paper used for money is made out of cotton because this is strong. The bills have to be difficult to copy, so they have a watermark and often a security thread in them.

Security thread

Watermark

You can see the watermark if you hold a note up to the light.

The watermark

The watermark is made by making the paper thicker in some places and thinner in others when it is still wet. Look out for them in other types of paper too.

An artist designs a new bill. An engraver cuts the design into a sheet of steel. This is used to make printing plates with many copies of the design on each one.

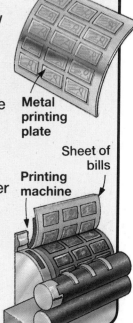

Metal printing plate

Printing

A machine presses the inked plates on to paper to make a sheet of bills. It can make 9000 sheets an hour in up to eight colors.

The sheets are then cut into single bills and packed.

Sheet of bills

Printing machine

Glass bottles

Bottles, jars and many other everyday things are made out of glass. When glass is very hot it becomes soft and can be made into different shapes.

2000 years ago people found out how to blow air into hot glass to make hollow things. Now this can be done by machines.

How glass is made

50% Sand
16% Soda
20% Cullet
14% Lime

The glass used for bottles is called sodalime glass. It is made by mixing sand, soda, lime and cullet (crushed glass).

The tanks in modern furnaces can hold over 2000 tons of glass.

This mixture is heated in a huge oven called a furnace to 2840°F. The mixture melts and makes red-hot liquid glass.

Gob

1. A lump of hot, soft glass (a gob) is taken from the furnace and dropped into a metal mold.

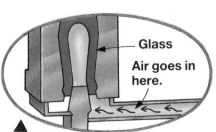

Glass

Air goes in here.

2. Air is blown into the glass. The bottle is then taken out of the mold and turned over.

3. It is put into another mold and more air is blown in through the top to form the final shape.

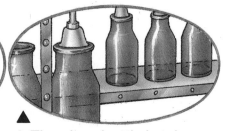

4. The glass bottle is taken out of the mold and put on a moving conveyor belt.

This machine can make over 200 bottles a minute.

The first automatic bottle-making machine was used in 1907.

Blowing glass

Until 100 years ago, blowing glass by mouth was the most usual way to shape things. Some people still do this.

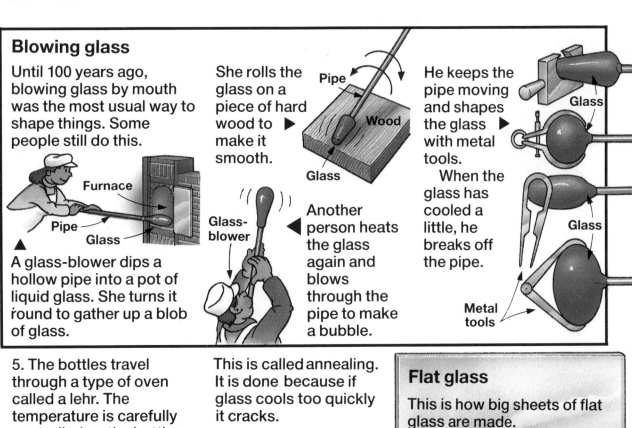

A glass-blower dips a hollow pipe into a pot of liquid glass. She turns it round to gather up a blob of glass.

She rolls the glass on a piece of hard wood to make it smooth. ▶

Another person heats the glass again and blows through the pipe to make a bubble.

He keeps the pipe moving and shapes the glass ▶ with metal tools.

When the glass has cooled a little, he breaks off the pipe.

5. The bottles travel through a type of oven called a lehr. The temperature is carefully controlled so the bottles cool slowly.

This is called annealing. It is done because if glass cools too quickly it cracks.

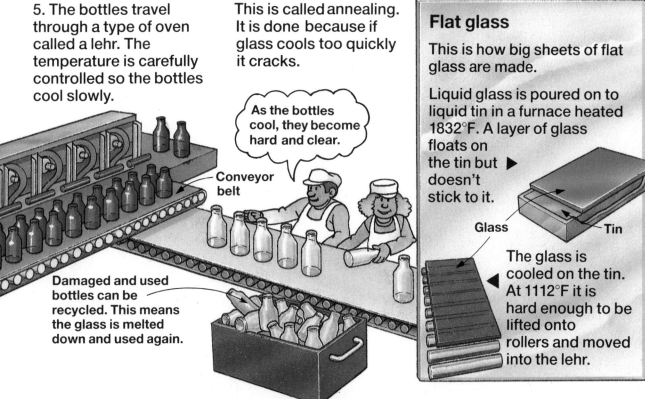

As the bottles cool, they become hard and clear.

Damaged and used bottles can be recycled. This means the glass is melted down and used again.

Flat glass

This is how big sheets of flat glass are made.

Liquid glass is poured on to liquid tin in a furnace heated 1832°F. A layer of glass floats on the tin but ▶ doesn't stick to it.

The glass is cooled on the tin. At 1112°F it is hard enough to be lifted onto rollers and moved into the lehr.

Food and drink cans

Most food cans are made from tinplate which is flat steel covered with a very thin layer of the metal tin.

Tin doesn't rust, but it is too expensive to be used by itself. A thin layer stops steel rusting and spoiling the food.

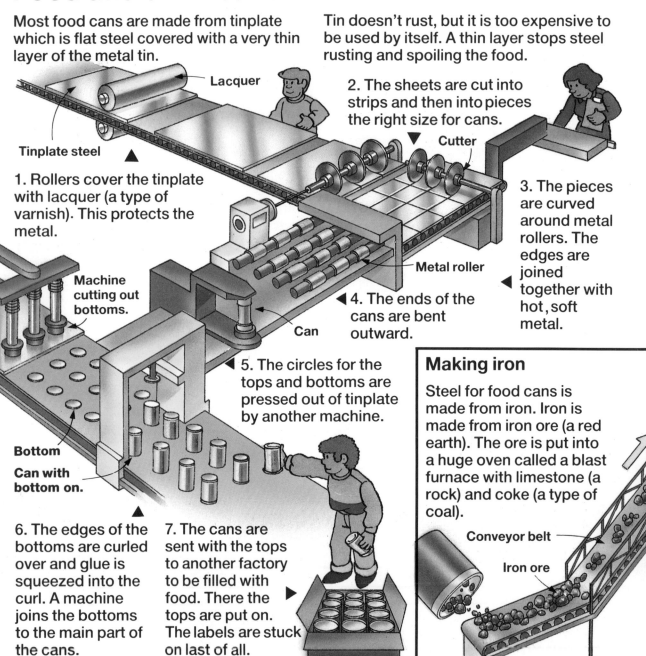

Lacquer

Tinplate steel ▲

1. Rollers cover the tinplate with lacquer (a type of varnish). This protects the metal.

2. The sheets are cut into strips and then into pieces the right size for cans.

▼ **Cutter**

3. The pieces are curved around metal rollers. The edges are joined together with hot, soft metal. ◀

Metal roller

Machine cutting out bottoms.

Can

◀ **4.** The ends of the cans are bent outward.

◀ **5.** The circles for the tops and bottoms are pressed out of tinplate by another machine.

Bottom

Can with bottom on. ▲

6. The edges of the bottoms are curled over and glue is squeezed into the curl. A machine joins the bottoms to the main part of the cans.

7. The cans are sent with the tops to another factory to be filled with food. There the tops are put on. The labels are stuck on last of all. ▶

Making iron

Steel for food cans is made from iron. Iron is made from iron ore (a red earth). The ore is put into a huge oven called a blast furnace with limestone (a rock) and coke (a type of coal).

Conveyor belt

Iron ore

Drink cans

Most drink cans are made from the metal aluminum which doesn't rust and is light and strong.

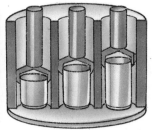

The bottom and sides are made on machines that can stretch one piece of metal upward to make a can without a join.

The design is printed on after the can has been shaped.

The top is put on when the can has been filled.

Top

Can facts

In the USA, one million tons of aluminum are made into cans every year – the same weight as two of the world's largest ships.

This house in Lesotho, in Southern Africa is made from old cans and paint pots.

Now cans are thinner, you can make 7000 more cans from one ton of aluminum than 10 years ago.

Old can
New can

Blast furnace

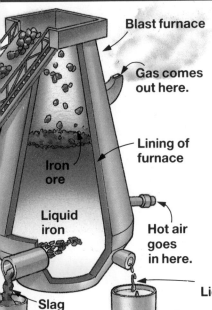

Gas comes out here.

Lining of furnace

Iron ore

Liquid iron

Hot air goes in here.

Slag

Liquid iron

Hot air is blasted into the furnace. At 2732°C, the coke mixes with the iron ore to make liquid iron.

The limestone mixes with the unwanted things in the ore making slag (waste matter). The iron trickles out at the bottom .

Making steel

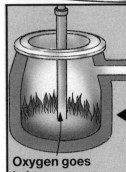

Oxygen goes in here.

Liquid steel

Most steel is made in a furnace by blowing oxygen into hot iron.

This makes liquid steel. The furnace can tip over and pour the steel out.

Steel for food cans can be rolled out flat while it is soft.

LEGO® blocks

Scientists separate out the different ingredients (chemicals) in things like oil, coal and gas and use them to make plastic. Different chemicals make different types of plastic.

Making plastic

Everything is made of millions of tiny parts called molecules. Each molecule is made up of even smaller parts called atoms. Plastic is made from some of the biggest molecules there are, but they are still too small to see.

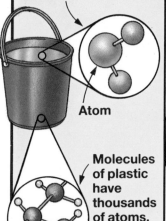

A molecule of water has three atoms.

Atom

Molecules of plastic have thousands of atoms. This is a small part of one.

Atom

The big molecules of plastic are called polymers.

The chemicals which are used to make plastic are made of much smaller molecules called monomers.

This is a monomer of a gas used to make plastic.

Scientists heat and press lots of these monomers together in long chains to make polymers.

Plastic is made in a factory called a chemical plant. When it leaves the plant, it looks like small colored lumps. These are called granules. Some are made into LEGO blocks.

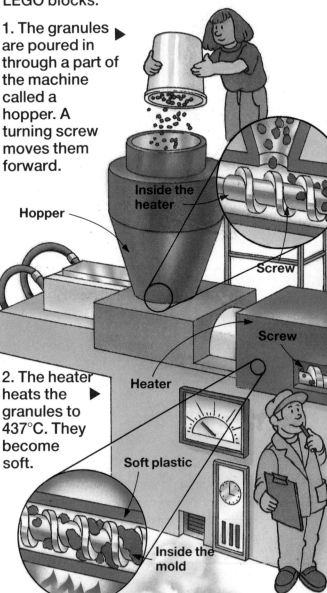

1. The granules ▶ are poured in through a part of the machine called a hopper. A turning screw moves them forward.

Inside the heater

Hopper

Screw

Screw

2. The heater heats the ▶ granules to 437°C. They become soft.

Heater

Soft plastic

Inside the mold

Plastic clothes

Some of the clothes you are wearing may be made from materials such as nylon or polyester or acrylic. These are called synthetic fibers. They are sorts of plastic.

Acrylic sweater

Nylon tights

Polyester shirts

Some materials, such as viscose, are plastics made from chemicals mixed with natural things like wood and cotton. These are called man-made fibers.

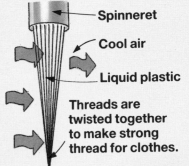

Viscose is made from wood pulp.

Viscose skirt

These fibers are made by pushing liquid plastic through holes in a machine called a spinneret.

Scientists got the idea for this by watching silkworms (see page 203).

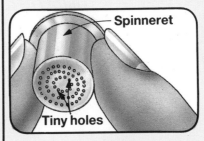

Spinneret

Tiny holes

These thin plastic threads are hardened in warm or cool air, or in acid, depending on the material.

Spinneret

Cool air

Liquid plastic

Threads are twisted together to make strong thread for clothes.

Look at the labels on your clothes. How many man-made or synthetic fibers can you spot? Clues on page 248.

100% ACRYLIC

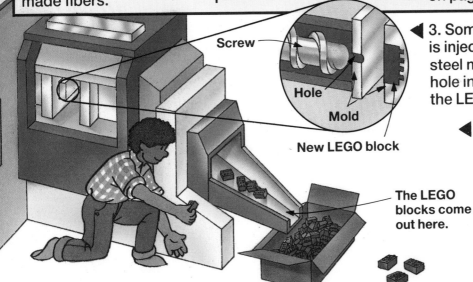

Screw

Hole

Mold

New LEGO block

◀ 3. Some of the soft plastic is injected into a cold steel mold that has a hole in it the shape of the LEGO block.

The LEGO blocks come out here.

◀ 4. The plastic cools and hardens in the shape of the mold. The mold is opened up and a LEGO block falls out into a box.

211

Bars of soap

Bars of soap are made from fats and oils mixed with a chemical called caustic soda. Until 30 years ago soap-making was done in open pans and took a week . Now it can be done in a few hours by machines that work non-stop.

A big soap factory makes a million bars a day.

Fats and oils in soap

Castor oil	5%
Palm oil	10%
Coconut oil	25%
Animal fat	60%

Oils from plants and fat from animals can be used to make soap.

1. The caustic ▶ soda, fat and oil are boiled together in a closed pan. The pan works like a pressure cooker. It cooks the soap in 15 minutes.

Boiling pan

Salty water

◀ 2. The soap has glycerin (a chemical) in it. This isn't needed, so salty water is added. Glycerin mixes with the water, but the soap doesn't.

3. A machine called a centrifuge spins the mixture very fast. This separates the glycerin mixture from the soap.

Centrifuge

Glycerin

Fitting column

How soap works

Soap is made up of millions of tiny parts ▶ called molecules. Each molecule has two parts – a head and a tail.

Head

Soap

Tail

Water

Dirt

Skin

◀ The head likes water, the tail doesn't. The tails stick to the dirt on your skin when you wash, and pull it away.

4. A machine called a fitting ▶ column removes any other chemicals that aren't needed in the soap.

212

Soap long ago

Today soap is quite cheap and there are lots of colors and types to choose from. 400 years ago soap was very expensive, didn't smell nice and was only dirty brown or grey.

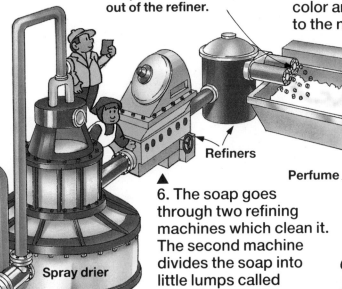

Some people used to make their own soap by boiling a mixture of fat and ash.

Elizabeth 1

In those days, people didn't wash very often. Queen Elizabeth 1 of England (1533 – 1603) only had a bath once a month – more often than most people.

Soap noodles coming out of the refiner.

7. Perfume and color are added to the noodles.

8. The noodles are pressed together and dried some more to make large rectangular pieces.

Refiners

Perfume

Rectangular pieces of soap

6. The soap goes through two refining machines which clean it. The second machine divides the soap into little lumps called noodles.

Cold air

9. The soap is cut into bars. These go through a tunnel of cold air to make them firm.

Spray drier

Soap

5. The liquid soap has now cooled a little. A spray drier heats and dries it to make it more solid.

10. A stamper makes a pattern on the bars of soap. They are then wrapped and packed in boxes.

SOAP

213

Pencils, paint, tape and toothpaste

On these pages you can find out how a few more everyday things are made.

Wooden pencils

1. The leads are made from ground-up graphite (a sort of ▶ soft rock), clay and water. This soft mixture is pressed through a small hole to make thin sticks.

2. The sticks are cut, dried and baked in a hot oven (kiln). ▼

Leads

Kiln

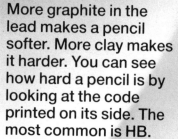

Types of pencil

More graphite in the lead makes a pencil softer. More clay makes it harder. You can see how hard a pencil is by looking at the code printed on its side. The most common is HB.

////////////	4B	Soft and black
////////////	B	Black
////////////	HB	Hard and black
////////////	H	Hard
////////////	2H	Hard
////////////	4H	Very hard
////////////	7H	Extra hard

Grooves

◀ 3. The wood is cut into flat strips. A machine makes three grooves in each strip. The leads are put in the grooves.

Join

Lead

4. Another strip of grooved wood is glued on top. The strips are pressed together firmly.

Paint

Stamp

5. A machine cuts the wood into three pieces and shapes these into pencils. They are then painted.

6. A machine stamps on the maker's name and type of pencil. The pencils are sharpened and packed.

Sticky tape

The tape is a type of plastic. The sticky stuff (adhesive) is made from synthetic rubber and resin.*

Liquid is put on one side of the tape. This will make it easier to unroll.

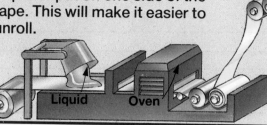

Liquid   Oven

A machine puts a very thin layer of adhesive on the other side of the tape.

*Real resin is sap (a liquid from inside trees). Synthetic resin is made from chemicals.

Paint

Paint is made from pigment (a powder) and binder (a liquid). The pigment gives the paint its color.

◀ Pigments can be made from things such as rocks and plants or from chemicals.

The binder is often ▶ varnish made from vegetable oil mixed with real or synthetic resin*. It can also be a type of plastic.

◀ All the ingredients are measured and mixed in a machine for many hours, before being put into tins, pots or tubes.

When you use paint, the binder dries to a solid layer that keeps the pigment in place.

Paint mixer

Paint

Toothpaste

These ingredients are put in a sealed metal mixer for three hours.

1. Polisher: powder made from bauxite (a sort of rock).
2. Humectant: stops paste drying up. Made from maize.
3. Binder: keeps paste well mixed. Made from wood pulp.
4. Detergent: cleans teeth and makes paste foamy. Made from chemicals.
5. Germicide: chemical for killing germs in paste.
6. Fluoride: chemical that helps keep teeth strong.
7. Flavor: makes paste taste nice. Made from plants such as mint.
8. Saccharin: makes paste sweet. Chemical made from coal.

The lids of the tubes are put on. The bottoms are left open. A machine fills each tube with paste. The ends are sealed by another machine.

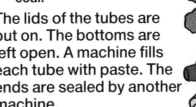

After each layer the tape goes through ovens to dry.

Jumbo roll

Oven

Tape

The adhesive cools and becomes solid and sticky. The tape is wound to make a 'jumbo roll.'

Finally, the tape is cut and wound on to smaller rolls.

A large factory can make enough tape in a week to cover 1000 swimming pools.

Facts and dates

Shoes

★ Shoe sizes were first used in 1792, in England. Before that, each pair of shoes was made specially for a particular person.

★ The most expensive shoes were bought by Emperor Bokassa of Africa for his coronation. They cost $85,000 (£38,000).

Glass

★ The first glass was made 5000 years ago in the Middle East.

★ The largest bottle is a 6ft whisky bottle that can hold 41 gallons – about the same as 555 cans of drink.

★ Mr. Pilkington invented the method for making flat sheets of glass (see page 39) in 1952.
The largest sheet of glass ever made was 65ft x 8ft.

Pottery

★ The first potter's wheel (see page 31) was used about 5,500 years ago. It was a flat table spun round by hand.

Silk

★ To make 2·2lb of silk, silkworms need to eat 484lb of Mulberry leaves.

★ Silk is so fine that it takes 3000 cocoons to make 1m of silk material.

Cotton

★ Pieces of cotton 8000 years old have been found in a cave in Mexico.

★ People only began to use cotton for sewing about 150 years ago. Before that silk or linen thread was used.

★ The top five cotton producers are:

	(Tons per year)
China	5,700,000
USA	2,913,000
USSR	2,400,000
India	1,250,000
Pakistan	860,000

Metal

★ The largest steel company is in Japan. It makes 27 million tons of steel a year.

Wool

★ The top five wool producers are:

	(Tons per year)
Australia	722,000
USSR	460,000
New Zealand	363,000
China	205,000
Argentina	155,000

★ In Australia there are about nine times as many sheep as people. There are 15 million people. How many sheep is that ?*

Paper

★ The Chinese made the first paper from wood, cotton and straw about 2000 years ago.

★ 412 newspapers can be made from one tree. About 14 million copies of the Japanese newspaper Yomiuri Shimbun are sold every day using paper from about 34,000 trees.

Plastic

★ The first plastic was made in 1862. It was called Parkesine.

★ The first man-made fiber (rayon) was made in 1884.

HOW THINGS ARE BUILT

How are tunnels made?
How are bridges built?
What is scaffolding for?
How do cranes work?
How does an oil rig work?

About building

This part of the book shows you how buildings such as houses, roads and bridges are built.

On the right are some of the different sorts of builders you will meet in this section.

The person who makes walls out of bricks is called a bricklayer.

The person who makes things with wood is called a carpenter.

What are buildings made of?

Buildings are made out of strong things such as concrete, steel and wood. You can find out more about these on pages 238-239.

This diver dives into the sea to work on the underneath of an oil rig.

This person is called a welder. He uses a very hot tool to join metal pieces.

The story of building

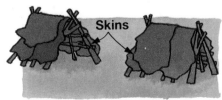

Skins

A million years ago, people built huts from branches. They hung animal skins over them to keep out rain.

Tree trunks

Later, they moved blocks of stone by dragging them over tree trunks. They kept moving the trunks to the front of the stone.

Earth slope

About 4000 years ago, the Egyptians built stone pyramids. They made earth slopes so they could drag stone blocks up to the top.

How buildings begin

Plan

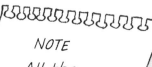

NOTE
All the buildings in this book can be built in many different ways. Usually only one way of building is shown.

Once somebody has had an idea for a building, a plan is drawn to show how it is to be built.

Engineers draw plans for buildings like bridges. They make sure these buildings don't fall down.

Architects draw plans for houses and offices. They work with engineers if the building is big.

Architects like to think of ways to make buildings attractive and pleasant to work in or live in.

When the plans are finished, a copy is given to the builders. The builders can then start.

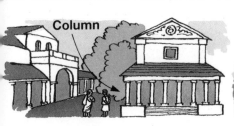

Column

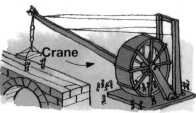

Crane

Over 2000 years ago, Greeks and Romans used stone columns to hold up buildings. The Romans are also famous for roads.

600 years ago, builders used cranes to lift loads. This helped them to build tall buildings like bridges and churches.

Now we have modern machines, twenty skyscrapers can be built in the same time that it took to build one pyramid.

Brick houses

Houses are built in many different ways. The builders you can see at work here and on the next two pages are building with bricks, concrete and wood. See if you can find out what your house is made from.

Preparing to build

The plan on the right shows what the house will look like and how big it is going to be.

Plan of house drawn by an architect.

Ground floor
105 Deer Park Street
Kitchen
Dining room
Hall
Lounge

Top floor
Bed room
Bathroom
Bed room

Side view (elevation)
Front view (elevation)

1. The builders ▶ work out how many bricks and other things they need.

2. Trucks take everything to the site.

3. The builders measure out the site from the plans. They use string to mark the edges of the house.

The string is fixed to pieces of wood.

Trench filled with concrete.

Drain pipe

Cement

Sand

4. A concrete mixer mixes sand, cement, gravel and water to make concrete. ▼

5. A digger digs trenches between the string lines. These are filled with concrete to make a hard base (foundation). It also digs trenches for pipes.*

220

*Find out more about pipes on page 231.

Building the walls

Bricklayers build walls on the foundation. First they make the corners and put string between them. This helps them build straight.

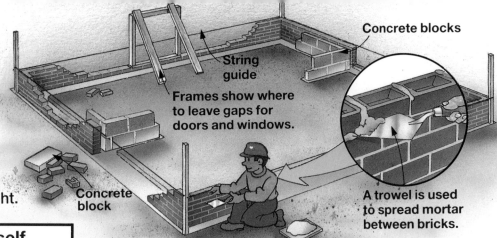

Concrete blocks

String guide

Frames show where to leave gaps for doors and windows.

Concrete block

A trowel is used to spread mortar between bricks.

The bricks are stuck together with mortar (see page 239).

The walls inside the house are made from big concrete blocks.

(see page 239).

See for yourself

Try this experiment to see how important the damp-proof course is.

1. Dip some kitchen paper in water. The water goes up it.

Wet Dry

2. Cut another piece in half. Tape the halves together with a small gap between them.

Tape

Gap

3. Dip it in water. The water cannot go above the waterproof tape.

Wet Dry

Water goes up through floors and walls in this way, unless stopped by a waterproof layer.

Keeping water out of the house

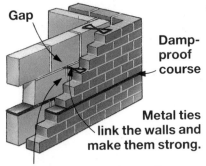

Gap

Damp-proof course

Metal ties link the walls and make them strong.

The air between the walls helps keep the house warm and dry.

◀ Another wall is built about 2 in inside the outer wall.

The bricklayer puts waterproof tar paper (see page 238) in both walls, just above the ground. This stops water soaking up. It is called a damp-proof course.

waterproof tar paper (see page 238)

Building the floor

The ground inside the ▶ walls is dug out. Concrete is poured over layers of stones, sand and plastic. The plastic stops water rising into the floor.

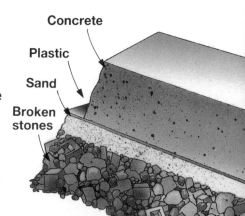

Concrete

Plastic

Sand

Broken stones

Building the upstairs

1. Builders lay pieces of wood (joists) from one wall to the other.

2. They nail wooden floorboards on top of the joists to make the floor.

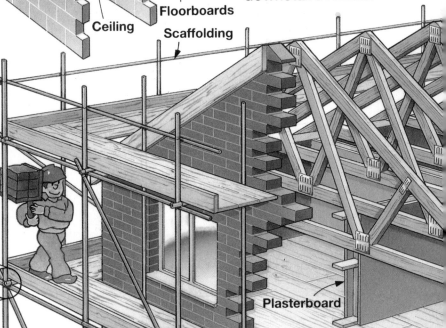

Joists

Ceiling

Floorboards

Scaffolding

3. They nail plasterboards (see page 239) underneath the joists. This makes a ceiling for the downstairs rooms.

Scaffolding

Scaffolding is like a huge climbing frame made from steel tubes. Builders stand on planks laid across it to reach the top of the house.

Clamps are tightened around the tubes to fit them together.

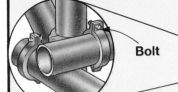

Bolt

Plasterboard

Houses with frames

The brick house on this page is held up by its walls. Other houses are held up by wooden, concrete or metal frames.

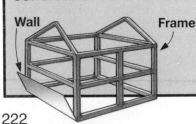

Wall

Frame

This often happens in the USA.

A wooden house which is held up by its frame can be moved on a truck.

Upstairs rooms ▲

Plasterboards are used to divide the upstairs area into rooms.

Making the stairs ▶

The carpenter builds the staircase. The top of each step is called a tread. The upright pieces are called risers.

Putting the roof on

1. The frame for the roof is made from wooden triangular shapes. They rest on the walls.

2. Roofing paper is spread over the frame. Strips of wood are nailed on top.

3. Overlapping tiles are nailed to the strips. Rain runs off them and into the guttering.

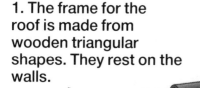

The tiles used along the top are called ridge tiles.

Battens

Roofing paper

Guttering

Floorboards

Riser

Tread

Building the chimney

The chimney is built up through the roof. A metal strip (flashing) is bent round it. This stops rain leaking between the chimney and tiles.

Flashing

Laying the water pipes

A plumber joins pipes together to carry water around the house.*

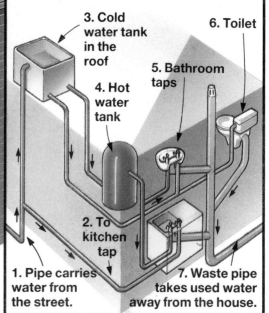

3. Cold water tank in the roof

4. Hot water tank

5. Bathroom taps

6. Toilet

2. To kitchen tap

1. Pipe carries water from the street.

7. Waste pipe takes used water away from the house.

Finishing off

★ A glazier puts glass in the windows.
★ An electrician lays wiring.
★ A plasterer covers the walls with plaster.
★ A decorator paints the house.

*This system is primarily used in foreign countries.

223

Skyscrapers

A skyscraper is built on a huge frame. This is fitted to a strong base (foundation).

Skyscraper foundations

A skyscraper is very heavy, so it needs a strong foundation. It has legs, called piles, which go deep into the earth.

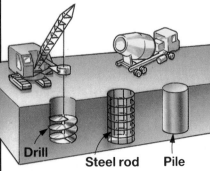

Drill   **Steel rod**   **Pile**

First, deep holes are ▲ drilled in the ground. Steel rods are put inside them. The holes are then filled with concrete.

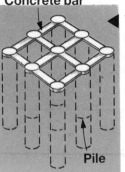

Concrete bar

Pile

◄ The tops of the piles are joined with concrete bars. This is called a pile foundation.

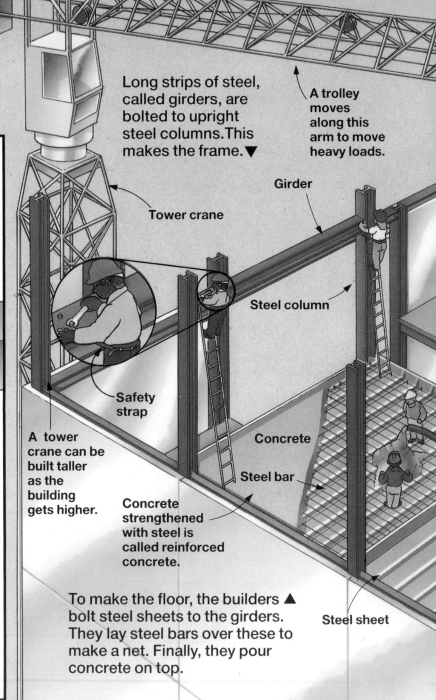

Long strips of steel, called girders, are bolted to upright steel columns. This makes the frame. ▼

A trolley moves along this arm to move heavy loads.

Girder

Tower crane

Steel column

Safety strap

A tower crane can be built taller as the building gets higher.

Concrete

Steel bar

Concrete strengthened with steel is called reinforced concrete.

To make the floor, the builders ▲ bolt steel sheets to the girders. They lay steel bars over these to make a net. Finally, they pour concrete on top.

Steel sheet

224

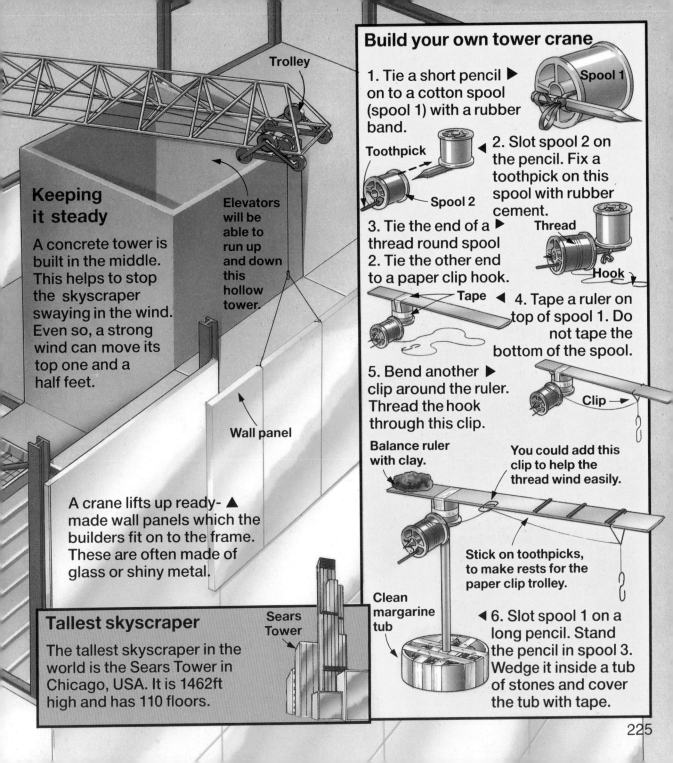

Trolley

Keeping it steady

A concrete tower is built in the middle. This helps to stop the skyscraper swaying in the wind. Even so, a strong wind can move its top one and a half feet.

Elevators will be able to run up and down this hollow tower.

Wall panel

A crane lifts up ready-made wall panels which the builders fit on to the frame. These are often made of glass or shiny metal.

Tallest skyscraper

The tallest skyscraper in the world is the Sears Tower in Chicago, USA. It is 1462ft high and has 110 floors.

Sears Tower

Build your own tower crane

1. Tie a short pencil ▶ on to a cotton spool (spool 1) with a rubber band.

Spool 1

Toothpick

2. Slot spool 2 on the pencil. Fix a toothpick on this spool with rubber cement.

Spool 2

3. Tie the end of a ▶ thread round spool 2. Tie the other end to a paper clip hook.

Thread

Hook

Tape ◀ 4. Tape a ruler on top of spool 1. Do not tape the bottom of the spool.

5. Bend another ▶ clip around the ruler. Thread the hook through this clip.

Clip

Balance ruler with clay.

You could add this clip to help the thread wind easily.

Stick on toothpicks, to make rests for the paper clip trolley.

Clean margarine tub

◀ 6. Slot spool 1 on a long pencil. Stand the pencil in spool 3. Wedge it inside a tub of stones and cover the tub with tape.

225

Roads

Roads are made up of several layers. They need to be strong, because of all the cars and trucks which go over them every day.

Clearing the ground

1. First, the builders clear the ground. They cut down trees and use bulldozers to clear the bushes and stumps. ▶

Roman roads

The Romans laid more than 48,000 miles of roads for soldiers to march over. Slaves had to carry earth and stones by hand to build up each layer. They put flat paving stones on top of their roads.

Bulldozer

These are called caterpillar treads. They grip bumpy ground.

These little metal feet stamp on the ground to make it firm.

◀ 2. Machines called scrapers and excavators dig out the bumps and fill in the hollows.

Compactor

3. A large roller called a compactor is rolled over the ground to make it hard.

This scoop can swing round to dump the earth.

Scraper

Excavator

Blades scrape up the earth into this box.

Starting to build

Crushed rock is spread over the soil. A machine called a grader levels this stony layer. ▼

Grader

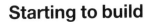

Flattening hills

Steep roads are difficult to drive on. Builders make a hill less steep by cutting out earth at the top and piling it up at the bottom.

Earth is piled up here.

Earth is cut out here.

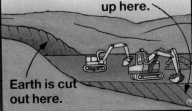

Finishing it off

1. Hot asphalt (see page 238) is poured into the front of a machine called a paver. The paver spreads it evenly over the road.

Paver

Asphalt comes out here.

Asphalt is used because it is soft when hot and gets hard as it goes cold.

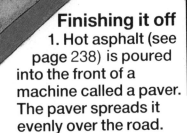

Record roads

The USA has the most roads (over three million miles). This length would go round the world 162 times.

Road roller

The road roller has smooth metal rollers instead of wheels.

2. A heavy roller follows the paver. It presses the asphalt down, helping it to set hard.

3. Several layers of asphalt are put down. Stone chips are scattered on the top layer. These make the surface rough so car tires will grip it safely.

227

Bridges

Bridges have to be very strong so that heavy trucks and trains can go across them.

On this page you can see how a bridge is built over a road.

1. First, concrete ledges (abutments) are built up on both sides of the road. Thick concrete walls (piers) are built in a line between them.
▼

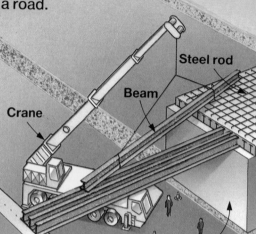
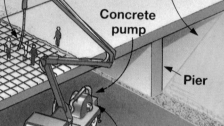

Crane

Beam

Steel rod

Concrete is poured out here.

Abutment

Concrete pump

Pier

Concrete is tipped in here.

Pier

Pier

Pier

Abutment

▲ 2. A crane lifts concrete beams on top of the piers and the abutments.

▲ 3. The builders lay a criss-cross of steel rods on top of the beams. Concrete is pumped on top of the rods.

Brick arch bridges

Arches

Bridges used to be built by making arches out of brick. Builders joined lots of arches together to make long bridges.

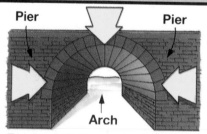

Pier   **Pier**

Arch

Brick arches are built between two thick brick piers. These stop the arch collapsing when weight is put on the bridge.

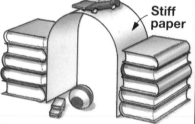

Stiff paper

Use two piles of books to keep a paper arch in place. The books will stop the arch from flattening even if you put a toy car on top.

Building over rivers

Building supports in a river is difficult and there are often wide gaps between them. Builders use several large concrete blocks to cross these gaps.

These strong wires help to stop the girder bending as the hoist travels along it.

The hoist travels along this girder.

Hoist

The blocks are floated towards the hoist on flat boats.

Support

Support

Concrete block

Concrete blocks are hollow inside.

A machine called a hoist lifts the blocks up to the bridge. The builders link them together with strong steel ropes called cables.

Boat

Strengthening the bridge

When all the blocks are in place, more cables are threaded through them. Steel plates are put on the ends of the cables to hold them in place.

A machine pulls the cables and squashes the blocks firmly together.

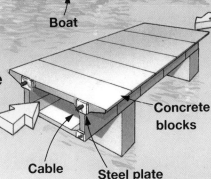

Concrete blocks

Cable

Steel plate

When blocks are joined like this, they will not fall apart, even when trucks go over them.

Suspension bridges

This is a suspension bridge. The road is hung (suspended) from two thick steel cables.

1. A concrete tower, ▶ shaped like a ladder, is built on either side of the river.

   The cables run across the tops of these towers. Their ends are fitted into lumps of concrete (piers) on the river banks.

Saddle

Tower

The cables go through metal grooves called saddles at the top of each tower.

Cable

One tower stands on each side of the river.

Steel deck

Pier

Bottom rung

2. A platform of steel (deck) stretches between the piers. The road is built on top of this.

The piers have to be very strong to stop the cables being pulled out by the heavy road.

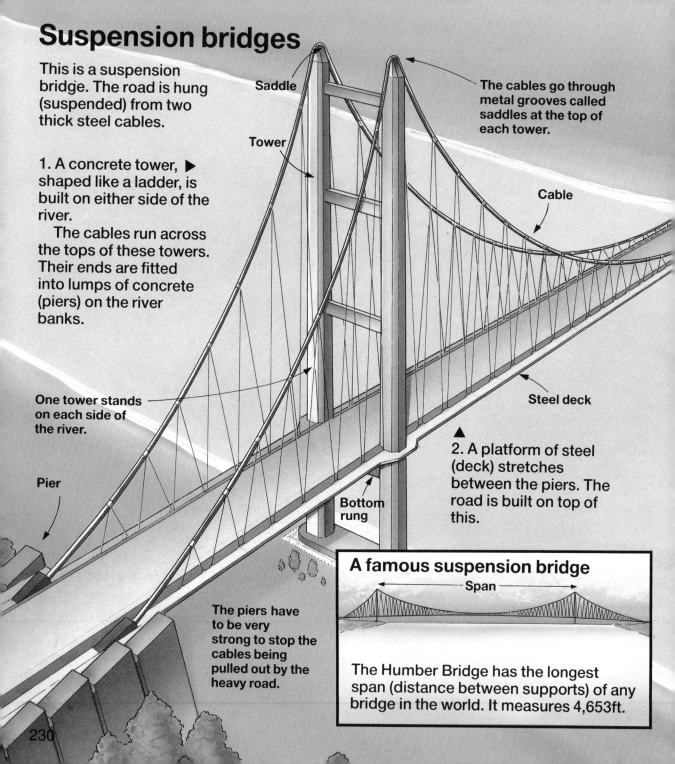

A famous suspension bridge

◄── **Span** ──►

The Humber Bridge has the longest span (distance between supports) of any bridge in the world. It measures 4,653ft.

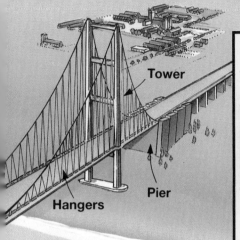

Tower

Hangers

Pier

▲
3. Hangers join the deck on to the cables. These hold the road up so that it doesn't bend or break.

Getting the deck in place

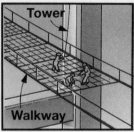

Tower

Walkway

Hangers

Cable

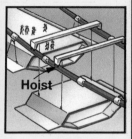

Hoist

1. Builders hang wire walkways between the towers. These are taken down when the bridge is finished.

2. They stand on the walkways to put the cables between the towers. They fit hangers to the cables.

3. A hoist lifts steel pieces up to the builders. They fit each piece to the hangers. This makes the deck.

Joining the deck together

When all the deck pieces are in place, some builders climb inside. They join pieces together with melted metal. This is called welding.

  Here is how they do it:

1. They put metal rods in the gaps between the pieces.

2. They use electric power to melt the rods.

3. The melted metal fills the gaps. It hardens as it cools.

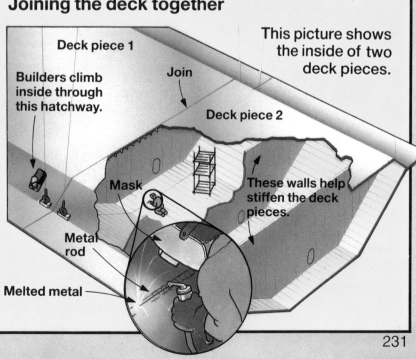

Deck piece 1

Builders climb inside through this hatchway.

Join

Deck piece 2

This picture shows the inside of two deck pieces.

Mask

These walls help stiffen the deck pieces.

Metal rod

Melted metal

Dams

Rivers overflow with water in winter but dry up in summer. Because of this, dams are built across rivers to store their water. A river blocked by a dam forms a huge lake called a reservoir.

Reservoir

This dam has a curved concrete wall. It is called an arch dam. It can hold back billions of tons of water.

Valley

Building the dam

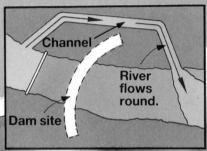

Channel

River flows round.

Dam site

1. The builders blast underground channels through the valley's sides.

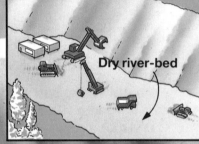

Dry river-bed

2. They use machines to dig out the river-bed until they reach a layer of solid rock.

Power stations

When water flows fast it has a lot of power. This is turned into electricity in buildings called hydro-electric power stations.

These are built below dams where steep pipes can carry very fast-flowing water to them.

Tower

3. They now build several tall concrete towers on the layer of solid rock. They spray cement into the gaps between the towers to make one enormous dam wall.

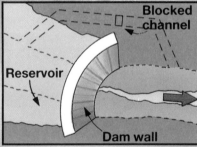

Blocked channel

Reservoir

Dam wall

4. Finally, the underground channels are filled up with concrete. The river flows back until is blocked by the dam. A lot of water builds up to form the reservoir.

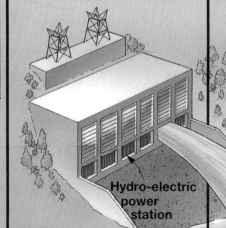

Hydro-electric power station

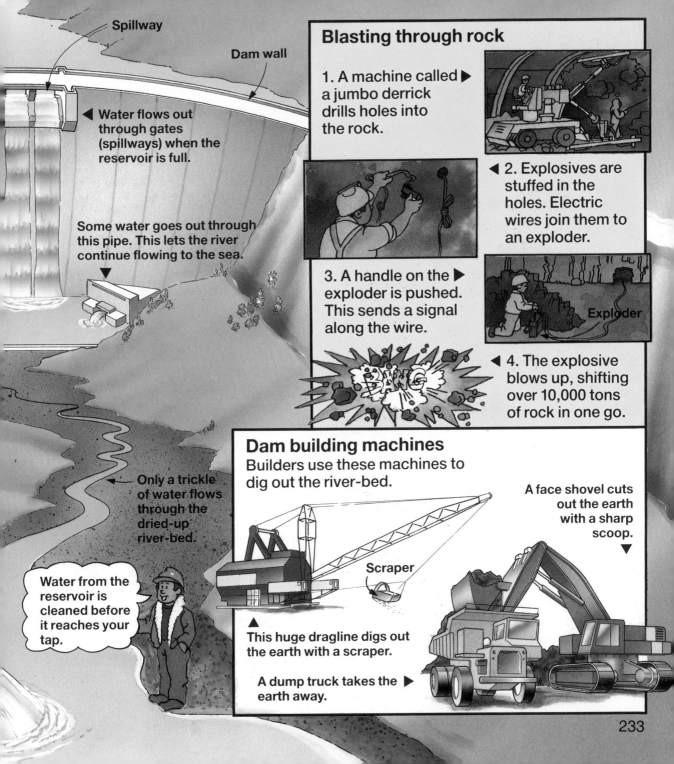

Spillway

Dam wall

◄ Water flows out through gates (spillways) when the reservoir is full.

Some water goes out through this pipe. This lets the river continue flowing to the sea.
▼

Only a trickle of water flows through the dried-up river-bed.

Water from the reservoir is cleaned before it reaches your tap.

Blasting through rock

1. A machine called ▶ a jumbo derrick drills holes into the rock.

◄ 2. Explosives are stuffed in the holes. Electric wires join them to an exploder.

3. A handle on the ▶ exploder is pushed. This sends a signal along the wire.

Exploder

◄ 4. The explosive blows up, shifting over 10,000 tons of rock in one go.

Dam building machines
Builders use these machines to dig out the river-bed.

A face shovel cuts out the earth with a sharp scoop.
▼

Scraper

▲
This huge dragline digs out the earth with a scraper.

A dump truck takes the ▶ earth away.

233

Tunnels

Tunnels are built deep below cities, rivers, mountains and even the sea. Some are large enough for cars and trains to go through.

Large tunnels are made by this machine. It is called a TBM which stands for tunnel boring machine. It bores through the earth.

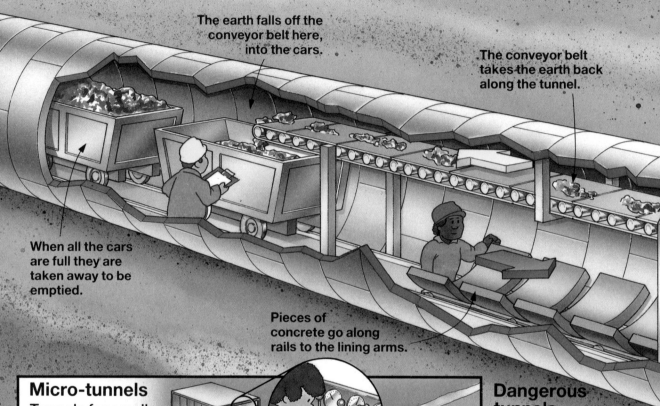

The earth falls off the conveyor belt here, into the cars.

The conveyor belt takes the earth back along the tunnel.

When all the cars are full they are taken away to be emptied.

Pieces of concrete go along rails to the lining arms.

Micro-tunnels

Tunnels for small pipes and drains are called micro-tunnels. Some micro-tunnels are dug by a machine called a remote-controlled drill. This is steered from a cabin on the ground above it.

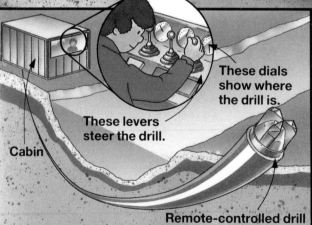

These dials show where the drill is.

These levers steer the drill.

Cabin

Remote-controlled drill

Dangerous tunnels

Freshly dug tunnels are often weak. Their sides could collapse, killing the builders. This TBM makes sure the tunnel does not collapse by lining the sides with concrete as it goes.

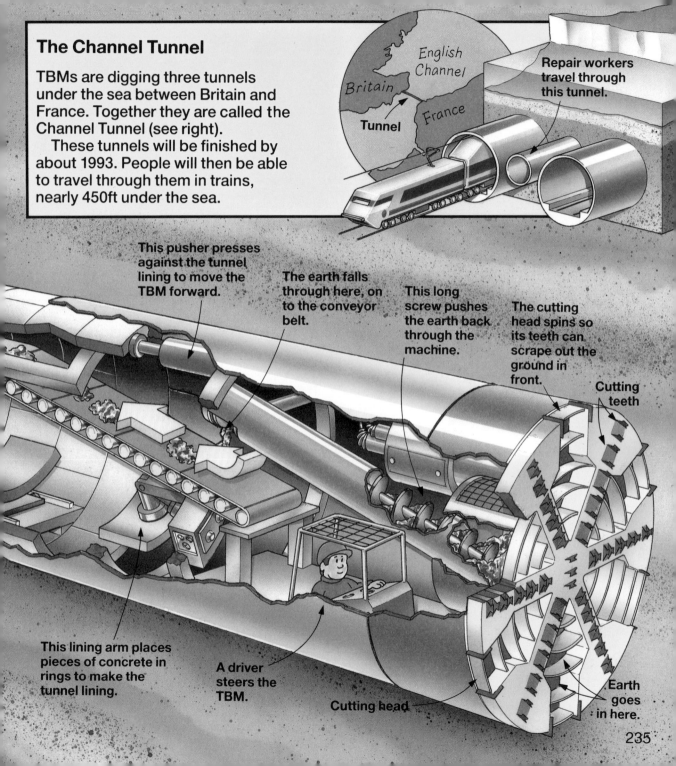

The Channel Tunnel

TBMs are digging three tunnels under the sea between Britain and France. Together they are called the Channel Tunnel (see right).

These tunnels will be finished by about 1993. People will then be able to travel through them in trains, nearly 450ft under the sea.

English Channel

Britain

France

Tunnel

Repair workers travel through this tunnel.

This pusher presses against the tunnel lining to move the TBM forward.

The earth falls through here, on to the conveyor belt.

This long screw pushes the earth back through the machine.

The cutting head spins so its teeth can scrape out the ground in front.

Cutting teeth

This lining arm places pieces of concrete in rings to make the tunnel lining.

A driver steers the TBM.

Cutting head

Earth goes in here.

235

Offshore oil rigs

These rigs are drilling machines that get oil from under the sea. They are fitted to platforms which stand on the sea-bed. Over 100 people work on a platform. It must stand firm in rough seas to keep them safe.

Helicopters land here to take people on and off the rig.

Helideck

Living quarters are high above the waves.

Workers live here for two or three weeks at a time.

Platform

The platform rests on these long legs.

The legs are often more than 650ft long.

Building the platform

Gates keep out the sea.

1. Workers build the platform at a place near the sea called a dry dock.

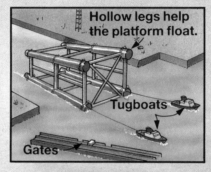

Hollow legs help the platform float.

Tugboats

Gates

2. Builders open the gates to let water into the dock. The platform is towed out to sea.

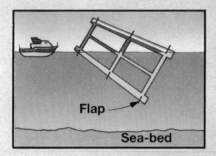

Flap

Sea-bed

3. Builders open flaps in the legs to let water in. The platform sinks and stands upright on the sea-bed.

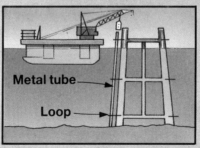

Metal tube

Loop

4. Tubes are hammered through loops on each leg. These go deep into the sea-bed to keep the platform in place.

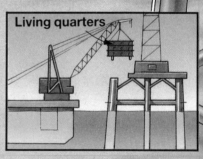

Living quarters

5. Boats carry out the rig and living quarters. A floating crane lifts them up on top of the platform.

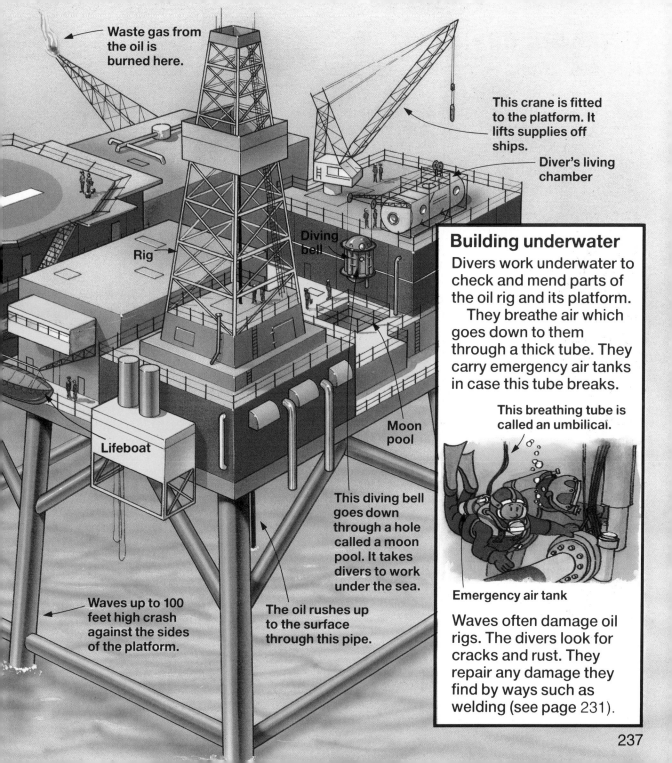

Waste gas from the oil is burned here.

This crane is fitted to the platform. It lifts supplies off ships.

Diver's living chamber

Diving bell

Rig

Building underwater

Divers work underwater to check and mend parts of the oil rig and its platform.

They breathe air which goes down to them through a thick tube. They carry emergency air tanks in case this tube breaks.

This breathing tube is called an umbilical.

Moon pool

Lifeboat

Emergency air tank

This diving bell goes down through a hole called a moon pool. It takes divers to work under the sea.

Waves often damage oil rigs. The divers look for cracks and rust. They repair any damage they find by ways such as welding (see page 231).

Waves up to 100 feet high crash against the sides of the platform.

The oil rushes up to the surface through this pipe.

What buildings are made of

Egyptians probably used cement in their pyramids.

Name	Where it comes from	What it is used for
Asphalt. Black, stony mixture.	It is made by mixing crushed rock with hot tar.	It is spread on roads to make a tough surface (page 227).
Tar. Thick, sticky oil.	Sometimes it seeps out of the ground. Sometimes it is drilled out by oil rigs.	It is mixed with crushed rock to make asphalt for roads.
Tar paper. Black, waterproof material.	It is made by spreading tar on rough paper.	It is used to stop damp rising up walls (page 221).
Brick. A hard block of clay.	Clay is shaped into bricks. These are put into a hot oven (kiln) to harden them.	Bricks are used for building walls (page 221). Bricklayers stick them together with mortar.
Cement. Fine powder.	It is made from clay and chalk. These are mixed, burnt and then ground up.	It sticks sand and stones together. It is used in concrete and mortar.
Concrete. A type of man-made rock.	It is made by mixing sand, broken stones, cement and water. It sets hard when dry.	Concrete is used to make lots of things such as blocks, towers, columns and foundations.

The fastest bricklayer in the world is Ralph Charnock of Great Britain. He once laid 725 bricks in an hour.

Thousands of years ago, builders used tar to stick bricks together instead of mortar.

The tallest structure in the world, the Warsaw Radio Tower, is made of steel. It is 2,131ft tall.

Name	Where it comes from	What it is used for
Mortar. Gritty paste which dries hard.	It is made by mixing sand, cement and water.	It is used to stick bricks together (page 221).
Plaster. Stiff paste which is hard and smooth when dry.	A rock called gypsum is ground to a fine powder and then mixed with sand and water.	It is spread over brick and concrete walls to make them smooth (page 223).
Plasterboard. Stiff board.	It is made by sandwiching plaster between two sheets of paper.	It is used to make ceilings and some inside walls (page 222).
Reinforced concrete. Very strong concrete.	It is made by letting concrete set around steel rods or bars.	It is often used to make bridges because it is so strong cars and trucks can go over it (page 228).
Steel. Very strong metal.	It is made from iron which has been heated in a type of very hot oven called a furnace.	Pieces of steel are joined together to make things such as bridges, oil rigs and skyscrapers.
Wood. The inside of a tree.	Trees are cut down and sawn up to make pieces of wood for building.	It is used to make floors and roof frames in many houses. Some houses are made just from wood.

Did you know that the largest concrete building in the world is the Grand Coulee Dam?

It is on the Columbia River, USA.

Building records

★The oldest buildings in the world are 21 huts in France. They were built about 400,000 years ago.

★The largest building in the world is in Holland. The floor covers 1,215,974ft or 50 football fields.

Houses

★The largest house is in North Carolina, USA. It has 250 rooms and a yard as big as 6,644 football fields.

★A cottage in Wales has only two tiny rooms and a staircase. The whole house is 6ft wide and 10½ft high.

Skyscrapers

★The first skyscraper ever was the Home Insurance Building in Chicago, USA. It was 172ft high and was built in 1885.

★The top six tallest skyscrapers are:

Sears Tower, Chicago USA	1462ft
World Trade Center, New York, USA	1356ft
Empire State Building, New York, USA	1257ft
Standard Oil Building, Chicago, USA	1140ft
John Hancock Center, Chicago, USA	1130ft
Chrysler Building, New York, USA	1050ft

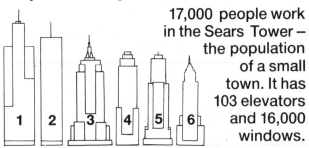

17,000 people work in the Sears Tower – the population of a small town. It has 103 elevators and 16,000 windows.

Roads

★The countries with the most roads are:

USA	3,819,354 miles
Canada	1,801,200 miles
France	901,200 miles
Brazil	847,161 miles
USSR	845,280 miles

★The busiest road in the world is in Los Angeles, California, USA. About 363 vehicles per minute travel along it.

Bridges

★The oldest suspension bridge (see page 62) that still exists was built in 1470. It is in Yunnan Province, China.

★A bridge in Japan that joins Honshu and Shikoku islands is 11,748ft long.

Tunnels

★The longest tunnel is the New York City West Delaware water supply tunnel. It is 101 miles long.

★London has 244 miles of subway train tunnels which carry 800 million passengers a year.

Dams and oil rigs

★The highest dam is the Nurek Dam (USSR). It is 990ft high – only 20in shorter than the Eiffel Tower in Paris.

★The tallest oil rig is the BP Magnus in the North Sea. It is 1,030ft tall.

Index

octopus, 116
offshore oil rig, 195, 236-237
oil, 77, 194, 210, 236, 237, 238
Olympus Mons, 157
orbits, 69, 74, 75, 87, 88, 122, 123,
    125, 127, 146, 150, 151, 161, 163
ox-bow lake, 80
oxygen, 83, 84, 95

P

paddle, 27, 36
paddle-wheel, 28, 29
paddy, 188
paint, 215
Pangaea, 94
paper, 204-205, 216
parachuting, 65
passenger terminal, 58
pasta, 187
Patrouille de France, 71
paver, 227
pencil, 214
periscope, 42
Persian Gulf, 82
phases of Mars' moons, 156
phases of the Moon, 151
Phobos, 156
pilot boat, 32
pinch pot, 199
piston, 6, 18
pit stop, 10
Planet, 161
planets, 122, 123, 128, 138, 139, 141,
    146, 147, 148, 154
plankton, 82
plants, 110-111
plaster, 198, 223, 239
plasterboard, 222, 239
plastic, 197, 210-211, 214, 215, 216
plates, 199
Pluto, 147, 160, 161
Poles, 74, 75, 88, 89
pollution, 115

pork, 182, 183
port, 30, 46
Post, Wiley, 67
potter, 175
potter's wheel, 199, 216
power boat, 26, 33
preserving food, 171, 192
printing machine, 205
probes, 138, 139
propeller, 52, 56, 66
pugmill, 198
pulses, 178
pumice, 107
punt, 37
purse seiner, 45

Q

Queen Elizabeth II (QE2), 30

R

radar, 39
radiator (car), 4, 6, 7
radio signals, 137, 138
railway, 18, 20
rain, 78, 79, 90, 91, 92, 93, 94, 98
rain dances, 171
rainbow, 85, 90, 91, 99
rallying, 13
recipes,
    for bread, 172
    for rice pudding, 189
    for yogurt, 175
recycling, 195, 205, 207
Red Giant Star, 165
reef, 82
reed boat, 37
reptiles, 94
reservoir, 232
rice, 171, 188-189, 192
rig, 34, 35
rings, 146, 159, 160, 161
rivers, 76, 77, 79, 80-81, 114, 115
road racing, 17

Answers

Page 173 - Pittas, chapattis, soda and naan
are all unleavened.

Page 211 - Polyamide, Lycra, aramid,
elastane, polypropylene, Terylene, Crimplene
and acetate are some other synthetic and
manmade fibers.

Page 216 - 135 million sheep